UNTRACEABLE

UNTRACEABLE

Aya de León

CANDLEWICK PRESS

Copyright © 2023 by Aya de León

Excerpt on pages 264–265 from *Song of Solomon* by Toni Morrison (New York: Vintage, 2007)

First edition 2023

Library of Congress Catalog Card Number 2022923580
ISBN 978-1-5362-2375-0

23 24 25 26 27 28 APS 10 9 8 7 6 5 4 3 2 1

Printed in Humen, Dongguan, China

This book was typeset in Warnock Pro.

Candlewick Press
99 Dover Street
Somerville, Massachusetts 02144

www.candlewick.com

For all the big girls

PROLOGUE

Los Angeles, CA

Riding on eight wheels turned out to be dangerous.

I knew how to ride a bike and a scooter, and even to skateboard a little bit, but I had no idea how to roller-skate. I wished I had learned earlier. I worried that going skating for the first time as a fifteen-year-old could get ugly. But I didn't have a lot of friends at school—no close friends at all—so when one of the few invited me to a roller-rink birthday party, I said yes, even though I was afraid I'd embarrass myself.

I had done gymnastics for several years, so I wasn't totally uncoordinated, but that was back in elementary school. I was definitely gonna be the only Black girl at the party, not to mention the only girl bigger than a size six (like, ten sizes bigger). And I'm tall, too. If I fell down, it would be a long way to the ground and a surefire invitation for someone to tell a fat joke.

Since there was no way I was getting on skates for the very first time at the party, I begged my mom to dig out her old quad skates so I could practice. Yes, that's right: quad skates, not Rollerblades. My mother was a teenager in the '90s, but in some ways, she seems like she grew up in the '70s—she is old school. Her feet were only a half size bigger than mine, so I figured the skates would fit with an extra pair of socks. The boots were scuffed black leather with red wheels. They had red toe stops and red laces. They definitely looked like something out of a 1970s disco.

I headed to the backyard. It wasn't much of a yard. More like an extended driveway—just a square of concrete with a small strip of grass on the side that was overgrown with weeds. Mom kept saying she was going to plant a garden, but all she had managed so far was to put up a plastic gardening shed. There wasn't a lot of room behind the house, but I didn't want to be on the sidewalk in front, putting on a comedy show for the white hipster neighbors this afternoon. I had almost an hour to practice before math tutoring, and I was determined to make the most of it. I planned to skate around our tiny yard, wheeling carefully on the concrete, while holding on to the fence for balance.

I pushed the door open and stepped out in my

double-socked feet. The skates were heavy in my hand, tied together and dangling from the knot clutched in my fist.

Standing on our tiny block of a back porch, I pulled out my phone for a selfie. I planned to take a picture of me holding the cheesy disco skates for posterity. I would have taken a video, but the storage was nearly full. My dad was a climate-change researcher who traveled a lot and sent me tons of photos and videos. Plus, I had videos of me and Dad together that I watched whenever I missed him, and I couldn't bring myself to delete any of them. It made my phone act buggy, but I didn't want to entrust a single one of my memories with my dad to any type of cloud. Maybe I'd go through and delete some of them when he got home. Or maybe I just needed more storage on my phone.

I put the phone in camera mode and was just about to flip to the selfie lens when I saw a man crouching by the shed.

He was Black, or maybe Latinx, with a cap pulled low over his stubbly face. He was medium height and stocky, dressed in dark clothes.

I gasped and clutched at the phone, reflexively snapping a photo.

At the sound of the camera shutter, the man leaped toward me, grabbing for the phone.

My dad often practiced self-defense with me, teaching me to push past fear and simply react—hitting, kicking, and punching. He also taught me to use whatever was nearby or in my hands as a weapon.

That would explain why I instinctively swung the roller skates at the man, looping them in a wide arc and letting them crash into the side of his head. They hit with a thud. I let go of the laces and he fell backward, the skates tumbling with him, his body crashing against our plastic shed.

What surprised me next was the look on his face. I expected to see rage, but his eyes were wide and his mouth was open in a grimace of pain. He looked afraid, upset, almost concerned.

But I didn't have time to worry about his feelings. I backed up toward the house until there was a good five feet between us. I kept my eyes trained on him, and my hand felt for the doorknob behind me. As he fell and crumpled, seeming to lose consciousness, I finally turned and rushed into the house, leaving him in the yard with the pair of skates, one of them on its side, a red rear wheel spinning.

"Mom!" I screamed, bolting the door behind me. I tried to call 911 on my phone, but it was frozen. I stabbed at it, trying to close the camera to get it to wake up.

"Yes, my love?" Mom asked as she came into the back hallway, wiping a trail of white flour off the brown skin of her cheek with a starched kitchen towel. "What's all the racket? Did you fall down?"

"A m-man!" I stammered. "He's still out there."

My mother rushed to the window and took in the man in dark clothes, staggering to his feet. In the fading afternoon light, I could see blood dripping down from beneath his cap.

Mom stood frozen, eyes locked on him.

For a moment, he looked up at us through the window, again with an expression that didn't seem right, and then he limped toward the front yard.

"Don't move!" Mom ordered. "Don't open the door!"

As if I would.

I just stood there, my heart banging in my chest.

She ran toward the front of the house—to call the cops, I assumed. I kept my eyes trained on the dark figure disappearing around the back corner of the house.

"Mom, he's—" I yelled in her direction.

"Stay there and watch!" she yelled back.

So I did. For a moment, I watched the spot where he'd disappeared around the corner. But then my eyes strayed to the shed, where a smudge of blood was drying on the plastic door.

My dad was a scientist. I imagined him taking a sample to his lab and using his tools to . . . maybe help identify him somehow? Who was this guy sneaking into our backyard? Was he trying to break in? Or just lurking around?

I had the sudden thought that maybe the guy was

homeless and just looking for a place to rest. But no. His clothes seemed too new. Too crisp.

I heard the front door open. Was my mother leaving?

"Mom!" I yelled, panicking.

"Stay there!" she commanded.

So I stood rooted to my spot.

My phone screen was still frozen in camera mode. In the lower corner was the last photo I had taken—a blurry shot of the shed with the man as a brown/black smear and my thumb taking up half the frame. I pressed the power button and restarted the phone, glancing only occasionally away from the window in the back door.

My phone still hadn't booted back up when I heard the front door slam, and Mom came running toward me.

"I wanted to see which way he went," she said. "I was hoping he had a car and I might get a look at the license plate. But he was on foot. Headed north, toward the gas station."

"Did you call nine one one?" I asked.

She hesitated. "I—I didn't."

"What?" I asked. Some strange guy was creeping outside our door, and she didn't call the cops? Leave it to my mom to act weird and ridiculous.

"I was going to," Mom said. "I picked up the phone and started dialing. But then I imagined giving the man's description to the police, and I realized it could describe your father. I've seen too many Black men get hassled by the cops in this neighborhood."

Like I said, ridiculous. There weren't many Black men in this neighborhood. Maybe a few coming home from work in suits. I doubted there'd be any in dark jeans and a cap.

"Did you remember the most important part?" I asked. "He's also bleeding from a head wound."

"I saw that," Mom said. "What happened?"

"I hit him in the temple," I said. "It was, like, whoa."

"Head wounds always seem worse than they are," Mom said. "I can use my professional network to see if anyone comes into the emergency room tonight that matches his description."

Mom's a doctor. She wasn't working emergency, but I guess there's some kind of doctor gossip network.

I sighed. "My phone snapped a photo of him, but it's blurry beyond recognition."

"Too bad," Mom said. "That might have been worth taking to the police." She asked me for a more detailed description, and I gave it to her.

"And what did you hit him with?" she asked.

"The roller skates," I said.

"*My* roller skates?" she asked.

"Yeah," I said. "It just sort of happened. One minute I was holding them by the laces, and the next minute they were sort of—"

"Knocking him upside his head," Mom finished.

"Yeah," I said, and a slightly hysterical giggle bubbled up from my chest.

My laughter sounded strange in the narrow back hallway. But once I started, I couldn't stop. I was sort of shaking but laughing, too.

It was infectious. Mom started laughing as well.

"Why am I laughing when I also feel really scared?" I asked between explosions of laughter.

"From the looks of it, *he's* the one who should be scared," Mom said, and we started cracking up again. "I can just see him explaining to the ER doctor stitching him up. 'Yeah, I was hit in the head by a teenage girl with a pair of roller skates.' He really learned that crime doesn't pay."

I rolled my eyes at her latest cheesy saying. Sometimes it felt like Mom only knew how to talk in clichés, but right now it was almost comforting. "I just hope . . ." I said, gasping through the peals of laughter. "I just hope he feels panic every time he sees a little kid go skating by."

The two of us sat on the floor in the back hallway, holding our sides and laughing, but I was definitely shaking the whole time.

After the laughter had subsided, we just sat there for a while. It felt kind of good to lean against Mom. I didn't do a lot of that lately. She just . . . got on my nerves so much. Everything about her was annoying. But it was good to feel close again, without actually having leaned on her on purpose. I didn't want her to think it was cool to start back up with hugging and kissing me all the time. One hug on the way out the door to school was plenty.

Finally, Mom stood up and helped me to my feet. We both looked out through the back window again. It was quiet. Nothing but a pair of roller skates and the smear of blood on the shed.

Mom quickly opened the door and ran out and grabbed the skates. When she came back in, I bolted the lock behind her.

"This is ridiculous," she said. "That man is long gone."

"I guess you're right about the cops, but I hate to let him get away," I said. I felt better after the laughter but still a little creeped out.

Mom was looking like she was just about to say something else when the doorbell rang.

"I'll get it," Mom said. "That should be Valerie."

Valerie was my math tutor. She's an engineering major at a nearby college. Mom opened the door and Valerie stepped in, wearing her typical ponytail and sweats. She greeted me with her usual bright smile.

Mom generally runs errands while Valerie's over.

I'm fifteen, old enough to stay home by myself, but Mom acts like I'm still in kindergarten. She likes someone to be home with me at all times.

"You know," Mom said, "I think I'll just go to the store tomorrow."

Okay, so maybe after the lurker guy, I wouldn't want to be home *alone*, but now I couldn't even stay with a glorified babysitter? What was next? Would my mother start going into the bathroom with me?

"Mom," I said, my voice getting a little higher pitched than I wanted. "We're fine. Just go ahead, okay? I really don't want tuna for my lunch tomorrow."

Mom looked from me to Valerie. "Okay," she said. "I won't be more than an hour."

On her way out the door, she looked back.

"I have my cell," she said. "Call if—if you need anything."

I mouthed the word "go," and she closed the door behind her.

After she left, Valerie and I got down to business. We were looking at math equations, but my mind kept wandering to the memory of the man I had hit with the skates. Who was he? And what did he want? Was he Black or Latinx? Or both? I guess you could be both. And even though he was lurking around, how come he had that strange look on his face? Also, how badly had I hurt him? Mom said he had headed toward the gas station. I kind of wanted to go look around. What if he was still there?

"Are you okay today?" Valerie asked. "Feeling sick or something?"

I blinked at her. "Yes," I said, an idea forming. "I do feel sick. To my stomach." I made a slightly nauseated face. "Let me look in the bathroom to see if we have anything for it."

In the bathroom, I made a noisy show of rummaging through the medicine cabinet.

"We're out of that pink stuff," I called. "Let's go to the gas station and see if they have any."

"I have my car," she offered.

"No, it's like a block away," I said. "And I need some air."

Valerie and I put on jackets and headed out. I turned on the alarm and locked the house.

By now, the sun had set. Our block was relatively quiet, in spite of people coming home from work. It was the kind of LA neighborhood where everyone pulled into the driveway of their pastel stucco house and walked directly inside. Like I said: lots of guys in suits, nobody on foot. No other Black guy would have been mistaken for the one I hit in the head. On the other hand, there wasn't a single person standing around outside who I could ask about seeing a guy limp by with a gushing head wound.

At the gas station, I walked up to the attendant in the little booth with the bulletproof glass. I pretended to be asking for stomach medicine, but instead I gave him a description of the guy. The man in the booth shook his head.

As we turned to go home, I noticed the restroom sign.

Mom had said the guy came this way. What if he went into the restroom and passed out on the floor from loss of blood? Then I would definitely call the cops.

"I have to go to the bathroom," I told Valerie.

"At a gas station?" she asked. "Can't you wait till we get back to your house?"

"I'm having stomach problems," I said, opening my eyes wide to make it look urgent.

Valerie knocked on the window of the booth and asked the gas station attendant for the restroom key.

"No key," the man said. "Just go around back."

As we turned the corner, I felt my heart thudding in my chest again.

Without a backward glance at Valerie, I rushed into the men's restroom. The light went on, and a quick glance told me it was empty.

"That's the guys' bathroom!" Valerie yelled after me.

"Can't wait," I yelled back, locking the door.

I turned slowly to inspect the space. It was just a regular gas station bathroom. Cleaner than many I had visited when our family took road trips. It smelled of bleach, and there was graffiti scratched into the mirror. But in the drain of the rusty sink, I saw a pale orange-pink smear.

I looked around. If he had come in and was bleeding, he had probably cleaned up in here. I walked over to the garbage can, which was full of paper towels. They mostly looked like they'd been used to wipe clean but wet hands. I peered into the can. I didn't want to use my hand to rummage around in the trash, but I wondered what I would find.

Beside the toilet was a cleaner brush. I wrapped some toilet paper around my hand and picked up the brush, then used it to stir up the towels in the trash. I was thinking that they should really compost these when I saw some bloody towels under the top layer.

I knew it!

It might be a DNA sample, I thought. I needed to get it.

I dug around in my jacket pockets and found an empty ziplock bag that had held some apple slices.

"Perfect," I murmured.

I turned the bag inside out and used it like a glove to pick up one of the bloody paper towels. Then I zipped it up.

I flushed the toilet and walked back out of the men's bathroom.

Valerie was waiting for me, looking worried.

"Are you okay?" she asked.

I nodded.

"Do you still need to get medicine?" she asked.

"No," I said, feeling the ziplock bag in my pocket. "I'm okay now."

I knew it wasn't like the police would do a DNA test on a paper towel found a block from a house where a man was lurking around and didn't even commit a crime.

And I couldn't ask Dad if he had a scientist buddy who could do it, at least not right away, since he was out of town doing fieldwork. But still. It seemed worth holding on to, somehow.

When we got to the house, Valerie excused herself to go to the bathroom, and I wet a napkin, wiped some of the blood off the shed, and bagged it. I labeled the plastic bags "shed door" and "gas station bathroom" with a permanent marker. I had no idea what I was going to do with these blood samples, but something about having them made me feel better anyway.

I told Valerie I just wanted to lie down.

In my room, I tucked the plastic bags into my toiletries case and opened my photos to look at one of my videos with Dad. There was the blurry photo of the man. I was just about to delete it when I realized it wasn't just a single photo but a burst. Apparently, I had unintentionally taken over a dozen shots in quick succession.

I touched the screen to open the bundle of photos. The one that the app had displayed was a blur with my finger in front, but it turned out there were thirteen photos. The ones at the beginning and the end were blurry, but two in the middle seemed to show the man in sharp focus.

I blew the image up.

Yes! He was clearly recognizable.

I called Mom, but she didn't pick up. What had she said? If I had a photo, I should go to the police?

I dialed 911.

Forty minutes later, Valerie was sitting on the couch, watching anxiously as a tall Black officer explained that he didn't really want my blood samples for DNA, but he would let me email him the picture.

I had just sent it when Mom walked in, carrying groceries and a bag of takeout. She glanced from me to the officer. "What's going on?"

"It turns out one of the photos is really clear," I said. "So I made a police report."

The officer handed her a card. "Here's the report number for your reference," he said. "Your daughter handled herself very professionally. She's observant and calm in a crisis."

Mom smiled her fake smile. "That's my girl."

◆ ◆ ◆

After the officer and Valerie both left, Mom's smile fell. "You called the police?" she asked. Her voice sounded unexpectedly tense.

"The officer was cool," I said. "You saw, he was Black himself. I told him about your concerns, and he totally understood."

"Why didn't you call me first?"

"I did, but you didn't pick up," I said.

Mom got that face she gets when she's exasperated but doesn't want to flip out.

"What?" I asked. "You said if I had a good photo I should call." I can't win with Mom. She doesn't want me to do anything, but she also gets mad when I do the exact thing she said to do.

"I know what I said." She shook her head. "I just— come on, let's eat this dinner."

I set the table for two, and Mom opened the takeout bag. It turned out to be Jamaican food. Oxtails and fried sweet plantains were usually her favorites, but she just picked at her plate.

Later that night, I got up to pee, and I thought I heard Mom talking in a low voice. Who would she be on the phone with at midnight?

When I came back out of the bathroom, I peeked my head into my parents' bedroom. Mom wasn't stirring, but next to the bed, a meditation was playing on her phone.

"Just release any tension you might have in your forearms," a slow, soothing voice—a woman with an Australian accent—said from the phone's speaker. That must have been what I heard.

I tried to go back to sleep but couldn't. I kept seeing the guy and the roller skates swinging, and then the blood. I went downstairs to double-check that the back door was locked, which was ridiculous. Mom always locked it. But as I twisted the already-locked dead-bolt, I looked out the window. In the bluish glow of the moonlight, it looked like the rest of the blood smear had been wiped away.

CIA Headquarters, Washington, DC

ALERT: "Forrest Kendall" "Carmen Kendall"
   MATCH FOUND
LAPD Report—attempted break-in
Address: 206867 Dracena Dr., Los Angeles, CA
Also: "Amani Kendall"

ONE

The next day, I knew something was wrong the minute my mom called me out of my last-period gym class for a doctor's appointment. I was sitting on a mat doing a combination of yoga and Pilates. The gym was high ceilinged, with tall windows that looked out on the school's manicured grounds. The teacher was having us hold our bodies in a plank position as long as we could. I was doing pretty well, but I had a lot more to hold up than the rest of the girls. In particular, most of my weight is in my posterior.

So when the sophomore from the office opened the gym door and walked across the room to hand the teacher a slip of paper, I was glad for the distraction from the burn in my midsection. And when the teacher looked at the paper and motioned to me, I thought it was a godsend. I relaxed out of plank, grabbed my backpack, and made my way to the front of the room.

The teacher had short gray hair and rimless glasses. She smiled and handed me the slip. But when I saw that it said *Doctor's Appt.*, I felt a clutch of panic in my chest. I hurried to the office.

I'd never had a doctor's appointment in my life. My mother was my doctor. You know how some kids are homeschooled? I'm home-doctored. So I read it as a distress code.

Which is the *only* reason I would ever have fast-walked across campus in my gym shorts, my thick brown thighs and big butt jiggling with every step. Apparently, Sir Mix-a-Lot has been thinking this is sexy for decades. But Sir Mix-a-Lot doesn't go to my Los Angeles prep school. I kept my head down as I strode out of the gleaming modern gym building and across the bright green soccer field. Penfield Academy's grass was always lush, even during the California drought.

The main office is in the original school building, built around the turn of the twentieth century, with bricks that managed to survive every quake, determined to mimic the buildings of Ivy League campuses, San Andreas Fault be damned.

"We're very late for your appointment," my mom said as soon as I walked in. "And the early bird catches the worm." She hustled me to the door of the front office.

Mom didn't look like a doctor today. Her hair was pulled back into a bun, with curls escaping at her temples. Her jeans were cut off just above the knees, and her toenails were unpainted in cheap flip-flops. An oversize Lauryn Hill T-shirt hid her curves. She had a paper shopping bag under her arm and smelled like cigarette smoke. Another parent in the waiting room gave my mother a scandalized look. Usually, I'd have been totally mortified to have my mom come to school looking homeless, but under these circumstances I was just worried.

"Is everything all right?" I asked.

"It's not a big deal, really," she said, taking my hand and leading me out of the office. "I'll explain in the car. Let's go by your locker to get your books."

"Just tell me," I said. "Is Dad okay?"

"Of course," she said. "This has nothing to do with him."

I breathed a sigh of relief. As a climate-change researcher, Dad traveled to Arctic environments for weeks or even months at a time, and it was hard to contact him when he was out in the field.

Mom hurried me down the wide hallway, past cases of academic and athletic trophies, past photos of distinguished alumni with mostly white faces.

I opened my locker, and Mom began scooping out all of my stuff.

"I only need my—" I began, but she cut me off.

"No time to pick and choose," she said, and handed me the double paper shopping bag. "Just grab it all."

I loaded the stack of books and my set of spare clothes into the bag, then looked up to see her rubbing a cloth along the edge of my locker door.

"Mom, are you wiping off my locker?" I asked.

"You know I clean when I'm anxious," she said, almost snapping.

"Does this have anything to do with that creepy guy behind our house?" I asked.

Mom's brows knit. "No, not at all." She nudged me forward. "Come on—time waits for no one."

The moment we stepped out of the school's front doors, I stopped moving. "Tell me what's going on," I demanded.

"In the car," she promised.

I refused to budge.

She looked me fully in the face for the first time. Her eyes were wide and imploring but also scared. I'd never seen her like this.

"My love, please," she begged.

I relented and we rushed down the school steps. Her phone started ringing, and when she glanced at it, I saw a number that had an unfamiliar area code. She shut the ringer off.

Our minivan was parked hastily in the red zone in front, an eyesore among the legions of luxury cars.

Mom opened the dented door, and a strong smell

of smoke greeted me. The back of our minivan was packed to the roof. It looked like she had stuffed in just about everything we owned. I felt panicked looking at a wicker basket that held all my baby pictures mixed up with a bunch of computer drives and chargers.

"What is this, Mom?" I demanded. "And have you been smoking?"

"Of course not—smoking is bad for your health," she said as we got in and buckled up. She reached out and took my hand gently. "There was a fire at the house today, my love."

"Are you okay?" I asked, my own eyes wide now.

"I'm fine," she said, speeding out of the school's driveway. "I got everything out that I could." She tilted her head to indicate all the stuff in the back.

"Is the damage serious?" I asked.

She nodded. "We won't be able to stay there for a while."

"How long?" I asked.

"I don't know," she said. "But it's going to be okay. And I got your fire suitcase."

Her reassurances did little to loosen the constriction in my chest.

The fire suitcase.

When my mom was a teenager, her house burned down and she lost everything. So from the time I was six, she insisted that I keep a suitcase under my bed packed with all my important stuff: my journals, my photos, my favorite books, my laptop, and a few baby things. "Anything that can't be replaced," she had always said.

I had humored her all these years. I figured, what are the odds that two generations of a small family would have fires?

Apparently, the chances were greater than I thought.

"Did you call nine one one?" I asked.

"Of course," she said. "But it was too late. By the time the firefighters came, it was almost burned to the ground."

Suddenly, I realized how lucky I was, and I felt like I might cry. My mom had survived two fires in her life. What if she hadn't escaped this time? What if I had lost her? With Dad away and out of range, what would I even have done without her? We stopped at a light, and impulsively I undid my seat belt and threw my arms around her. "Mommy, I'm so glad you're okay!"

She squeezed me tight in the awkward car hug, and we held on for a moment, until the truck behind us beeped. I went back to my seat, and Mom wiped her eyes as she sped down the street.

Had I really just called her "Mommy"?

Her phone rang again, silently this time. That same unfamiliar area-code number. She powered the phone off and dropped it into the compartment between the front seats.

I opened my mouth to ask about it, but then she wiped one hand across her eyes. Was she wiping away tears? Or just soot? Either way, she definitely looked shaken.

"Where are we gonna go?" I asked instead. We didn't have any family in Los Angeles, or any close friends, really. We had lived here when I was a kid, but in fourth grade, we'd moved away to DC. We had come back only six months ago, and by then, nearly all of our old friends had moved away. We had to start over, which was even more of a challenge because Dad had been away for most of that time—his most recent trip had been months already. Mom worked long hours at a local clinic, and I was drowning under the hours of homework at Penfield. Neither of us had much time for a social life.

Penfield Academy was a really academically intense school, and I had a scholarship to maintain. My parents had said they picked it because it was especially strong in science, and they were both in STEM fields. The school was known for graduating "well-rounded" kids to the Ivy Leagues because they had every single sport, every single kind of science club, ten different debate teams, and several student councils to focus on different areas of the school. As a result, each year they graduated thirty athletic team captains, five student council presidents, twenty debate team coleaders, and seventy-two club presidents. There were only two hundred kids in the school, and most of them were on ten different clubs in name only. Half of the clubs, like the Antiquities Society, never even had meetings.

I wasn't the only Black girl at Penfield; I was just the only Black girl who didn't fit in. There were long-haired, willowy Black girls with designer clothes and BMWs who fit in just fine. Some had actress moms or athlete dads, or both. But none of them was rushing to befriend the sophomore-year new arrival, the plus-size Black girl who wore African braids like something out of *National Geographic* because her mother wouldn't let her flat-iron her hair. Mom always says that beauty is in the eye of the beholder, and I try to tell her that the kids at Penfield *be holding* ideas of beauty that don't include this Black girl. But even if I did flat-iron my hair, the lowest tips would only graze my shoulders. It grew that long, and no longer.

My phone chimed, and I glanced down and saw an alert that I was a contest winner.

I didn't think anything could possibly lift my mood, but I picked up the phone and forgot our troubles for a moment.

"Mom! I won tickets to a Deza concert!" Deza Starling was my favorite rap artist. She had been a little more rough and sexy in her early work, but she was really positive now, rapping about the need for Black women to get respect and even about the climate crisis.

I thought Mom would offer one of her pat sayings: "See? Bad times don't last forever" or "The sun always comes out again." But instead, she snapped, "Let me see your phone."

I handed it over, and she powered my phone off with one hand as she turned the wheel with the other.

"Mom, what are you doing?" I asked.

"Dad has some equipment in the back that doesn't interact well with cell phones," she said. "You wouldn't want your whole phone wiped, would you?"

"No, but what's going on? There's something you're not telling me," I insisted. "I gotta turn off my phone? You keep getting calls from some weird number? Our house burned down? What the hell, Mom?" She was scaring me. Normally she was like a Stepford mom or something, all empty words and calm smiles. But now she felt . . . intense.

"You're right," she said. "I'm trying not to freak you out, but I can see it's not working. I'm scared the fire might have been set deliberately."

"Who would do that?" I asked, bewildered.

"I don't know," she said. "As a climate-change scientist, your dad gets threats from time to time. Corporations stand to lose a lot of money if we break our fossil-fuel dependence."

"You think they'd come after Dad?" I asked. "Burn our house down?"

"I have no idea," Mom said. "I just know that if someone's intentionally targeting our family, I don't want them to be able to track our phones."

"Track our phones?" I asked. I looked at Mom's cell phone and realized it wasn't the usual one she used.

"I'm not saying someone is," Mom said. "I'm just saying they might. I don't know yet. Please, love. Please just be patient with me. Everything's going to be okay. We just need to get where we're going so I can think."

"Where the hell are we going?"

"Do you remember Sister Niema?" Mom asked. "We're going to her house. We're going to stay there. I think she can help me figure this out."

Everything about the last half hour had been almost surreal. A fake doctor's appointment. Our house burned down. Don't use the phone. We'll stay with Sister Niema. Dimly, I recalled a Black woman with her head wrapped in African cloth who used to run a sort of Afrocentric Saturday school.

While my Jewish friends went to Hebrew school and my Chinese friends went to Mandarin school, I went to Harambee Girls Leadership, where we learned that Black people invented science and that the fortunes of the West were built by the labor of enslaved people.

I think my parents expected it to have more of an effect than it did on my everyday life. But when a group of skinny, wealthy white girls are laughing at you when you're squeezing into the largest-size gym shorts and they barely fit, you can't exactly yell back, "Your great-grandfather's money came from my people sweating in the cotton fields, and Africa brought indoor plumbing to Europe!" And when every boy you like in middle school likes a pretty white or mixed girl with long, wavy hair, you can't exactly say, "Queen Nzingha kicked the asses of Portuguese slave traders and colonizers in West Africa and was a symbol of fierce Black beauty, so will you take me to the spring dance?"

I know my parents meant well, but if they thought that African art and Black books in our house were gonna counteract all the messages I got in prep schools, they were wrong. Even in pre-K and elementary, when I went to hippie schools where we got to run around without shoes and the teachers asked the kids what we wanted to learn, I was still that raisin in the oatmeal. You can't really feel good about being Black when you're busy being Black all by yourself. Two hours on a Saturday isn't enough. I really liked some of the other girls, but we lived so far from one another that I almost never saw them. They came to my birthday party one year, and it was awkward. The Harambee girls sat together, and my white/Latinx/Asian/mixed friends from school sat in a separate cluster. I ran back and forth between groups.

◆ ◆ ◆

We finally got off the freeway sometime after 6 p.m. We exited in a part of Los Angeles that I only vaguely recalled. Some of the buildings looked familiar, but the place was really run-down. I had never realized it when I was little, but I definitely noticed it now: Sister Niema lived in the hood.

I felt a little anxious as we drove through the streets, past liquor stores and knots of guys hanging out on the corner. Eventually, we came to a single-story bungalow with peeling tan paint. I expected my mom to pull up in front of the house, but instead she reached into our van's glove compartment and pulled out an automatic garage door opener. Why did she have a remote for someone else's garage? There was something my mother wasn't telling me. I heard a grinding sound, and the wood-paneled garage door slid up, beckoning us inside.

Two

Mom let herself into Sister Niema's house with a key—another weird sign.

"Mom, how come you—?"

"Please, love," she said. "Just give me a moment to land before all the questions."

Okay, fine. She could have a moment to land. But I wasn't going to let her put my questions off all night. With the anxiety humming in my chest, there was no way I would be able to sleep till I got some answers.

If the outside of Sister Niema's house was run-down, the inside was the opposite—cozy and inviting. It was the smell that hit me first. A deep woodsy frankincense that took me back to when I was in single digits. Back then, I ran a little wild, but at Harambee, in Sister Niema's house, there was none of that. Not that she was strict; just structured. We always felt safe and secure. I recognized the decor: she still had a giant ebony ankh mirror; a golden bust of Nefertiti; and a Mount Rushmore–style painting with the heads of Malcolm X, Sojourner Truth, Marcus Garvey, and Ella Baker.

Sister Niema came out from the kitchen, looking pretty much the same, except that the wisps of hair that stuck out from her African head wrap were now streaked with gray, and her peanut butter skin had maybe a few more wrinkles.

"Carmen," Sister Niema greeted my mom. "What's going on?"

"And why do you have a key to Sister Niema's house?" I asked.

"Every woman should have someone else's key in case of trouble," Sister Niema said. She turned back to Mom. "So what's the trouble?"

"Our house burned down," I said.

"Lord help us," Sister Niema said. "I thought I smelled fire. You all better sit down and let me make you some tea."

I went to the bathroom first. I hadn't realized I'd been sort of holding it through the ride.

When I came back, Sister Niema sat us down on her burgundy-colored couch with steaming mugs of some home brew that was supposed to relieve stress.

The couch was firm, but the upholstery was faded and worn. I remembered it from before.

"A fire at your house, you said?"

Mom nodded. "But there's a little more to it than that."

"What more?" I asked. Absently, I tried a sip of the tea and burned my tongue.

Mom fidgeted with the seam on the couch's upholstery. "Amani, I've been with your dad a long time," she began. "But of course, I had boyfriends before him."

"Yeah," I said. I ran the tip of my tongue along the inside of my teeth. "So?"

"So one of them wasn't a good guy," she said. "And he—he turned up."

"And burned down our house?" I asked, setting the mug down.

"I got a message on the way here that made me almost sure it was him," she said.

I felt a knot of panic in my chest constrict. "Oh my God," I said. "Did you call the police? You need to report him."

Mom looked at Sister Niema. "He works in law enforcement," she said.

"It's not really safe to talk with the authorities in a situation like that," Sister Niema said.

"We need to lie low for a little while until we can make a plan," Mom said.

"You can stay here as long as you need to," Sister Niema said.

"Wait!" I said. "Was it the guy from the backyard last night?"

"The guy from—" Mom began, then stopped herself. "Oh God, no. I saw the photo on your phone. Definitely not him. I—I have no idea who that guy was."

So there was more than one guy prowling around the house? What was going on? "Okay," I said, trying to keep calm. "So we stay here. But what about school?"

"You won't be able to go back right now," Mom said. She took several large swigs of the tea in her mug. I was still reeling. This guy was so dangerous that we couldn't call the police? He had burned down our house?

Sister Niema wrote something down on a sticky note and handed it to my mom. "Here's the information so you can enroll Amani in the high school down the street."

I was going to a different school? What? Because he might find me and get to Mom?

The panic in my chest became unbearable. It felt like all the air was being squeezed out of me. "No, no, no!" I said. "This is too much. I can't deal!"

I tried to leap up off the couch, but Sister Niema held on to me. At five feet eleven inches, I was taller and heavier, but her arms were surprisingly strong. She sat me back down and pressed one hand on my chest.

"You're safe, Amani," she said, looking me straight

in the eye. "You're gonna stay here, and your mom and I are going to keep you safe."

I burst into tears.

"Amani." Mom leaned over to hug me.

I crumpled onto the familiar burgundy couch and sobbed.

I put my head in Mom's lap, and Sister Niema put her arms around me.

"It's going to be okay, my love," Mom assured me in a voice that didn't sound completely confident.

"Yes," Sister Niema said in her soothing contralto voice. "It's gonna be fine, after a while. With a loss like this, there's some grieving to do. You've both been brave until now, but no need to be strong. Let yourself go, Carmen."

It took me a minute to realize that Mom was crying, too. She didn't sob like I did, but I could hear a little catch in her breath from time to time. When I looked up, her face was wet.

After we'd both had our meltdowns, Sister Niema walked us into the narrow kitchen. I remembered eating snacks at the long wooden table off metal plates that had safari animals on them. Now she served up dinner in ceramic bowls.

"Why don't you all eat while I unload the car, okay?" Sister Niema asked.

I nodded. The cry had left me spent and hungry.

We sat down at one end of the battered wooden table. In the bowls was some kind of bean and kale concoction. I tasted it tentatively. The spices were different but good. It needed salt, but there wasn't any on the table.

Mom pushed her food around with a faraway look in her eyes. I didn't ask for salt.

Eventually, Sister Niema came back in to join us, and Mom leaned back from the table, abandoning her food. Then I was facing three Black women: Sister Niema, Mom, and Lauryn Hill, looking out from Mom's T-shirt. Mom always said she got that shirt at a concert in New York City, Lauryn's hometown. Which was kind of weird because wasn't Lauryn Hill from New Jersey? Besides, I could never quite picture Mom at a concert like that, because she's sort of like a Black TV mom, with her doctor job and her perfectly rectangular meat loaf. But here we were at Sister Niema's because some dangerous ex of my mom's might have burned down our house, so obviously she was more complicated than I thought.

By the time we finished dinner—I ate two bowls and Mom barely finished half of hers—it was almost ten o'clock. Mom took a shower, and I went up to our room to get ready for bed.

Against the wall, Sister Niema had stacked up all the stuff from our van. I pulled out some pictures from the wicker basket, lay down on the queen bed, and spread out the photos. There I was as a baby, wearing a yellow onesie, in a room with periwinkle-flowered wallpaper. The next couple of shots were just me lying on the bed with different expressions, and then one of my parents holding me. Mom and Dad looked young and bright-eyed. I missed Dad so much.

I picked up my phone to email him and remembered again what had happened. Wait. Did he know?

I stepped into the steamy bathroom. "Mom, does Dad know about the fire?"

She stuck her head around the shower curtain. "I sent a message," she said. "I'm just not sure how soon he'll get it."

A few minutes later, Mom came into the bedroom, a towel over her hair and no longer smelling like smoke.

She collapsed onto the bed and leaned in close. Her arm was touching mine, her skin still moist from the shower. How come Mom's skin seems glowy, but after I take a shower, I feel sort of clammy?

She lay on her back, exposing her loose belly, complete with stretch marks. Mom just really didn't care about modesty. It was her one trait that was totally out of character with the Perfect American TV Mom thing. You'd think she was like one of those dolls that had underwear molded into the plastic. But one minute my mom was baking cookies that were all the same size, and the next she was acting like some hippie nudist.

Thankfully I never had friends over anyway, so I didn't have to worry about explaining her to them.

"Hey, Mom," I asked. "Who were you messaging in the car?"

She yawned. "Sister Niema."

"But she has a local LA area code." She'd given me her cell number in case of emergency. "Who was calling from that other number?"

Mom shook her head. "Telemarketers," she said. "Really robocalls. 'You're a finalist to win a vacation to Hawaii! Just sign up for this service . . .'"

That reminded me of the Deza tickets I'd won. The message said they were sending them to my email. My main account was AKAK213@yeemail.com, because Mom, always overprotective, insisted I had to have fake names on my personal email addresses.

"At least I really did win those concert tickets," I said.

Mom sighed. "I'm sorry, my love," she said. "That's just more bad news. You can't go. And we need to stay off email for a while."

I opened my mouth to protest. The chances that going to the concert would lead to danger seemed laughable. But then again, any guy who would burn our house to the ground and send Mom on the run was not to be tested.

THREE

Roosevelt High was huge compared to any school I'd ever attended before. It was made up of several long gray buildings that were basically boxes with a big stripe of windows across the middle. It would have looked like a college if it weren't so run-down.

The traffic in the school parking lot was congested, but an SUV playing loud rap pulled away from the curb as we approached, and Mom took their parking space for our minivan. She locked the car, and we walked toward the scraggly lawn.

Several city buses had stopped at the curb, and a steady stream of brown kids emerged, laughing and talking loudly. We were surrounded by more Black teenagers than I had ever seen in one place. I had hoped to have this experience at the Deza concert, but I guess that wasn't gonna happen. Still, one of the girls was playing Deza so loud in her headphones that I could hear it from a few feet away.

We moved with the crowd to the double doors of the building, but things slowed down a bit when we had to walk through a metal detector. Most of us got to walk through with our backpacks, but a few kids got pulled aside, their bags searched. I'd heard about schools with metal detectors before, but I'd never experienced it.

Once we got through the security checkpoint, we followed the signs that said MAIN OFFICE. There were lockers along the walls, with slightly mismatched patches where they had clearly painted over graffiti. In the hallway, the talking, shouts, and laughter were punctuated by the banging sound of locker doors slamming shut.

We ducked into the front office, where all the seats were taken and several students were standing. At the desk, a young man was trying to convince the school secretary that his note was not a forgery. "For real, it's my mama signature right there."

"I know your mama doesn't spell absent with an *i*, Cornelius."

"Come on, Mrs. J. Call me Neal like everybody else."

"Just give it up, bruh," one of the boys on the chairs said. "She ain't gonna excuse you. Now other people got business here."

Neal let out a sigh that was half growl and snatched his note off the counter.

Mrs. J turned to my mother. "New student?" she asked.

My mom nodded.

Mrs. J opened the low gate. "Right this way." She motioned for us to wait outside the vice principal's office.

As we stood there, a police officer stepped into the main office. He pointed at one of the kids waiting in line.

"Me?" a young Black man asked, and the cop nodded. "What?" the boy demanded. "I didn't do nothing!"

"Come on." The cop made a beckoning motion.

"This ain't fair," the young man said. "I want the restorative justice lady."

Before we could see any more, the office door opened and two young Latinx women walked out. They looked directly at me, their stares challenging. I dropped my eyes to the floor.

When I glanced back up, the VP motioned us in and closed the door behind us. He was a harassed-looking Black man in his forties, with a bald spot on top of his head. He wore a rumpled white shirt and an African mud-cloth tie.

Mom handed him my forms, and we sat down as he flipped through them. Mom had coached me in the car on the way over. My name would be Imani instead of

Amani: close enough that I would answer but not the same, so it wouldn't be found in a search. And instead of Kendall, my last name would be Kennedy.

"Your daughter's been homeschooled all this time?" the vice principal asked. "Why the change?"

"Sister Niema has been encouraging us to consider it," Mom said.

The VP smiled. "Niema and I go way back."

"We wanted Imani to have more social opportunities," Mom said.

Outside the window, I heard a girl say to her friends, "I told her, I'll slap the smile right off your ugly face."

"Well," the VP said. "There are lots of social opportunities here at Roosevelt."

Mom just smiled and nodded.

Next, I needed to get a schedule. The computer was down, so Mrs. J in the front office set it up for me. By the time she was done, first period was nearly over, and the school was much quieter.

Mom glanced out at some boys clowning around in the hallway.

"I'm tellin' you they took all that fool's money," the first boy said, laughing.

"Aw, hell naw," the second one said, laughing just as loud.

My mom turned to me. "It's only temporary," she murmured. "Just lie low and we'll figure it out, okay?

I'll be here at three thirty to pick you up. Will you be all right?"

I could tell she needed me to be. "I'll be fine," I said, ignoring my heart banging against my ribs so loud I thought she might be able to hear it.

"Okay, my love," she said.

We both stood, and she gave me a quick tight hug, but I pulled back. Did she have to embarrass me on day one? This didn't look like a school with a lot of cookie-baking, hug-giving moms.

Just as she stepped into the hallway, the bell rang for second period, and my mom was swallowed up in a crush of students.

"Um, excuse me," I asked Mrs. J. "Do you have a campus map or something, so I can find my class?"

She peered at my schedule. "I'll have my second-period office aide take you. She can show you to your locker as well."

The aide turned out to be a petite Asian girl named Linda who barely spoke a word. She had a few tasks to finish after the second bell rang, so it was about half-way through the period by the time she finally guided me to my locker, which was near the front office. It took a few tries to open it, but I managed. It was warm in the school, so I took off my jacket and stuffed it in. I had on the jeans from my old locker. I'd tried to wear the same T-shirt as yesterday, but it was red, and Sister Niema said you couldn't wear red or blue at Roosevelt.

She had loaned me a black shirt that read BLACK AND PROUD. It fit more snugly than I was used to, but it was all I had. Today Sister Niema was washing the smoke smell out of the clothes my mom had saved.

Linda escorted me down the long corridor and out onto the wide cement yard. Apparently, the history classes were in another building.

As we walked across the concrete, I heard some boys yelling out.

"Hey, girl! Can you slow down?"

"Why don't you come and talk to us?"

I did a sort of double take, realizing they were looking our way.

"Hey, you! Pretty girl! Come talk to us."

"Do those guys harass you every day?" I asked Linda.

She busted out laughing.

"What's so funny?" I asked. "Sexual harassment is not a joke. It can interfere with your education."

Once she could contain her laughter, she looked me in the face. "Don't you know they're talking to you?"

"What?" I turned to the boys, horrified.

There were three of them leaning on the edge of a cement planter, the tree inside spindly and dry.

"Yes, you, the thick one," one of them said.

I whipped my head back around, feeling my face flaming hot. We were at the doors of the Humanities building, and I tugged desperately at the door handle.

Linda pushed the door on the right, and it opened. I practically ran over her trying to get into the building.

"Always walk on the right," she said.

I nodded, not trusting my voice to speak. I wished I had a camping tent to hide in. Mostly to hide my butt.

"Here's your history class," Linda said, and she turned to walk back to the office.

I thanked her and lingered outside the class for a moment. The hall was empty, and I pressed my face to the cool metal of the locker.

I heard a door open, and a girl walked past.

"Tryna look in your man's locker?" she asked.

"No, I—"

"Let me save you some trouble," she said. "All these boys is cheaters. Dump his ass."

"B-but I don't . . ." I stammered after her, but she was already out the door.

My face had cooled off somewhat. I pulled out my phone and checked my face, using the dark screen as a mirror. I was medium brown-skinned, so the blush didn't show. I twisted the door handle and walked into class.

Thirty desks faced the chalkboard, which read "Cause and Effect." Below it was listed "WWII," "Civil Rights," and "Women's Movement." Students sat at their desks with eyes up, down, or sideways. The teacher was a Black guy, and my schedule said he was Mr. Iroko. He had a familiar face, like an actor who you've seen in another show but can't place.

"Nobody?" he said. "Nobody can tell me anything about cause and effect here?"

He turned to me. "Yes, can I help you?"

"I'm new," I said, and handed him my schedule.

He nodded. "Class, meet Imani," he said, and indicated that I should take a seat on the far left.

"She can share my desk!" a young man in the back volunteered. "Maybe she could sit on my lap."

The class laughed, and I felt my face burning again.

Mr. Iroko looked sharply at the young man. "That's your second warning," he said as I slunk into the indicated seat.

"Nobody read the chapter last night?" Mr. Iroko asked. "Everybody's getting an F for the day? Can one person tell us how this relates to cause and effect?"

"That's not fair," one girl said. "I tried to do that boring reading, but it didn't really say anything about civil rights or the women's movement."

I glanced down at the textbook. It was called *The Roots of Our Melting Pot*, and it looked like it was from the 1980s.

"That's right," the teacher said. "I need you to use your critical thinking skills to make the connections. What did it say about women and African Americans in the war?"

Another boy piped up: "Rosie the Riveter and the Tuskegee Airmen."

"You're getting warmer," the teacher said. "If anybody can get the answer, you can use your phones until the end of the period."

"Oh my God," said one girl. "I seriously need to message my boyfriend. Anybody who can answer this damn question would be *'saaaaving . . . two hearts from breaaaaking,'*" she said, singing a line from a current pop song.

I slowly raised my hand.

"Yes," Mr. Iroko said, looking down at my schedule. "Imani?"

"Well, women went to work, and Black men fought in World War Two. It raised their expectations. Then, in the next couple of decades, the larger society tried to push them back down. But people had a taste of equality, so both groups organized to fight for their rights."

"Bam," Mr. Iroko said, dropping the eraser like it was a microphone. "That's how you do it. Ten minutes of phone time. And I'll be coming by, so make sure it's safe for work."

"Show-off," mumbled the girl who wanted to message her boyfriend.

I couldn't believe it. Didn't she ask for someone to step in? Ungrateful much?

I pulled out my phone, which was still on airplane

mode at Mom's insistence. I flipped through photos. There was one of me and Mom at the beach that Dad had taken. Mom and I both had on tankinis, and I studied our bodies. She wore her weight more in the middle. Meanwhile, my body was so mismatched that my tankini top was three sizes smaller than the bottom. We bought them in a big ladies' catalog.

Mom didn't seem to care that a strip of brown was showing between her top and bottom with fine, silvery stretch marks across the soft skin. I wanted to reach through the picture and tug down her top to cover it.

I enlarged the photo so I could see my own body more clearly. Usually I didn't look at myself this closely, but I was trying to see what the boys saw. My shoulders were narrow, and my torso was long. My chest was—I don't know—between small and medium? My stomach was flat, but my butt, hips, and thighs were big. Then my legs tapered down to narrow ankles.

In the bathing suit, I was way bigger than any bikini models I ever saw. My behind was bigger than even the models in the plus-size catalog. I looked more like some bigger girls I'd seen once in a rap video. But that video was more mortifying than affirming, with the sexy way they were dancing and the camera cutting back and forth between their backsides and their chests. It didn't feel anything like me.

I shrank the photo back to normal size and looked at me and Mom, laughing and splashing in the waves, until I felt a shadow over my desk. I looked up to see Mr. Iroko. "So," he said as he handed back my schedule. "What school are you coming from?"

I almost said Penfield Academy, before I remembered my story. I kept my voice low. "I was homeschooled."

"Oh," he said, his voice decidedly *not* lowered. "Homeschooled. Your parents did a good job with critical thinking skills."

"I guess . . ." I said.

I heard a few kids around me mumbling "homeschool?"

Thankfully, the bell rang.

I picked up my backpack and checked my schedule, grateful to see that my next class was in the same building, one floor up.

As I squeezed out of the classroom door, someone pressed in next to me. It was the boy who'd invited me to sit on his lap. "Homeschooled?" he said. "Yo parents was scared to let a girl fine as you out in these streets."

I couldn't speak. I just swallowed and shook my head rapidly from side to side, my cheeks aflame.

When the lunch bell rang, it took me a minute to get my bearings. I hurried to my locker and put my jacket back on. The coat was too warm, but it was better than dealing with the comments chasing after my butt and the fire in my face.

As I stood outside my locker, I could hear a girl a couple lockers down whispering into a phone.

"I swear to God," she raged. "If she really messing with my man, I will—" She broke off as she saw a police officer appear farther down the hall. She turned toward her locker and continued in a whisper. "I will snatch that ugly weave out her head so fast . . . Did *you* see her in the car? You know yo cousin like to start drama. I'm not tryna get expelled from school if the girl was just standing next to his damn car."

I quietly closed my locker and zipped up my jacket. I had my lunch bag in my hand but had no idea where I should go to eat.

I walked out past the cop—the same guy from the office that morning. Did the school have its own police officer?

In the cement yard, I looked around. No grass. A few spindly trees. Weeds grew up through cracks in the asphalt. To my right, several boys and a girl played basketball. To the left was something that looked like it used to be a fountain but was now just a cement ring that kids sat on. A line of benches curved around it. Most of them were filled with clusters of kids eating pizza. An express snack bar at the far end of the yard did a brisk business in slices.

I found a spot under a tree to eat the lunch that Sister Niema packed for me: sunflower butter and apricot jam on multigrain bread. It was a far cry from what

I was used to in the gourmet dining hall at Penfield: organic salads with roast beef and sweet potato fries. But the sandwich was comforting and familiar. I ate it and tried to become invisible.

The rest of the day was more of the same, but I kept my coat on and my mouth shut. I don't think I've ever been as happy to see my mom's face as I was at three thirty.

"So?" she asked. "How was it? Why do you still have your coat on? It's blazing."

I reached forward and turned on the AC. "It was awful," I said. "The students don't care about learning. The teachers have the world's lowest expectations. The textbooks are decades out of date. And the grounds look like a postapocalyptic landscape." I unzipped my jacket. "And I kept my jacket on because, apparently, I have a neon sign on my butt that says 'Check me out! Extra points for nasty comments.'"

Mom blinked. "Oh, I'm so sorry, my love."

"I didn't like Penfield, but at least they had a decent library that I could escape into. I'm not going back to Roosevelt. We said I was homeschooled, so if I can't go back to Penfield, then I'm ready to be homeschooled."

"Mmmmm," Mom said noncommittally. "Let's not put the cart before the horse. First off, remember how you always used to say you were fat, and I always said you were curvy? Well, you're finally in an environment where people agree with me."

"Mom, I weighed almost twice as much as the other girls at Penfield. 'Curvy' is a word people use to your face when they say 'fat' behind your back."

"I get that Penfield was a body-shaming environment," she said. "The truth is that the word 'fat' shouldn't be an insult anyway. Every human body has fat on it or the person would die. I know that as a doctor." She put a hand on my shoulder. "But as a mom, I'm sorry I wasn't paying attention this morning. We'll get you something less formfitting. But I can't homeschool you. I've got to work at the clinic."

"Is that safe?" I asked, suddenly worried. "Can that guy find you?"

Mom shook her head. "No way. They have me on call out in the field. Nobody has the location but my boss, and she knows what's going on. So we're safe, my love."

"What about Sister Niema?" I asked. "Can she homeschool me? She always used to tell us to read books."

"She works, too."

"I can stay home by myself, then. I'm fifteen and a half."

"I don't want you falling behind in school."

"Did you hear what I said?" I asked. "I'm not learning anything anyway. And you said this is only temporary."

She shook her head. "I'll ask Sister Niema if she has ideas on how to make Roosevelt work."

"Mom, I'll go to the public library," I pleaded. "I'll check out books for all my subjects. I promise to read them all. I swear I'll learn more that way than if I stay at Roosevelt."

"You need to stick it out, my love," Mom said. "If at first you don't succeed, try, try again."

I should have known better than to ask Mom. She's practically a robot. It's like she doesn't even care.

We came to a freeway entrance, and I expected Mom to get on the freeway we usually take to our house. But then she passed the entrance, and I remembered that we no longer had a house. Just a stack of boxes and baskets and a couple of suitcases of our most prized possessions. The loss hit me all over again.

"I'm really tired, Mom," I said. I cranked up the AC and pulled the hood of my jacket over my head. I leaned my face against the passenger window. I wasn't tired. I just didn't want Mom to get all worried and upset if she saw me crying. I didn't sob or hiccup. Just let the tears slip down. At one point, I reached in my pocket to take out my phone to call Dad. Then I remembered I couldn't. So I just cried some more.

After dinner, I felt restless and bored. When I went to Penfield, I had hours and hours of homework. Now I had almost none, and I wasn't allowed to use my phone.

I sighed and went looking for my old backpack from Penfield to find the book I was reading. Everything was all jumbled together, and while I didn't find my backpack, I came across a familiar purple notebook. My cipher book! It was a game my dad and I had played since I started kindergarten. Every time he traveled, he would send me coded letters, and I would figure out how to decode them. Obviously, they had gotten harder over the years.

The first one of the latest series that he had given me had looked like this:

BNBOJ J DBOU XBJU UP HFU IPNF UP TFF ZPV.

The BNBOJ was the key. I'd realized that my name, AMANI, was likely to show up in his message, and the repeated letter in AMA would be a clue. Here, BNB could become AMA if each of the letters was one later in the alphabet. It decoded to AMANI I CAN'T WAIT TO GET HOME TO SEE YOU.

The second in the series was more difficult, and I hadn't cracked it yet. First of all, he didn't put my name at the beginning. Second of all, he also used numbers.

9 I51CCP D9MM RFN 1D1E9.

I pulled out a pencil and played around with it for a bit, finally zeroing in on the 1D1. I realized that maybe he had used my name again, and 1D1 could be AMA, too. It didn't take much longer to deduce that he had started his alphabet with numbers 1–9 and then continued with the alphabet from A. So, 1 = A, 2 = B, 3 = C, until 9 = I. And then A = J. It decoded to I REALLY MISS YOU AMANI.

I looked back over the ciphers. Somewhere out there, probably on a block of ice, my dad was missing me. Maybe even making up a new code for me to crack. It cheered me up a little.

FOUR

I lay awake in bed the next morning feeling leaden. It was like the shock was lifting and reality was setting in. Our house had burned down. Dad might not even know yet because he was out in the field. Mom had some old boyfriend stalking her, and we were on the run. It was too much. I stared at the horizontal stripes of morning light filtering in between the blinds. In my old room, I had soft cotton curtains in a bold shade of turquoise. They must have burned as quickly as paper.

Mom opened the door to our room and tiptoed in. I closed my eyes as soon as I heard the doorknob turn and pretended to still be asleep. I didn't even need to open my eyes to know Mom had taken a shower. I could smell the shampoo in her hair and feel the steam from the bathroom rising off her body. She toweled off, and I could hear her creeping around getting dressed.

Mom has always, you know, loved me and taken care of me, but she's really . . . well . . . boring. I mean, her personality is so bland. Other than the love, what is there? I love her and everything, but I don't always really feel *connected* to her. I couldn't imagine her having some stalker ex-boyfriend. Mom's like a news anchor or something. She has this standard accent. She doesn't curse. There's nothing quirky about her. She's a great cook and gives good hugs, but when she talks, it's full of clichés. It's like she's a singer for a foreign pop band, singing in English. Like she doesn't know the language and is just singing phonetically.

And it's also weird that she's so comfortable in her own body. Like how she just roams around the room naked. Who does that? It's like she walks past the same magazine covers that I do, but she's miraculously immune to every ounce of LA pressure to look like a Barbie doll. Why can't she be more like a normal mom?

She put on a long-sleeve cotton shirt and jeans for work and left the room, leaving the door open a crack. Eventually, the smell of cinnamon and honey drifted in—not just oatmeal but some kind of baked thing.

I didn't feel like getting up. But I had to pee. And at the other end of that smell was something I wanted to eat. I shuffled out to the kitchen by way of the bathroom and found Sister Niema and Mom sitting at the table with a half-eaten cinnamon roll in front of each of them and a steaming pan between them holding a half dozen more.

"Good morning," I said, reaching for one.

Mom swatted my hand. "You need to eat some protein first."

I grabbed the one from her plate. "Just one bite," I said. It was delicious: flaky, sweet, and spicy, with a little clove and ginger.

"Oh my God, that's so good," I said through the mouthful of dough.

"Not bad, considering it's gluten-free," Sister Niema said.

I wanted to take back some of my liking, but it was too late. And too good.

Mom got up and went to the stove, stirring some scrambled eggs.

"So what's this grand plan?" I asked Sister Niema. "Mom said you have some ideas to improve my school situation?"

"You need reinforcements at Roosevelt," she said.

"I need them to tear Roosevelt down and start over," I said.

Mom froze, the bamboo spoon hanging in midair, covered with pale yellow flecks of egg. Sister Niema closed her eyes and took a deep breath.

What did I say wrong?

"That seems pretty wasteful," Mom said lightly,

like she was trying to make a joke. "You recycle your leftovers, but you want to put a whole school in the garbage?"

Her efforts didn't reduce the tension in the room at all.

"Amani," Sister Niema started quietly. I remembered that voice. Back when we were kids, she had used that voice when one of the most rambunctious girls had broken her lamp.

I looked up at her, a chunk of cinnamon roll in my hand. I wanted to pop it in my mouth, but it was clearly time to sit still and listen.

"Amani, there are over four thousand kids at that school. How many did you meet yesterday? Meet and actually talk with?"

Some of the cinnamon roll's sugar was sticking to my fingers.

"Even one?" she asked.

I dropped my eyes. Suddenly I'd lost my appetite for the cinnamon roll.

"No . . ."

"So you've prejudged a whole school based on what? The clothes they wore? A little street language?"

I pressed my index finger and thumb together and then pulled them apart, feeling the resistance of the sugar's stickiness.

"I told your parents not to send you to those bougie white schools for just this reason," Sister Niema went on. "You need to learn how to live among your people."

My mouth was tight, and I could feel the tears coming. Mom sat down next to me and put her arm around me. I wanted to shrug it off, but I also kind of didn't, so I just stayed put.

"I know some of those kids are a little rough around the edges," Mom said.

"A little rough?" I said. "Do you know what the boys were saying to me? All day. Not just one boy or two. It seemed like every single one was looking at me like a piece of meat."

I set the chunk of cinnamon roll back down on Mom's plate.

Sister Niema nodded. "Okay, that's real," she said. "I hadn't thought about what it would be like to have the sexual harassment ramp up from where you used to live."

"Ramp up?" I asked. "At my old school, nobody ever said anything about my butt, except that it was in need of surgical reduction."

Sister Niema shook her head. "All that plastic surgery and dieting talk is from white people with too much money and nothing to do."

"But I can see how it would give you whiplash to go from Penfield to Roosevelt," Mom said.

Sister Niema nodded. "I guess I got toughened up to it. Or not. Maybe that's why I wear loose dresses to this day."

"I want to take self-defense," I blurted out. Some guy creeping around our backyard. Some guy stalking my mom. Guys harassing me at school. I wanted more than my dad's occasional fighting tips. I wanted to know how to systematically kick some ass.

Sister Niema agreed. "We need to get you into capoeira class."

I had never done capoeira, but I remembered seeing videos of people doing it at Harambee. It was like martial arts but slower and mostly kicking.

I had been thinking more like mixed martial arts, but capoeira was a start. I nodded as the doorbell rang.

Sister Niema smiled. "That'd be your reinforcements," she said, standing up.

From the kitchen, I watched Sister Niema open the door and let in a tall, dark brown girl around my age. She had glasses and wore a pair of bright green overalls with sneakers, and her hair was in two dozen cornrows.

"Hey, Sister Niema," she said, and they hugged.

The two of them walked into the kitchen. I was sitting there with my hair uncombed and wearing one of my dad's torn-up Howard T-shirts with leggings, but it was too late to make a better impression.

"Hey, girl," the young woman said, and waved awkwardly.

"Imani," Sister Niema said. "You remember Ella from Harambee, right?"

"Of course," I said, wiping my hands on a napkin,

in case we were supposed to do some kind of hand-shake. I vaguely remembered her as one of the three Harambee friends who came to my birthday party, but she had changed so much in, what? Almost a decade.

Mom introduced herself as well.

I kept rubbing my hands on the napkin, trying to get the stickiness off my hands, but really just spreading it around.

"I thought Ella could show you around at school, help you get your bearings," Sister Niema said. "I wish I'd thought of it yesterday, but I was so busy pulling strings to get you in right away."

"Cool," I said. "Let me get dressed."

I washed my hands, brushed my teeth, and put on a loose blouse and maxi skirt. Then I combed my hair back into an Afro puff. When I returned to the kitchen, Ella was looking at my schedule.

"This is ridiculous," she said. "They got you running back and forth across campus, plus these are some of the worst classes. Can you send a note that she needs to be challenged more, academically?"

"Shouldn't I just come to the school?" Mom asked.

Ella shook her head. "If a parent comes, then the vice principal will handle it personally. He'll say there's no room in those classes. But Mrs. J knows how to work the system."

Sister Niema nodded. "Ella can handle it. And you all need to get going, or you'll be late."

"Okay," Mom said, and gave me a kiss. She handed me my lunch and a hastily scrawled note. "Good luck today."

"You're not gonna drive us?" I asked.

"It's only about a twenty-minute walk," Ella said. "The drive is longer during rush hour because of the one-way streets, plus you gotta go around the freeway."

"You girls can get to know each other again," Sister Niema said.

Great, I thought. *Just what I need. Twenty minutes with a strange girl I'm supposed to remember.*

We headed out the door. In spite of the peeling tan paint, Sister Niema's house was one of the neatest on the block. Her lawn was tidy and had some yellow flowers planted in rows beside the steps. But the apartment building two houses down was a mess, with a heap of garbage in front.

Still, kids in bright outfits and adults in work clothes and uniforms emerged on their way to school and jobs. Their neatly combed hair and lotioned skin stood in strong contrast to the dilapidated buildings.

When we stopped at the light on the corner, Ella glanced down at the paper bag. "Don't tell me," she said. "Sunflower butter and some randomberry jam on multigrain."

"You've had it before?" I asked.

"We've stayed over a few times," she said. I wondered if her mom had the key to Sister Niema's house, too. "The sandwiches aren't that bad. It's just those hard little things from the bread that get caught in your teeth."

I grinned. "What are those? Nuts? Grains? Rocks?"

"Pieces of Powerful Black Knowledge of Self you just can't digest yet?" Ella asked.

I busted up laughing.

"Sister Niema is over the top sometimes," she said. "But she's always there in a crisis."

I nodded. Mom hadn't told me what I could or couldn't tell Ella, so it was safer to stay quiet.

As we walked across the street, a pair of boys zipped past us on a dirt bike, one on the seat and one on the handlebars.

"So . . . what have you been doing since Harambee? You guys moved to DC, right?" Ella asked.

"We were there for a few years," I said. "Then I came back and was . . . homeschooled."

"My mom homeschooled me and my brother for a while in elementary," Ella said. "But we all got sick of each other. I went to an alternative school for a while, but it only went up to sixth grade."

A car slowed down next to us, and a guy leaned out the window. "Hey, schoolgirls," he said, leering. "Need a ride?"

Ella turned and looked him right in the eye: "My Black brother, we are descendants of kings and queens in Africa. I choose to walk to maintain my power and fitness. But I thank you for your offer, and have a blessed day. A blessed day, my brother. Stay Black."

He blinked and retreated a bit into the car. "Yeah, okay, sis . . ." He sped off.

I looked from Ella to the receding car. "Oh my God!" I said. "How did you do that?"

"If you ignore them, they get louder," she said. "If you tell them off, they just call you the B-word. This way, they usually don't cuss at you."

"So what do you do?" I asked, ready to learn the formula. "You look at them and say 'Black and proud' stuff?"

"Two things," Ella said. "Make really direct eye contact. And your voice needs to be strong and preachy, but your words need to be familiar and affirming: 'my brother,' 'beautiful.' You gotta make a reference to royalty. And say 'blessed' as often as you can, but with emphasis. It's gotta be like a gunshot."

"Blessed," I said sharply.

"Yes!" she said. "Blessed! Blessed! Blessed-blessed-blessed! How can they call you ugly names when you're machine-gunning blessings at them?"

We cracked up. "You're a genius," I said.

"I got it from my mom," Ella said. "She thinks these guys are just looking for some kind of engagement. They know you're not gonna get in their car."

"Does it work at school?"

"It's harder at school, because the boys are yelling from so much farther and across the crowded hallway and stuff," she said. "But if you do it when you can, word will get around that you're one of the 'conscious' girls, and they'll tone it down eventually."

"Thank goodness."

"But it only works when you're dressed modestly. Don't try it in booty shorts."

"I don't plan to try anything in booty shorts," I said.

"I'm just saying," Ella said. "Nobody deserves to be harassed, no matter what they're wearing. I had a friend who would say, 'Go ahead and look, but if you touch me, I'll kick your ass.' She said she only wore tight clothes on days when she had the energy to manage a lot of male attention."

I agreed with that in theory, but I wasn't going to test it. I planned to stay with the maxi skirts for the foreseeable future.

When we got to the main office, Ella took my arm and sauntered us in past the gate.

"Wassup, Mrs. J?" Ella said, and took us to the office aide's computer. She pulled up my schedule and started tinkering with it. In five minutes, she had me in advanced English, eleventh-grade history, physics, and second-year algebra.

"Does that look about right?" she asked.

"Amazing," I said.

"I couldn't get you into eleventh-grade history with Mr. Iroko and still manage a yoga class, but this'll do," she said. She printed out the schedule and walked it over to the school secretary.

"Hey, Mrs. J. You remember this new student, Imani?" she said. "Her mom says she needs more challenging classes, and here's a schedule that works."

Mrs. J punched some codes into the computer.

"The program won't accept it," Mrs. J said. "There's no room in the algebra class."

Ella nodded. "It says it's full, but one of the students got arrested last week, and I don't think he'll be back anytime soon."

"Okay," said Mrs. J. "I'll approve it. If he gets bailed out, we'll work it out somehow."

"Somebody in the algebra class got arrested?" I asked. "For what?"

"Shooting somebody," Ella said. She was writing us two hall passes to get to class late.

"Did he do it?" I asked.

"Definitely," she said. "But the guy didn't die, and the kid who shot him was also selling drugs. He might be back if the higher-ups in the drug trade bail him out and put him back to work. Plus, he's actually a nice kid. He's only selling drugs to support his mom. She got injured in an industrial accident, but the company won't pay." She took my arm and led me out of the office. "Thanks, Mrs. J!"

Ella put her hand on my back and steered me down the hall to algebra.

FIVE

The day was much more bearable than the one before. Ella was in some of my eleventh-grade classes, and kids in all of my classes cared about the material. I learned a few things. I got less attention in the skirt, and I dropped blessings on harassers like grenades.

Okay, so maybe Mom and Sister Niema were right. Maybe I had looked at Roosevelt High through prejudiced glasses. And had made generalizations about *all* the kids. It was a big school with lots of different things going on.

I ate lunch with Ella, and I picked out the hard grains from Sister Niema's bread. Ella handed me her straw, and I shot a few of the grains through it at some pigeons. One of the birds went over and pecked at the grain, then took it in its beak and promptly spit it out. We laughed so hard, I nearly peed.

Throughout the day, my thoughts wandered a few times to worrying about Mom and about our whole situation. But mostly it was just great to have school to take my mind off things.

The next day, when Ella rang the doorbell, I was already dressed and ready to go, cinnamon roll in hand. As I went to let her in, I took a huge bite.

"See you later, Mom," I said with my mouth full as I swung open the door. Which is why I had a half-chewed bite of cinnamon roll clearly visible in my open mouth when I came face-to-face with Ella and a tall handsome guy. I closed my mouth, swallowed, and nearly choked. My eyes bugged out, and Sister Niema showed up to hand me a cup of water.

"Good morning, children," she said to them. "Good to see you, Dexter. I don't think you've met Imani."

"Pleased—" I began, but the "to meet you" turned into a sputtering cough. My mom has always said that coughing is an indication that the person is not indeed choking to death, but I might have welcomed death at that moment. By the time I could nod hello, I was flushed, my face covered in a sheen of perspiration.

"Nice to meet you," he said. "I think we saw each other a few times as kids, when we came to pick up Ella from Harambee. You used to wear that shiny turquoise jacket, right?"

I blinked. How could this handsome boy have remembered anything about me?

"Come on," Ella said. "We don't want to be late."

Suddenly, I felt dowdy in my long skirt and loose blouse. Not that I wanted to be wearing booty shorts. Just something . . . I don't know. Cute. Teenager-ish. A skirt and leggings? A scoop-neck T-shirt with a sassy slogan? I felt like somebody's mother.

"Yeah," I said. "Let's go."

For a half block, we walked in awkward silence.

"So," I said to Ella. "You mentioned you had a brother, but not that he went to our school." I turned to Dexter. "Where were you yesterday?"

"Out of town for a track meet," he said.

Great, I thought. *He's totally cute and an athlete.* Could he possibly be even more out of my league? Maybe if he had a car.

"I lost," he said.

"Huh?" I asked.

"At the track meet."

"Sorry to hear that," I said. But that was a lie. I was glad that at least he wasn't a *star* athlete.

"You two have a couple of classes together," Ella said. "She's a sophomore like you." She had me tell the story about the pigeon to Dexter, and he laughed as hard as we had. His laugh was infectious, and I found myself laughing just because he was laughing.

By the time we got to school, I realized not one creepy guy had said a single thing to us. I had to restrain myself from begging Dexter to go with me everywhere I went.

I've always hated that place in the movies where the girl gets all wide-eyed and asks the boy to rescue her. And I've always been mad when the guy is like, "I'll protect you." But I guess I never had a lot of creeps after me before. What I'm trying to say is that it was nice to have a break from all that. And if that break came in the form of a tall, brown-skinned, handsome guy with dark eyes under his round glasses and long, muscled limbs, then all the better, right?

SIX

The next day was Saturday, and Mom took me shopping after lunch. I needed an arsenal of maxi skirts and blouses. I was open to some palazzo pants as well.

I also needed leggings and a top for capoeira class, which was starting on Tuesday. And—joy of all joys—these had to be white. I'd learned that both Ella and Dexter were in the class, so Dexter would see me in the least slimming color in the universe, where each ripple on my skin or line of my underwear would show through. Maybe we could also put a neon sign back there saying "Pluto isn't a planet; my butt is."

"This is cute," my mom said. She held a bright magenta sundress out to me. It had spaghetti straps and the skirt hit at my knees.

I shook my head. "Too formfitting."

"Just try it on, okay?" she asked. I rolled my eyes but took it from her.

In the dressing room, the maxi skirts were all fine. What was really to try on? *Long?* Check. *Loose?* Check. *We have a winner.*

I liked maybe half of the blouses. Some looked a little too senior citizen. I didn't want to look like someone's grandma if I was walking to school with Dexter. I liked a few T-shirts. None too tight.

The capoeira clothes were a nightmare. Even the largest-size pants dug into the flesh at my hips and made bulges.

In order to try on the sundress, I had to take off my bra, but it had a little built-in support.

I looked at myself in the mirror. The sundress did look cute. I stepped out of the dressing room.

"Oh, it's gorgeous, my love," Mom said. Suddenly she folded her lips in and started to cry.

"Mom, what's wrong?"

"I'm just realizing I had a pretty dress I had put aside for you for your Winter Dance. It must have burned in the fire."

"It'll be okay, Mom," I said. "It's just a dress. We got out all the important stuff."

"Of course we did," she said, wiping her eyes and pulling herself together. "I just wish your dad were here."

"Me too."

"But I have good news," she said. "I heard back

from someone today who can probably get our message to him. Let's buy some new phones so he'll be able to contact us."

She didn't have to tell me twice. I changed back into my clothes while she bought the new stuff. We skipped the capoeira pants and instead bought white leggings at a plus-size boutique, and then we headed to the electronics store.

As we crossed the mall, I saw a large display for the Deza concert—the one I had won tickets to but couldn't claim. My heart sank for a moment. It was all so unfair.

Mom picked out a pair of prepaid cell phones and paid cash for them. The guy went to get them out of the locked cabinet, and I started talking to her about something the teacher had said in my physics class. I was just about to get to the funny part when I saw her attention shift abruptly to her left and she stiffened. She looked over her shoulder and across the counter.

"Mom? Are you with me here?"

She turned to me and smiled. Her face was calm, but the smile was fake.

I froze, feeling anxiety descend into my gut.

Mom reached into her pocket and pulled out the car keys. Then, keeping her hand low, she pressed them into my palm.

"I need you to bring the car around, my love."

"The car?" I closed one hand around the keys and blinked at her, confused.

She smiled and tilted her head to the side. "Yes, of course. Our car."

"Mom, you wouldn't even let me get my permit. Even though I turned fifteen and a half last month," I said. "First you told me driving was too dangerous. Then you said the cops were too hostile to young Black people. Then you said it was bad for the environment, and you wanted to wait till we got a more eco-friendly vehicle."

Mom's smile stayed pasted on her face. "Exactly," she said. "You're not accustomed to remembering where we parked, but it's in section A-three, right near the north exit stairs. So I need you to go get it and bring it around to the mall door just outside this store. Beep twice. It's an automatic, so you should have no trouble driving it, sweetheart."

Sweetheart. She had never before called me that. It sounded metallic and strange coming out of her mouth. She always said "my love," which is embarrassing and overly romantic sounding, but she'd used it my whole life. As she spoke, I could see her palm, covered by the sleeve of her sweatshirt, rubbing the edge of the counter where we'd both just had our hands.

"Hurry now," she said. "Before the clerk comes to

wait on me. You know how angry men can get when women keep them waiting." She tilted her head to the left.

Over her shoulder, I saw a man in the headphone aisle. He was Black and had on a navy blue hoodie and big shades. The graying stubble on his jawline made him too old for that look. He had pulled the headphones on over his hood.

Angry man. Guy in a hoodie. I got it. A fake smile bloomed on my face. I reached to put the keys in my pocket, but the maxi skirt didn't have pockets. I gripped the keys in my palm and forced my body to look relaxed.

I strolled casually over to the virtual reality headsets. There was a display of two young women—racially ambiguous, maybe Asian, maybe Latinx, maybe mixed—wearing VR headsets. If I hadn't been so freaked out, I would have laughed. My mother always said that brown women don't have the luxury to walk around completely unaware of their surroundings.

When the guy in the hoodie turned to try on a different pair of headphones, I slipped out the door. Back in the mall, I walked as fast as I could without attracting attention. I looked for the nearest exit and headed toward the parking lot.

Mom was right. I wasn't used to remembering where the car was parked. A3, she had said. Near the north exit stairs. Unfortunately, I was near the west exit stairs. I knew that only because a sign said WEST EXIT. I stepped out into the parking lot and began running north.

The maxi skirt got in my way, so I grabbed the fabric up in one hand. The skirt pulled tight on my butt, my bare legs showing.

"Hey, hold up, big girl," a guy said, but he was just a blur in my peripheral vision.

I could feel my chest burning as I ran the length of a couple department stores, then I hit the corner of the mall, and the north side came into view.

Near the exit, I saw our blue van. Mom had probably parked near the exit intentionally. Mom was probably thinking about this stuff all the time. Maybe the danger had never really subsided. She had just been protecting me. Trying to make things seem normal when they really weren't.

I came up alongside the van and opened my fist to get the key. It was covered in sweat. I tried to push the unlock button, but my thumb slipped in the moisture and I hit the alarm by mistake. Loud, rhythmic beeping filled my ears. I hadn't thought my heart could beat any faster, but I realized there was a difference between winded and panicked. I hit the lock button, then the unlock button, and at last, the alarm stopped.

I pulled the door handle, but it was still locked. Fingers shaking, I pressed the unlock button again, and the car finally opened.

I slid into the driver's seat, heart hammering. *How the hell do I do this?*

But I had watched my parents drive the car thousands of times. I slid the key into the ignition and turned it. The car started and the stereo came on, blaring one of Deza's songs: *"Sepia girl, you can do anything!"* I turned the music off and heard the hum of the engine.

I had never sat in the driver's seat before. The steering wheel made me feel claustrophobic. I felt for the gas and brake pedals and pressed on both to get the feel of them.

You had to change the gears to go; I knew that much. The car was in P for park. I tried to move the stick down, but it wouldn't move. There was a button on the side. I tried pressing that, and it moved. Mom had backed in, even though most of the cars had parked front ways in. Maybe this was part of her strategy, too. Reversing out always took longer, but Mom was poised to go. Poised for *me* to go. I put the car in . . . what gear? The panel said PRND21. I knew P was park and R was reverse. Which should I do?

I put it into "1," and the car made a low grinding growl and jerked forward. That didn't sound right. I tried to slam on the brakes and accidentally hit the gas. The minivan lurched forward again, nearly hitting a car going by. As the driver honked and yelled something at me, I felt desperately around with my foot until I found the brake. The car stopped. I put on my seat belt.

I closed my eyes and took a breath. I remembered Dad letting me steer the car sometimes around a parking lot when I was little. He did the pedals. I did the steering wheel. What had he said? D was for drive.

Okay. I put the car in drive and kept my foot on the brake. I took it off slowly, and the car began to move. A little more gas and I was easing forward. Okay, time to hustle. I got into the lane that led around the mall and headed back to the west exit.

The adrenaline was pumping. I stopped at every stop sign, fully and completely. I didn't see any mall cops, but it wouldn't do to get pulled over when I was young, Black, and unlicensed. I'd be getting hauled away, if not beaten or shot.

Just past the west exit, I saw the outer door of the electronics store. Mom had said to beep twice, but there was no need. She was right by the window, admiring some karaoke machines, holding one of the microphones and fiddling with the display.

The moment she saw me, she dropped the mic and slipped out the door. Once she got outside, she sprinted to the van.

Through the plate-glass window, I saw the clerk and the guy in the headphones look up.

Mom jumped in and yelled, "Drive!"

"Don't you want to take over?" I asked.

"No, just go!" she demanded as she buckled her seat belt.

I hit the gas, and we shot forward down the road that wrapped around the mall.

"Turn left!" she yelled, and I turned into the underground parking lot.

"Where are we going?" I asked, slowing to let an elderly woman finish crossing to her car.

"In case they come out and look for us, I don't want them to see us exiting."

She directed me to the south exit, and just before we came up from underground, we changed places.

I felt so relieved when I was no longer in the driver's seat.

With Mom behind the wheel, we went twice as fast. She sped out of the mall parking lot and onto the freeway. Then she got off two exits later and drove into a municipal parking garage. It was nearly empty of cars on a Saturday. At the entry, she punched the button, and a ticket spat out as the gate went up to let us in.

We wound our way up to the third floor, where she pulled into a dark corner and stopped the car.

"Where are we going?" I asked.

"Just a quick change of clothes," Mom said.

I reached for the bag from the mall, not sure why our clothes were going to be important.

"Leave that," she said, and opened the door for me to come out.

She walked me around to the side of the van that faced out into the parking garage. "Cough if you see anyone coming."

I nodded and kept an eye out.

Then, to my astonishment, Mom reached under the back bumper of the van and began to peel off the blue paint in a single thick layer, like it was a rubber glove. Underneath, the van was red.

I gaped at her.

"Keep a lookout," she hissed.

I swiveled back to my duty, but there was nobody.

A few minutes later, she had an armful of blue that she threw in the trunk, and soon we were driving back out in a red van. She paid cash to exit the parking garage, and we drove to Sister Niema's house at a normal speed.

"Are you okay?" she asked.

"I don't know what I am," I said. "Was that him? Was that the guy?"

"I think so," Mom said. "In the hood and shades, I can't be certain."

"But how could he have found us in the first place?" I asked.

"It was my fault," she said. "This morning I looked up prepaid phones at that store, and I must have activated my account."

"He could find you through that?" I asked.

"Like I said, my love, he's law enforcement," she said. "He can access all their resources to catch criminals. If a mass murderer used his Walmart discount, you'd want them to be able to track that, right?"

"I guess," I said. I stared blankly out at the traffic on the wide boulevard. A family was next to us in a station wagon. The mom was driving, with the dad in the passenger seat and three kids in the back. They were all singing some pop song at the top of their lungs.

Mom smiled. "You've been saying you want to learn to drive," she said. "You got your wish."

"Are you really going to joke about that when we just ran for our lives? And then you changed the color of our van like it was nail polish?" I asked. "No, actually. Nail polish would've taken longer."

"I'm sorry, my love," she said. "It's important that we stay off the grid. We need to be untraceable."

"I was so terrified when you sent me to drive the van," I said. I could feel myself shaking in my seat.

"I know," she said. "I never wanted to have to lean on you like this. But I knew you'd be great in a crisis. You're so mature and brave. I'm really proud of you."

The shaking didn't stop, but along with the waves of fear, I also felt a new warm feeling. Mom was proud of me? She thought I was brave? She'd said nice things to me before, but they'd always just sounded like those clichés she loved so much—I'd never really believed them. "Thanks, Mom," I said, teeth chattering a bit. "I got your back."

I kept shaking, but by the time we got to Sister Niema's, the shaking had turned to a few tremors.

I lay back on the bed in the guest room and programmed the phone, which took only a few minutes because it was a flip phone. It had basic features like calling, texting, and even a music player and a voice recorder, but it was pretty bare-bones. I put Mom's new number into the phone, and then Ella's and Sister Niema's. It was so weird that I had only these few people in my life now.

SEVEN

Tuesday after school, Ella, Dexter, and I met at a dance studio down the street from Sister Niema's house for capoeira. It was a converted bungalow with hardwood floors and big windows. At the curb in front, two women were loading several drums into a small hatchback.

We opened the door and made our way down a dim hallway. Ella showed me to the girls' dressing room, a windowless pantry that had been repurposed. I felt shy about changing in front of her and one other girl from school, whose name I learned was Celeste.

Celeste was a sophomore like me, and her body was short and boyish, with a flat chest. She had worn her white T-shirt, so she was just changing her pants, sliding jeans off slender hips and pulling up the white cotton bell-bottoms.

Ella was tall and had smooth muscled limbs. She wore a heavily structured athletic bra because she needed one. On her, the capoeira uniform looked graceful and sleek.

I changed into the white leggings and T-shirt that I'd bought with Mom over the weekend. Pulling them out of my backpack, I recalled the guy in the sweatshirt, the wild escape, and driving the car.

"Aren't you gonna get dressed?" Celeste asked.

I mumbled a yes and turned my back to them to change my shirt. I put on a tank top underneath and my cotton tee on top. Then I turned around to change my pants. As I put on the bottom of the capoeira uniform, I pulled out the wedgie I'd made of the new underwear Mom had bought me.

I breathed slowly as I stepped into the studio wearing my uniform. I felt so incredibly awkward with Dexter seeing the shape of my body for the first time. Did I want him to like it? Did I want him to ignore it?

I caught his eye and then looked quickly away.

I glanced around the studio, which had been built out of the house's old living and dining rooms. Someone had scraped the paint off the walls and the linoleum off the floors but hadn't properly finished either. There was a barre below a pair of dusty windows that looked out onto an unkempt lawn. Across from the windows were large posters of Dance Theatre of Harlem and Alvin Ailey, including the famous black-and-white photo of the Ailey dancer Judith Jamison wearing all white, with a skirt that whips around her like a raging sea.

Though Jamison's skin was dark, her body, like those of all the dancers in the posters, was long and slender. I felt completely out of place. Thank goodness the teacher was full-figured, with wide hips, a big bosom, and a belly. She made me look thin by comparison. Her hair was buzzed off on the sides, with short curls on top. Her skin was a light brown, and she had hazel eyes and big teeth in a ready smile.

"I'm Amber," she said, shaking my hand. "Have you done capoeira before?"

I shook my head. "I did gymnastics through middle school and danced on and off." I didn't mention that I had done yoga and Pilates at my previous school. It sounded too bougie.

"You'll be fine," she said, and proceeded to lead us through a series of warm-up stretches. When we got to the basic capoeira step, the ginga—pronounced with a soft first g, like giraffe—I caught on quickly.

She then demonstrated moves that all had Brazilian names. There were a bunch of kicks that were unlike anything I'd ever done before. She even did a cartwheel, which she called "aú." Capoeira definitely included a lot of martial arts. Between my training in yoga and gymnastics, I mostly had the flexibility to follow along.

But when she had the class get into actual gymnastics, it all felt strange. I had done these moves before, but in a different body. My middle-school chest had been completely flat, my hips narrower, and my butt a fraction of the size.

It had been years, but with a few tries, I found I could still do a back walkover.

"Nice!" Amber said. "We're gonna work with that a little later."

We did some singing—in Brazilian Portuguese. Not that I was very good at it, but I faked my way along. Ella and Dexter knew all the songs. Ella in particular sang out strong and had a really nice voice.

Amber accompanied us on an instrument that looked like a bow that could shoot an arrow, but it had a little gourd thing connected to it. She called it a "berimbau" and used a rock to strum it.

She had us practice several different kicks, and then we did a bit of paired work. First, Amber partnered with me and Celeste to assess our skills. While she paired up with us, Dexter played the berimbau. In capoeira, you pretend to kick the other person, but it feels more like a dance. You move in time to the music, and they get out of the way. With the partner work, I didn't have time to think. My body just took over. It some ways, it was pure fun. I was excited, in the moment, eager to see what would happen next.

Ella and Dexter were both pretty good. Celeste was new but catching on quickly.

"Let me pair you up," Amber said. "I'm going with weight compatibility. I'd say Ella and Celeste, Imani and Dexter."

Was I blushing? I tried to keep my face neutral. Was I embarrassed that she mentioned my weight? Or excited to be with Dexter? Or both?

If it was fun and effortless with Amber, it was awkward with Dexter.

It got better when I threw in a cartwheel. Cartwheels felt good. I remembered doing strings of them across the grass in the park when I was a kid.

The eye contact was hard. You are supposed to look at your partner to tune in. After all, you don't want to be kicking each other for real. But I found Dexter's big brown eyes distracting, and the glint of his teeth between his smiling dark lips even worse.

Slowly, I got the rhythm of working with him. I did more cartwheels. I did them fast, throwing myself from one spot in the floor to another. I tried them with one hand and found that I could still do them on my right side but not on my left.

The music sped up a bit, and Dexter and I sped up, too. After a while, I just stopped thinking and let myself respond—almost unconsciously—to the connection with his movement and with the music. At one point,

I did a cartwheel with no hands—what we called an aerial in gymnastics. I didn't mean to; it just happened.

When the music finally stopped, Dexter and I fell out laughing.

"That was amazing," Amber said to me. "Can you do that again and add a kick?"

"Do what?" I asked.

"The aú with no hands," she said. "Can you end it with a kick?"

"I don't know if I could even do it again," I said.

"But I just saw you do it," she said.

I shrugged. "I used to do them all the time, but that was back in junior high," I said. "Back then, I was . . . littler."

"What?" Amber said. "What? You think you can't do it because you got a big butt now? Because you got hips?"

"No," I said, even though it was like she was reading my mind. I was definitely blushing.

"Girl, you better use that booty," she said. "Move your butt, and you move your center of gravity." And then, to all of our surprise, she did it. Big bosom and belly and all. She took two flying steps and sprung up from the mat, did the aerial, and kicked out at the end.

I was incredibly relieved that her acrobatics took the attention away from me, my body, and my butt.

She smiled at us and breathed heavily. "More mass

just needs more muscle and skill to lift it," she said. "I want you all to practice this week. Ella, work on that kick with the turn. Celeste, get that fan kick. Dexter, get that aú on the left, and, Imani, I wanna see that no-hands aú and kick next week."

I felt exhilarated. Just watching Amber do that move made me excited about what my new body might be able to do.

"So what are you about to get into?" Ella asked on the way home.

"Nothing," I said. "Where are you all going?"

"Our mom signed us up for this pro-Black nerd gathering," Ella said.

"It's not a nerd gathering," Dexter said defensively. "It's a Diaspora Game Night at the new Black comic bookstore."

Ella mouthed, *Black nerd.*

"What's the game?"

"Triángulo," Dexter said.

"Trianga-who?" I asked.

"See?" Ella said. "International Black nerds."

"It's a slave rebellion game that started in Latin America," Dexter said. "It's fun."

"I'm all for slave rebellions," I said. "I'm in."

The store was called Wakanda Comics and Books, and it was a half mile past the school, away from Sister Niema's house. The small storefront was squeezed between a hair salon and a cell phone store. Just inside the door, there was a life-size cardboard cutout of Chadwick Boseman as Black Panther. Someone had pasted a halo on him at an angle, like a low-slung golden crown.

The place was about half the size of a standard classroom and packed tight with comic books and graphic novels. Dexter walked us back to the rear of the store, where a few Black teens and young adults were crowding around a table.

"Welcome, welcome!" said a college-age-looking guy with a scraggly beard, locs, and a septum piercing. "We're just getting started. My name's Warren, I use he/they pronouns, and I'll be your tour guide today."

We all introduced ourselves. I was she/her and Dexter and the pair of young adult guys at the other end of the table were he/his. But I was surprised to learn that Ella was comfortable with either she or they pronouns.

"Thanks, everyone, for coming out tonight," Warren said. "Glad to see some of our Magic: The Gathering folks. If you like Magic, you gonna love Triángulo. We've been surprised here at Wakanda that there aren't more of our people playing, even though it's a very unapologetically Black game. We think maybe it's just because it comes out of Latin America. So we decided to do these intro nights and get a game started here."

Warren continued with his speech: "Triángulo is a

trading-card game and a comic book slash graphic novel series that began in the late nineties and has become immensely popular in Latin America, and increasingly in the US, with the crossover success of the superhero Arantxa. Even though Arantxa herself is not Black, the Triángulo universe has a slavery abolition origin story. It begins on a fictional Caribbean island in the early sixteen hundreds, and it's about three characters who create a spell that allows enslaved Africans to fly and breathe underwater to escape to a Maroon colony. The game is played with each team attempting to free the captives from enslavement in the seventeenth century and to defeat a supervillain in the present era. Players take turns. Each team plays cards to reach their own goals and attempts to block, delay, or obstruct their opponent from reaching the same goal in their parallel world.

"So these are our main players: Arantxa, the Basque Witch; Olumide, the Yoruba Priest; and BaguaNi, the Taino Bohique."

Arantxa had olive skin and wild curly hair. She wore a tattered soldier's uniform where the wide-legged pants had been converted into a skirt. Olumide was a chocolate brown, and her hair and body were wrapped in matching indigo cloth. She had a necklace of blue and clear beads. BaguaNi had jet-black straight hair. He wore a long loincloth of tan animal skin. He had an

X of cloth and feathers that hung across his otherwise bare chest.

"So far, they've done a comic series for Arantxa and BaguaNi, but next year Comicultura is doing an Olumide series, so it's about to get very Black very soon."

He opened up the game box. Inside was a thick piece of laminated cardboard folded in quarters. He unfolded it and put it on the table. It was like a map with intricate designs of all the locations in the story: the Maroon colony, the sugar plantation, the modern-day world. And in the middle, where it said TRIÁNGULO, he placed a tiny triangle-shaped stone in the center of the letter *Á*.

After that, Warren brought out a small pack of cards that had illustrations of people on both sides. He explained that these were basic character cards. "And if you buy any Triángulo merchandise tonight, it'll be twenty percent off," Warren said. "Your basic starter kit is the game board, the pack of character cards, and a second pack of cards that constitute different power moves to make things happen."

As we watched Warren fan out the cards, Dexter whispered to me, "When you play, your goal is to free everyone from enslavement. You get them initiated with the necklace, then they can get to the triangle stone and breathe underwater to get free." There was a little underwater area on the board, near the Maroon colony.

"We've got a few boards," Warren said. "Go ahead and get to work freeing your people."

Warren handed us a second board, and Dexter opened it up.

"So can three of us play?" Ella asked.

"Two teams," Dexter said. "It should be me against you and Imani because I've played before."

"Is this gonna be a replay of the tic-tac-toe tragedy?" Ella asked. "Where I beat you and you end up crying?"

"Oh my God, Ella," Dexter said. "I was five."

"This is a game about knowing your history," Ella said. "That's all I'm saying."

"Moving on," Dexter said. "The game is being played simultaneously in the early sixteen hundreds and in present time. A really powerful card is the one that switches you to the past or to the present. If you know you're strong in the other time, you can play a time-travel card, and you might be able to take your opponent down."

"We gonna take you down," Ella said. "Right, Imani?"

"Definitely," I said.

We didn't exactly take him down. Dexter had read the comic books and understood the game better. But just as he was about to beat us, Warren came by and told us to use the Middle Passage card to send a new group of Africans for Dexter to have to free.

"Warren!" Dexter said. "How you gonna take sides?"

"My brother," Warren said. "I'm just trying to create fans. Fans who wanna come and play here. You can't be running them off like that."

It would have taken Dexter another hour or so to free all his people again, but we needed to get home in time for dinner. So nobody won.

"Check out our calendar and come on back for our Triángulo game night," Warren said.

We all promised we would.

When I got home, there was good news. Sister Niema said Mom had left something for me.

She handed me a typewritten envelope with a smudge of soot on it. It was addressed to me and had a sticky note from Mom: *This came for you the day of the fire. It was so hectic, I forgot to give it to you.*

Could it be from Dad? I wondered, ripping it open. It could! Another cipher!

I ran to our room and unfolded the paper on top of my cipher notebook.

JUF BKVBXR AFFM RP OQPVC PE XPV BLBMJ RSBX RSQPMF

Come on, Dad. I caught the BLB right away. *A* changes to *B*, so *M* changes to—wait. It didn't work. I tried the rest of the cipher with every letter one later, and it didn't make sense. I stared at it for a moment until the words swam in front of me.

Suddenly, I was incredibly irritated. I'd been so

excited to get something from my dad, but this cipher just added more confusion to my already-confusing new life. I had to figure out this new school. All this creepy attention from boys. Being on the run with Mom. The last thing I needed was something else to figure out.

EiGHT

Unfortunately, Ella and Mrs. J hadn't been able to get me into Spanish class. In all my other schools, I had taken Spanish and picked it up quickly. It was seriously effortless. I figured I was just good at languages . . . until I had Latin at Penfield. It was sort of like Spanish and sort of not. It made my brain hurt. Here at Roosevelt, the only foreign language class with space in it was intro to African languages. It was also taught by Mr. Iroko, my history teacher.

If I thought Latin was foreign, this was *really* different, and stepping into it in the middle of the year was worse. Thankfully, the class was reviewing the Yoruba alphabet, which was similar to the English alphabet but with accents and dots. Everything was pronounced differently. It was tonal, so words meant different things depending on whether your voice went up or down. In

English, tone only matters if you're asking a question. In Yoruba, it matters for everything.

I remembered once in DC I was wearing an African dress on culture day. A white kid asked, "Are you African?" I said yes—probably recalling Sister Niema talking about "our people on the Continent" at the Harambee Girls Academy.

"Speak to me in African," the white kid had said. Even at the time, I knew something was wrong with his question, with his whole attitude.

And now, studying an African language, I learned that the African continent has like two thousand languages. None of them is called "African." So even if I mastered Yoruba, I'd only be speaking to a small fraction of "our people on the Continent."

Mr. Iroko had us reading words aloud.

"Alafia," the class chorused.

"Which means?"

"Peace."

As we worked through the column of words on the board, all my instincts for pronunciation were wrong. Neither English nor Spanish could help me.

I sighed and made more phonetic notes on my paper.

"You not used to having a hard time in school, huh?" Katanya, the girl in the desk in front of me, asked over her shoulder. She was dark brown and had on bright lipstick.

"What?" I murmured, looking up.

"You used to knowing the answer all the time, huh?"

"I don't know," I said, speaking to the back of her coral ombré weave. But she was right.

"I bet you mostly been going to white schools," she said. "They ain't gonna help you in this class."

Mumbling something that was neither agreement nor disagreement, I focused on my paper.

I struggled through the final fifteen minutes of the period. When the bell rang, I was right behind Katanya as we walked into the hallway.

She was tall, like me, and had a figure like mine but with a bigger bust. She wore her shape proudly in tight fuchsia pants and a matching cropped sweatshirt.

Boys gave her a ton of attention. One even tried to press up too close to her, but she elbowed him hard. "Girl, you look good today. Come give me a hug," he said. He was walking with a knot of other boys. I trailed behind her, thankfully invisible in my maxi skirt and loose blouse.

"I don't have time for little boys," she said. "Come back when you got something to offer a grown woman."

His friends laughed at him, and he fired back at her, "Ugh, I didn't like you anyway, wearin' clothes that been outta style since middle school. Where you get that? A garage sale?"

But his words just rolled off her shiny polyester pants.

Later that night, I was sitting between Mom's knees on the edge of the bed, and she was cornrowing my hair. I dug my toes into the carpet as she combed out the tangles.

"You sure are quiet tonight," she said.

I considered telling her more about the harassment at school and my troubles in Yoruba class, but she just wasn't the kind of person you could talk to about stuff.

"Roosevelt is really different from Penfield," I said instead.

"You know, Sister Niema was right about some things," she said, going back to doing my hair. "Prep schools are really white and can set Black kids up to feel isolated."

"I know," I said. "And I see where I was too judgy when I first got here. But why can't there be a school where there are kids of color and also . . . you know . . . nice stuff?"

"That's the racism, love," Mom said. "Schools in our communities don't get the same resources. And well-resourced private and even public schools are notoriously white."

"But it's not just about having nice things, really," I said. "It's also about kids being nice. I mean, kids at Penfield were mean in one kind of way, like snobby—"

"And body shaming," she put in.

"Yeah, but kids at Roosevelt are kind of—I mean,

there are fights. And kids saying really brutal things to each other. And stupid stuff. Like, why does it matter if you got your clothes at a garage sale? Fast fashion is killing the planet. It's good to reuse and recycle."

Mom sighed. "You're right," she said. "But we live in a society that shames and blames people who are poor. And with an economy that makes it really difficult for people to get out of poverty. So if people don't have access to the kinds of good-paying jobs and resources to stop from *being* poor, the culture encourages them to use their money to buy things that will keep them from *looking* poor. And then instead of criticizing the system, it encourages people to criticize each other. People treat others brutally if they or their families have been treated brutally."

She shook her head. "We sent you to all those alternative elementary and middle schools where they were telling you to be yourself, no matter where you went," she said. "But then, I guess we sent you to a high school that stressed conformity. And now Roosevelt is a whole different ball game."

"Different in a lot of ways," I said. "Was it like that at your high school in Virginia?"

"That was such a different time," she said. "And a different culture. You can't really compare them."

Mom was always vague with the details of her own schooling.

"One thing that seems to be the same in both

Penfield and Roosevelt is that a lot of the girls seem kind of obsessed with boys and whether or not boys like them," I said. "Stupid."

"Don't be so quick to say 'stupid' about boys liking you," she said. "One of these days soon that won't sound like such a ridiculous idea."

"Whatever," I said. It already didn't sound ridiculous if the boy was Dexter. But I certainly wasn't going to tell that to my mother.

NINE

Thursday after school, I went with Ella, Dexter, and Celeste back to capoeira class.

When we got to the studio, there was a note for us from Amber.

Sick today. Sorry. But you all should stay and practice.

"Practice?" Ella said. "I've got a history test tomorrow. I need to study."

"Come on," Celeste said. "Let's practice for ten minutes to say we did."

The three of us changed in the girls' dressing room and met Dexter in the main room.

"Let's take a selfie and text it to Amber," Celeste suggested. The four of us crowded together in our white uniforms.

I felt Dexter's arm around my waist, his fingers just below my ribs. The smile on my face reflected that nervous excitement I always felt when I was close to him.

Celeste snapped the picture, and then we dispersed. Ella led us in a quick warm-up, and we paired up on different sides of the studio.

Dexter and I faced each other and began doing our gingas. It was hard not to grin at him, so I just tried to focus on my breathing and did a few minor kicks.

Dexter did a kick and spin. "You're in trouble now," he said. "I've been practicing."

"Really?" I asked, continuing to do the gingas. I couldn't kick and talk at the same time.

"Not at all," he said. "I'm just trying to psych you out."

"It's working," I said.

"If anyone should be psyched out, it's me," he said. "With that little flippy-flip thing you do."

"That flippy-flip thing is called an aerial," I said. "And I can't do it."

"You did it that one time," he said.

"That was a fluke," I said. "I just got caught up in the music and had a lot of momentum going. I can't replicate it."

"Sure you can," he said. "Let's make that our goal for today. We don't leave until you can do the aerial."

"I don't agree to that goal," I said.

"I think that's a great goal," Ella said from across the room. "That way, Amber will think all of us stayed and worked hard, not just you two."

"Wait," I said. "Don't leave. How did I end up being the one who has to work hard on everyone's behalf?"

"Just think of the schedule you had before I went to Mrs. J," Ella said. "You owe me, Kennedy."

It took me a moment to remember that Kennedy was my last name.

"I'll be exerting myself, too," Dexter said. "Bringing out excellence in others is hard work."

"Nobody's asking you to flip over with no hands," I said.

"See you all at school tomorrow," Celeste said, and the two of them waved goodbye and left.

"Seriously," I said to Dexter. "I can't do this."

"Start with what you can do," he said. "Do a cartwheel."

"Fine," I said. "Only if you do one, too."

I did a perfect cartwheel, my feet flying over my head, limbs extended, toes pointed.

"Okay," he said. "Prepare for the worst cartwheel ever."

He put his hands on the ground and swung uneven bent-kneed legs and flexed feet over his head. He landed in a sort of crab position.

"Come on," I said. "You did it that badly on purpose."

"Wow," he said. "Adding insult to injury."

"Sorry," I said. "That's really your best?"

"Keep digging," he said. "You'll eventually find some buried treasure." He mimed using a shovel.

"Oh my God," I said, shaking my head. "That sounded really bad. Ahem. Do over!" I fixed my face into wide-eyed cheerful encouragement. "This is great raw material. Let's build on what you can already do. Go, Dexter!"

"Nice clean-up job," he said, brushing the imaginary dirt back into the hole and patting the ground. "But now that I've embarrassed myself, the least you can do is try for real excellence."

"Okay, fine," I said. I did a one-handed cartwheel.

"Look, you're fifty percent there!"

"Ha ha," I said. "One-handed is very different from no-handed."

"Well, first of all, when you did the flippy-flip thing, your legs snapped over your head more quickly."

"That's because the aerial is more like a roundoff than a cartwheel," I said, and did a perfect roundoff.

"Try that with one hand," he said.

"Okay," I said. The first time I tried, I had to put my other hand down for a second at the end.

"What happened?" he asked.

"I guess I got scared," I said.

"You had it, though, didn't you?" he asked.

"I don't know," I said.

He looked around and brought a big mat over.

"This way if you do fall, you won't actually get hurt," he said.

I tried it a few more times, and it got so I could do it every time with just one hand.

"You got it!" he said.

"Yeah, but like I said, from two hands to one is much easier than one hand to zero."

"Well, build up to it," he said. "Like that first time when you put your hand down at the end."

I took a deep breath. Then I did the roundoff, putting my one hand down at the last minute and pulling it up quickly.

"Yes!" he said. "You're seventy-five percent there!"

I shook my head.

"Let's take a break," he said. "Get some water."

I was sweating. I mopped my forehead with my sleeve and hoped I smelled okay. The last thing I wanted to do was to be like my mom, who never worried about sweating and would spread her post-workout stinky self everywhere, trying to hug me no matter what she smelled like.

I pulled my water bottle out of my backpack, and Dexter filled up both our bottles from the bathroom down the hall.

"Why are you pushing me so hard to do this?" I

asked when I had finally caught my breath and taken a long drink.

"Because," he said, "as a Black man, it is my duty to help my people achieve!"

I laughed. It sounded like something Sister Niema would have us memorize and recite back in Harambee.

"Up, up, you mighty race!" I agreed.

"Facing the rising sun . . . !" He sang a line of the Black national anthem, and we both laughed.

"But seriously," I said.

"Seriously?" he asked. "Because I think you really want it, but something's holding you back. And it seems like boys get told to sort of just—you know—go for it with every kind of sport. Not to let anything hold us back. But not girls. Like, Ella's older than me, and we used to play tackle football when we were little. But then we spent this one summer with our grandparents, and the girls didn't play football. Only the boys. Grandma said it wasn't ladylike. After a summer of being sidelined, Ella got self-conscious or something, and now she only plays soccer. I see her watching sometimes when I play tackle football with our cousins. She looks like she wants to play, but she doesn't jump in, even though she used to be better than all of us. It doesn't seem fair. I try to talk to her about it, but she doesn't take her baby brother seriously."

"Wow," I said. "I hadn't thought of that." I thought about all the ways I focused on how my body looked or what people had to say about it and not on what it could do.

"Okay, fine," I said. "I'm gonna do this. I'm hella gonna do this."

I stood up and tried harder than I had before, keeping my hand up till the last minute. But then I got scared and put it down too late and fell down on my butt.

"Yes!" he said. "That was great!"

"Your powers of observation do include noticing that I fell, right?"

"Yeah, but you really went for it," he said.

"But now I'm scared again."

"Hold on," he said, pulling out his phone. He found a DIY video on how to help someone do an aerial, featuring two skinny tween blond girls. They showed us how he could put one hand on my stomach and the other on my back while I do the aerial.

"This is great!" he said. "Now I can really help."

We tried it a bunch of times. Each time I could feel him helping a little bit less. Finally, I did it and didn't feel his hands holding any of my weight.

"You did it!" he said. "Now try it by yourself."

I tried it but put my hands down at the end.

"It's a mental thing," he said.

"No, it's an I-need-help thing," I said, and pulled him toward me with both hands.

"Nuh-uh," he said. "You got this."

He tugged away, and I tugged him toward me. He stepped back and tripped over the edge of the mat, pulling me down as well.

We sat up quickly and were shoulder to shoulder, my leg tangled over his.

Unexpectedly, he leaned in and kissed me. Just a soft peck on my lips.

I was so startled, I just stared at him wide-eyed.

"I'm so sorry," he said. "I thought—"

"Don't be sorry," I said. "It was . . . wow."

We heard voices in the hallway and scrambled to our feet.

"Hey," a young woman said, sticking her head into the studio. "We have Congolese dance in here in five minutes. Is your class done?"

"Yes," Dexter and I said in unison. He grabbed his backpack.

"I gotta go," he said, and dashed out of the studio.

I rushed after him but then turned back to get my backpack. As I ran out into the street, I could see him disappearing around the corner.

Just as I took a breath to call out to him, I heard a car's horn beep. "Damn, girl," a guy said, leaning out of an SUV. "You can wear white after Labor Day anytime, baby."

I backed into the studio. Dammit. I wished I had asked Ella for Dexter's number. But I had hers. I sent a message:

Thanks for abandoning me at capoeira today. But tell
Dexter I really appreciated his help, especially the
breakthrough at the end.

I hoped she would pass it on.

As I changed into my maxi skirt and blouse, I
looked at myself in the mirror. Did this just really happen, or did I make it up? Was it really possible that a
boy liked me? Like-liked me? Enough to kiss me? And
not some creepy guy on the street but a boy I actually
liked back? It seemed too good to be true.

But maybe those feelings were Penfield Amani.
Roosevelt Imani was different. I stood there for a
moment, remembering the pressure of his lips on
mine. It had been a few minutes since the kiss, but the
feeling of it lingered.

Curvy. Cute. My mom had said all these things
about me. Wow. Maybe they were actually true.

When I got home, Mom was still at work, but Sister
Niema was there, making sushi rolls with brown rice
and avocado.

On the kitchen table, her cell phone lit up, and I
noticed that the number had the same strange area
code that was calling Mom the night of the fire.

"Looks like you're getting a call from a telemar-
keter," I said.

Sister Niema hit "decline" and shook her head.

"Just more foolishness trying to take up my time. But how was your day?"

I wanted to say, *Amazing! Best ever! Dexter kissed me!* But instead I said, "Cool. Can I have a sushi roll?"

She nodded and handed me one. How was I eating a roll with the same mouth that had just been kissed by the boy I liked?

I was dying to tell someone, but I couldn't tell Sister Niema. I certainly couldn't tell my mom, either. I couldn't tell Ella because . . . I don't know. He was her brother! I guessed this is why girls wrote in diaries. Because things happened that you needed to tell someone. Or express somehow. I pulled out some of the colored pencils Sister Niema kept in the living room and drew for hours. Nothing obvious, just curlicues that I colored in shades of red, purple, pink, and brown.

By the time Mom came home, I had gotten a message back from Ella.

Thanks for staying. Dex says he was glad to help. Anytime.

Anytime.

TEN

I was sitting in first period, staring out the window. The sky was gray and overcast. It looked like it might rain later. The teacher had just finished taking roll when I heard what sounded like thunder. Then some shouts and a squeal of tires. The next thing I knew, all the kids were jumping up and running out of the class.

"I didn't excuse anyone!" the teacher yelled, but nobody was listening.

I turned to Ella. "What happened?"

"I think it was a shooting," Ella said.

"Are we safe? Why is everyone running away?" I asked.

"No, Imani," Ella said. "They're running to see."

By then, the teacher was standing in the doorway of the class, looking out into the hallway.

Ella walked up to him. "Can we be excused to go check on my brother?" she asked.

I looked at her anxiously. Was Dexter in some sort of danger? Or was she just saying that as an excuse?

He nodded. We were the last two students in the class anyway.

The halls were full of students calling back and forth, and Ella pushed through them to her locker and pulled out her cell phone. Nothing from Dexter, but she showed me a message from Celeste:

Did u hear that? Sounded like it was just outside the gym.

"I don't like this," she said. "Dexter has gym this period. I mean, he's probably fine, but—"

We heard sirens in the distance.

The vice principal and several security guards were striding down the halls with their arms stretched wide. "Go back to class, everyone."

We heard Mrs. J on the loudspeaker. "Attention, all students, you need to return to your first-period class-rooms at this time."

But Ella cut around the corner and pulled me along into a run. We ducked into a stairwell and went down a flight to the ground floor.

In the hallway, more security guards were corral-ling students back to class. Meanwhile, outside, the sirens got louder.

The emergency vehicles finally stopped moving, and from what I could hear, Celeste was right. They seemed to be outside the gym.

"Come on," Ella said, and she pushed open the exterior door. Pulling me along, she cut across the concrete yard to the gym building.

"Go back to class," a distant adult voice shouted through a bullhorn.

I turned to see a blue uniform.

"We need to stop or we'll get in trouble," I panted.

"He's not close enough to identify us," Ella said.

It hit me that she was right. At Penfield, a security guard could have identified me at practically a football field's distance. Not here.

We dipped around the corner to the side of the gym. The day was so dim with the cloud cover, it almost looked like late afternoon. I could see trees and cement and cars, washed with flashes of red and blue from emergency vehicles.

At the corner of the gym was a hole in the chain-link fence. You couldn't really see it unless you knew it was there. Ella pulled it open and slipped out.

I stuck my head and shoulders through the hole. I saw an ambulance and five police cars. A pair of cops was setting up a police line. Several others were pushing the students back. One had a bullhorn and was barking commands: "Students need to return to class. Those who fail to return may face suspension."

Students were yelling back, but I couldn't distinguish any words except "What the hell?"

I stuck my foot through the hole in the fence, but halfway up my thigh, it got stuck.

"I don't think I'll fit through there," I said.

Ella looked from the fence to my hips. "You can make it; you just need to push hard."

I stuck in my other leg and began to heave my hips. Maybe I could fit through, but the process would be seriously undignified.

"I can't," I said.

"Okay," she said. "Keep watch. I'll go see what I can find out."

For the second time that week, I kept a lookout.

I pulled my legs back out through the fence. From there it was too hard to see the scene in the parking lot. Instead, I peeked back around the side of the gym toward the academic buildings, but the cop who had called to us was long gone.

I kept scanning for Dexter. Was he okay? There were thousands of students at Roosevelt. He was probably fine. If he'd been in gym class, he wouldn't have his phone to text that he was okay. Still, I worried.

I walked back to the fence and saw a pair of paramedics carrying a still form on a stretcher, under a white cloth. They were in no hurry.

Did that mean someone was really dead? My heart beat faster as I looked at the form, telling myself that the span from the top of the head to the feet was much too short to be Dexter.

And then, as if to confirm it, he walked over to me with Ella. I took a deep, relieved breath.

"It was a junior," Dexter said in a low voice. "Lil Troy. They think it was a gang shooting."

"The cops think so?" I asked.

"Not the cops," Dexter said. "They're not saying anything. This kid who saw it. Three guys in a car with automatic weapons."

"Is he dead?" I asked.

Dexter nodded. I felt him reach for my fingers through the chain link.

I dropped my eyes. Ella didn't know about us. Not that there was really anything to know. Just a kiss and now a few fingers curled around each other.

I felt my heart hammering, and I tried to shift my thoughts. A kid was dead. My possible romance seemed unimportant in comparison.

"Let's get back to class," Ella said.

Dexter stepped away and let go of my hand. The two of them slipped in through the fence, and we made our way toward the academic buildings.

Dexter squeezed my arm before he peeled off to go to back to gym.

When I returned to class, the teacher had a yellow slip for me.

"Miss Kennedy, the front office wants you."

Between the shooting and the tingly feeling in my fingers and arm where Dexter had touched me, it took me a moment to realize Miss Kennedy was me. Then I panicked. Why would the administration want to talk to *me*? Was it somehow connected to the shooting? I thought about Mom's stalker being in law enforcement. I tried to connect the dots there but couldn't make any sense of it.

By the time I got to the front office, I was totally freaked out.

"Amani!" I looked around and saw my mom, wild-eyed and rushing over to me, calling me by my old name. "You forgot your medicine," she said.

She held out a tube of aloe vera gel. She had used it for a burn last month.

"Thanks, Mom," I said.

As she handed it to me, she leaned in. "I heard there was a shooting," she said. "I've been calling and messaging to make sure you were okay."

"They don't let us use our phones in class," I said. "I'm fine. They think it was gang related."

I could see her relax. "Okay," she said, hugging me tighter than usual. "Love you."

"No problem," I said. "I love you, too."

A moment later, Ella walked into the office.

The student aide pointed to my mom. "Your aunt is here to see you," the aide said to Ella.

Ella frowned in confusion.

Mom looked flustered. "I just sort of panicked and requested both of you," she said. "When I heard about the shooting. I—I thought maybe they'd have trouble finding Imani. Because she's new. I was just so worried."

Ella looked at my mom with a slightly "are you crazy" look and then nodded slowly. "Okay, *Auntie Carmen*," she said. "We're both just fine. Your *nephew* Dexter, too."

"Thank goodness," Mom said. "So sorry to call both of you out of class for no reason."

"It's cool," Ella said. "Just that kind of day."

Mom hugged me. God, did she really have to? And then hugged her "niece" Ella—which was not quite as awkward as I expected it to be.

Then she walked out of the office, and Mrs. J gave me and Ella hall passes back to class.

"No offense," Ella said. "But is your mom always this . . . overprotective?"

"Basically, yes," I said. "And it's been extra-extra lately."

"Got it," she said. "Glad we're 'cousins' now."

"Young ladies," one of the security guards said as the bell rang. "You need to head to class."

We showed him our hall passes. He sent Ella in the opposite direction to the science cluster.

My path to class passed by my locker. The hall was empty, so I opened my locker and checked my phone. Sure enough, I had a dozen missed calls and messages from Mom. I also had a message from an unfamiliar number. Dad!

He'd sent a picture of a polar bear mom with her cub. They were playing in a bank of snow. So cute!

> Miss my family so much. Glad I got to see these two today, reminding me that I do this for another important family. Thinking of you today, sweet girl. Working my way home as fast as I can. Love, Dadiki

I felt my heart leap. Dadiki had been my baby name for him. Mom had gotten through. Dad would come as soon as he could. Everything was all right.

At least for me. I recalled the gunshots that had sounded like thunder. There were never any guns at Penfield. But I thought about what Mom said about racism. There weren't knives at Penfield, either, but that school had sliced me up from day one. Still, that form on the stretcher. Lil Troy. I shuddered and hurried back to class.

Later that day, someone pulled the fire alarm. It was during the final period, and everyone headed out into the yard. Teachers were trying to tell the students that they didn't have permission to leave campus, but everyone was already shook from the shooting.

I looked for Ella and Dexter but couldn't see them, so I just pulled my hood up and started for home. I walked with my head down and my earbuds in, ignoring shouts that might have been aimed at me.

It took a lot of focus to ignore everything around me, which is why I actually walked past Sister Niema's house. A few houses down the block, I realized I had gone too far. And when I turned to look back, I saw a man coming down the steps of Sister Niema's porch.

Instinctively, I turned and walked to the entryway of an apartment building and pretended to study the doorbells.

Peeking out from under my hood, I glanced at the guy. I think my heart nearly stopped. I could have sworn it was the same guy from behind our old house. The one I hit with the roller skates.

By then he had turned and was walking away. Had I imagined it? I carefully scrutinized him from behind. He had the same general frame, although today was hotter, and he was wearing a T-shirt and jeans. The guy behind the house had been limping with an injury, and this guy had a spry walk. He had on a baseball cap, so I couldn't see his face or check for some telltale sign on his head where I'd hit him.

I pulled my jacket hood down over my face and trotted after him.

He turned the corner, and I jogged to catch up. Just as I edged past the liquor store, I saw him open the door to a nondescript gray-brown sedan. I stood in front of the liquor store, my hood pulled low over my eyes.

His car was parked facing me. As he opened the door and slid into the car, I got a good look at his face.

My skin went cold. It was definitely the same guy.

He was parked tightly between two cars, and as he edged out, I caught the license plate. The seven letters and numbers burned into my eyes, and I recited them over and over in my mind like a litany. Or like a rap song to the instrumental music blasting on a loop in my earbuds.

Not till he had made a left at the next intersection did I turn around and head back to Sister Niema's house.

But what about Sister Niema? Was she somehow in league with the guy?

Suddenly, there was a young man standing in front of me.

"I see you," I could hear him say loudly, over the music in my ears.

I pulled out the earbuds. "Excuse me?" I said. He stood in front of the liquor store, drinking from a bottle inside a brown paper bag. He had his shirt off and hanging from his low-slung belt. It was warm today, but it wasn't that warm.

"I see you," he said to me again, with a smile. "Walking by a few times. You like what you see?"

"Huh?" I said, blinking, confused. Still chanting the license plate in my mind. "No!"

"Why don't you stop and talk to me?"

I put the earbuds back in and pushed past him.

He yelled something after me, but I had cranked the volume all the way up and didn't hear. When I turned the corner back on to Sister Niema's block, I peeked over my shoulder. Thankfully, he hadn't followed.

What should I do? I walked down the block and sat on the apartment building steps. I called Mom but got no answer. I messaged her to call me. I tried the front desk at the clinic. If she was there, I'd just go and wait till her shift ended.

The receptionist said she was off-site.

Maybe I should be more specific about what had happened. But what should I say? *I just saw roller-skate guy. Sister Niema might be in league with him. Scared to go back to her house?*

"Imani!" I heard someone calling my name.

I looked up to see Sister Niema carrying a bucket of water down her driveway. She beckoned me over.

I thought about running away, but she was in pretty good shape, and she knew the neighborhood better than I did. I figured if she was in on it, I didn't want her to know I knew.

"Can you help me carry this water out to the front lawn?" she asked. Sister Niema bailed out her bathwater and used it on her garden.

"Sure," I said, trying to sound cool.

I carried two more buckets out. Sister Niema poured them into an old-fashioned metal watering can and was watering the yellow flowers.

I messaged Mom again:

Something's up. Please come home ASAP.

Sister Niema finished watering the flowers. "You're home early," she said. I listened for a note of accusation in her voice but didn't find one. "I'm surprised," she went on. "They don't usually close the school when there's a shooting."

"You heard about that?" I asked.

She picked up the watering can and walked up the driveway. I tagged behind her, contemplating if maybe I should make a run for it.

"It was all over the news," she said. "You must be scared to death."

She set the watering can down beside the back porch and put an arm around me. I sort of tensed up. She gently led me to the kitchen.

"I made some gingerbread," she said.

It was so weird. Sister Niema seemed like the same caring older woman she'd been that morning. But that creepy guy was definitely coming out of her house. What did I really know about her? Why did Mom trust her?

The silence between us had stretched to the awkward point. I fumbled for something to say.

"Someone pulled the fire alarm," I said.

She just nodded. The smell of the gingerbread was filling the kitchen. Cinnamon, ginger, clove. I could feel my mouth watering. There were also veggies out on the counter, like she had started dinner.

On the kitchen table was an actual cookie jar. She took off the lid, and I saw that she had iced the gingerbread. Well, I didn't think she was going to poison me, did I? I took one and bit into it.

"Oh my God," I said almost involuntarily through a mouthful of cookie. "Sooo good."

She smiled at me, then went back to cooking. She chopped up some garlic and put it in a skillet on the stove.

On the table were two glasses. One had an interior coating of green liquid with flecks of red in it pooling in the bottom. Sister Niema's afternoon kale smoothie. The other glass was clear.

His water glass?

I set my cookie down on a napkin and casually carried both empty glasses to the sink. Mom had encouraged me to be helpful around the house. I had done the dishes a few times. Why not again today?

Sister Niema had her head in a low cupboard, hunting through pots and pans. Swiftly, I hid his water glass behind the toaster and brought out another one.

By the time Sister Niema pulled her head out of the cupboard, I was washing her glass and the new glass.

She had a large skillet in her hand. "Making a stir-fry tonight," she said.

"You're kind of an amazing cook," I said, wiping one of my hands and taking another bite of the cookie.

"Those are dairy-free," she said. "Sweetened with apple juice concentrate."

Maybe it was the apple juice concentrate that emboldened me. "So was that your boyfriend I saw walking out of the house?"

Sister Niema laughed. "That young man, David? No, baby, he's just a young activist I work with."

I nodded and put the two clean glasses into the dish drainer.

As I started washing the blender she used to make the smoothie, I tried to make my voice sound casual. "So if David's not your boyfriend, what's your boyfriend's name? Is he closer to your age?" I washed the bottom part of the blender, the blades, and the little rubber ring.

"Somebody is all up in my business today," Sister Niema said, laughing.

She put the lid on the cookie jar. The gingerbread was conspiring with her easy laugh to make me think I had imagined it was the same guy.

But I knew what I had seen.

I doubled down on my playful tone. "I'm just saying," I said. "I come home early from school, and there's a young guy walking out of your house with a bounce in his step. What was I supposed to think?" I rinsed the large pitcher of the blender.

"As a woman of a certain age," Sister Niema said, "I'm flattered that your mind even went there."

I set all the pieces of the blender in the drainer beside both glasses. Then I picked up the cookie and took tiny bites, stalling, hoping for a chance to be alone in the kitchen.

Sister Niema ambled through the room, taking out gluten-free soy sauce and pasture-raised eggs. She hummed as she worked.

I took a second gingerbread cookie and began to eat it.

Sister Niema added some of the vegetables and stirred the contents of the skillet, then turned to me.

"Baby, would you mind watching this pan for me?" she asked. "That raw kale goes right through me."

"Sure," I said. Why did adults have to give TMI about their digestion?

But the moment the bathroom door closed, I got the water glass from behind the toaster. Taking a napkin, I wiped around the rim of the glass. I even poured the few drops of water from the bottom onto the napkin. Then I put the napkin in a ziplock bag and stuffed it into my pocket.

Finally, I poured some water into the glass and put it in the sink, as though it had been my water glass.

Then I stirred the garlic and veggies in the skillet.

A few minutes later, when Sister Niema came back, the garlic was turning light brown.

"Thanks, baby," she said, pulling a storage container filled with brown rice from the fridge.

"Anytime," I said, taking another cookie, then walked to the bedroom.

I dug in my toiletries bag and pulled out the ziplocks with the bloody paper towel and napkin from the gas station and the shed. I added the ziplock from today. Maybe one day I'd have the technology to compare them. Meanwhile, at least I had collected the evidence. I was about to stash them back in my toiletries bag when Sister Niema knocked on the door.

I quickly stuffed them into my jacket pocket. "Come in!"

She peeked her head through the door. "Dinner's ready," she said. "Come on down."

When we got to the table, I realized the corner of a ziplock bag was sticking out of my pocket. Thankfully, Sister Niema left the room to get some cilantro from the garden, and I moved the ziplocks from the lower pocket to the inside pocket, which zipped shut.

I had the jacket tied around my waist when she came back in.

The stir-fry was pretty good. I wolfed it down, followed it up with some more gingerbread, and asked to be excused.

Back in the bedroom, I went to write down the

license plate number. It began with a seven—7CV . . . Or was it 7VC . . . Damn! I had spent so much time with Sister Niema between the glass and the dinner that the license plate number had gotten hazy in my head. How was that even possible? When I was chanting it in my head along to the music, it had seemed I'd never forget it. I needed the music.

I put my earbuds in and turned on the music.

From the moment the beat started, the numbers came back to me: 7CVJ . . .

I wrote down the license plate number and went online to see what I could find out.

Turned out that the car had only one owner and had not been in any accidents. Apparently, it's easy to find info for buying a car but harder to find out who owns it.

I lay on the bed. I had a thousand different thoughts and a clash of feelings. There'd been a shooting at my school. I was sure I'd seen the guy who'd been creeping around my old house. My burned-down house. Sister Niema might be lying to me. Yet my belly was full of the world's best gingerbread.

Mom just needed to hurry up and get home. Home? This wasn't home. I looked at my phone for the thousandth time. Mom wasn't messaging me back. What if Sister Niema really was in league with that guy? David? How was she on a first-name basis with the guy who had tried to—what? Break into our house? Grab my phone? What had he really been trying to do? None of it made sense. Everything was calm and orderly here in Sister Niema's house. But was something sinister happening under the surface?

I felt panic in my solar plexus. Why didn't the spare bedroom lock? I slid the chest of drawers in front of the door. It wouldn't keep someone out for any length of time. But it would slow them down while I jumped out the window. I unlocked the window and waited.

I sat on my bed, looking from the door to the phone. Nearly an hour had gone by when I heard someone in the hallway outside the door. I walked swiftly to the window.

The knob turned, and the door bumped against the bureau.

"Amani?" It was Mom's voice. "What's wrong with the door?"

"Hold on," I said, and slid the bureau out of the way.

"What's going on?" she asked. "Why are you crying?"

I hadn't realized I was crying. I put a hand on my cheek and found it was wet with tears of relief.

She pulled me into her arms to comfort me.

I stepped away. "I saw the guy," I whispered sharply. "The one from behind our house. I just know it was him. I got his license plate."

"Are you sure, my love?"

"Yes, and he was coming out of the house," I said. "Sister Niema knows him, and his name is David. We have to get this license plate number to the police."

Mom opened her mouth.

"If you say we can't go to the police, then fine," I said. "But I won't stay here. Sister Niema is somehow involved with him."

"No," Mom said. "It's not—"

"Stop it!" I yelled. All the tension that had built up suddenly exploded. "Don't tell me I'm wrong. I saw him. I know it was the same guy. And I will not spend one more night—one more *minute*—in this house until we know what's going on."

Mom sighed. "It's not what you think, my love."

"Well, what is it?"

"That guy," she said. "David. I know him, too."

I had so many thoughts and questions that nothing could come out of my mouth for a second.

Into the pause in our conversation, a third voice spoke. "Is everything okay?"

I turned to see Sister Niema in the doorway. I took a step toward Mom.

Mom hesitated.

"What were you really doing with the man who was sneaking around our house?" I blurted out.

Sister Niema's eyebrows rose, but other than that, she didn't react.

"I was just trying to tell her that she couldn't send his license plate to the police," Mom said. "I was telling her that I know David, too."

Sister Niema looked from Mom to me. She appeared to be sizing me up. Finally, in a quiet but firm voice, she said to Mom, "Carmen, I think it's time we tell her."

Tell me what? Suddenly, I was more scared than when I'd seen the guy.

"I—well, your father and I—" Mom began, but Sister Niema cut her off.

"Your father does research," she said bluntly. "But not on climate. He often works as part of intelligence operations."

I don't know what I'd expected. That Mom was having an affair with David? That David was the stalker? That he was a roller-skating coach my mom had hired as a surprise? It was as if, hearing the real explanation, my mind needed to go back and come up with every other possibility. I would be more ready to believe that Dad was a werewolf, a shape-shifter, or an extraterrestrial before I could imagine that he worked as some type of spy.

I looked up and saw that Sister Niema's mouth was still moving, but I hadn't heard anything she'd said.

"Your father and my ex-husband were working together," Sister Niema was saying.

She had an ex-husband? What? Focus. Why did my mind keep shooting off on to tangents?

"They were involved in a case and made some powerful enemies."

"Wait," I said. "Is my dad a secret agent?"

"No, my love," Mom said. "Like Sister Niema was saying, your dad is a researcher. He sometimes goes on assignments, but he doesn't work undercover. Her ex-husband is the one who works in the field."

"They were both involved in an operation that made some members of a drug cartel very angry," Sister Niema said. "The cartel wanted revenge. We're not sure how, but they were able to access their identities and may have gotten some personal information about your family. David was assigned to watch your house, to protect you."

Something clicked in my head. The expression on David's face. The sort of worry and concern. Yes, it made a lot more sense now.

"I guess . . ." I blinked, trying to take it all in. "I guess I owe David an apology."

Mom spoke, her voice surprisingly thick. "David said that he told your father about you hitting him, and your dad was so proud. 'That's my girl,' he said."

Suddenly, I started to cry, too. "I miss Dad so much. Is he okay? Is he safe?"

Mom shrugged through her tears, unable to speak.

"He's fine," Sister Niema said. "He's just lying low for a while. His access to communication is limited, but that's for his own safety."

"That guy we saw at the mall," I said. "He was from the drug cartel?"

Mom glanced quickly at Sister Niema. "I think so," Mom said. "I wasn't a hundred percent sure."

"Did our house really burn down?" I asked.

Mom nodded. "That's the thing," she said. "The fire department still hasn't ruled whether or not it was arson. We didn't want to take the chance."

"So Dad's not a climate-change scientist?" I asked.

Mom laughed through her tears and shook her head. "Baby, there were so many times we wanted to tell you the truth. But the agency insists that people keep quiet about what they do."

"Which agency?" I asked. "FBI? CIA?"

Mom shook her head. "Neither one. It's an independent intelligence agency. That's all I should really tell you right now."

I nodded, feeling strangely calm. I didn't like it, but at least everything added up now. Things finally made sense. "So how long does Dad need to lie low? And how long to we need to stay here?"

"The agency is figuring that out right now," Mom said.

"But how come we can't trust law enforcement?" I asked.

"The agency isn't part of the US government, and they don't know where the leak is," Mom said. "Until they do, we can't trust anyone."

"They're hoping they can eliminate the threat," Sister Niema said. "But worst-case scenario, they'd give all of you new identities and relocate you as a family."

"Like witness protection?" I asked.

"That's basically the situation," Sister Niema said. "Your dad is a researcher who witnessed something having to do with this drug cartel. And they want to make sure the two of you are safe."

My mind clung to the idea that whatever happened, we'd get to be back together as a family.

"I know this is a lot," Mom said. "I'm so sorry you had to find out this way."

"Well," I said slowly. "I'm glad Dad's safe. And I'm glad there's a plan B." Suddenly, I had the vision of David looking worried about us, even as he was half passing out. "And if David's one of the good guys, I'm glad I didn't kill him with your roller skates."

Then the three of us laughed, and for a moment, I felt like myself again.

For the next few days, I walked around in a daze, trying to process what I'd been told. It wasn't until I was walking to school with Ella almost a week later that the rage set in. It wasn't a slow boil or a gradual warming. It was like flipping a switch.

"You seem quiet today," she said. "Is everything okay?"

And I suddenly wanted to scream: *No! My dad works for some spy agency, and a drug cartel is after him, and my parents have been lying to me my whole life!*

Mom and Sister Niema had emphasized that I couldn't talk about this with anyone, not even Ella and Dexter. But I had to say something.

"My dad works as a climate researcher," I said. "And . . . like . . . my parents aren't really honest about his work. I mean . . ." I searched for the words. "My dad has been sugarcoating global warming. Now that I'm older and doing my own research, I can see that . . . we're in . . . in a lot of danger. And I'm scared about it. Really scared."

"Yeah," Ella said. "Climate change is real. But you know all hope isn't lost, right? If the people rise up and demand change, we can still stop the worst of climate collapse. People say we're doomed, but it's not true. We just have to make big changes."

"Like, huge changes," I said. "Super massive."

"Right," Ella said. "And there's no guarantee."

"Exactly," I said. "So why is he acting like everything's fine? And my mom, too. I mean, she's . . . she's a doctor, and she deals with people who have been victims of violence. She also really . . . plays it down. Like . . . this guy was targeted by a drug cartel. And they . . . they almost killed him."

"LA can be a really dangerous place," Ella said.

"Yeah," I said. "And if my mom is working with their victims, I mean, who knows? She could be in danger or something."

"I don't think they usually go after the doctors," Ella said.

"It's the principle of the thing," I said. "They act like I'm a baby, and they paint a picture of the world as some cartoon planet with everyone holding hands and singing in harmony. But I'm fifteen, and I know there's a lot that needs changing."

I knew life was complicated, but I didn't know why it had to be so unfair. Not just the climate crisis, where the people who didn't create the problem—Black people—were the ones being hit worst. But also, on a more personal note, what if the only way to get back to my dad would be some sort of witness protection program? I'd get to keep my family, but I'd have to say goodbye to Ella and Dexter and Celeste. Roosevelt wasn't that bad. I mean, it was a mix, but it was worth it to have friends who really got me and were also Black. And there were other kids, like Katanya, who shared a couple of my classes. She wasn't exactly a Harambee type, but she seemed cool, too. Because of my parents' choices, I'd had to leave Penfield, and now I might have to leave here?

I could feel the tightness in my jaw as I said, half to

Ella, half to myself, "I wish they would just tell me the truth."

I was still mad, but it felt good to have said something.

Ella nodded. "My mom works in Hollywood, right? It turns out she was sexually harassed. She told us before it all came out on social media. I guess it went on for a few years, from when I was ten to, like, twelve. I knew something was going on but not what it was. Sometimes I would hear my parents up at night whispering, all tense."

We were walking under the freeway. I had to strain to hear her over the echoing sound of the cars going by.

"When she eventually told me," Ella said, "I felt a lot of different things. But I was mad that she hadn't said anything earlier. Then she explained she had been trying to protect me. Shelter me, you know? But it hadn't really worked. I had been totally anxious because it was a big secret. Since they weren't slick enough to actually keep me in blissful ignorance, I would have liked to know what was wrong."

But my parents *had* actually been slick enough. Some strange spy agency. I shuddered, and we hurried to the end of the block, out from under the freeway's shadow.

ELEVEN

I **saw Dexter for only a minute** after school. He had track practice. But we did manage to exchange numbers, and that afternoon he messaged me emoji updates. The little guy running track. Smiley faces. Pictures of food. I messaged Dexter various emoji back. The only text with words he sent was all business, letting me know that Amber wasn't feeling well and capoeira was canceled the next afternoon. I began to wonder: Were emoji-only texts a sign that he couldn't be bothered to write words? Or was he just busy? Or was he not allowed to message during practice, and it meant he was gallantly risking punishment to communicate? I had no idea. But I stuck close to home as I did homework.

"I hear a lot of beeping on your phone," Sister Niema called from the kitchen. "Everything okay?"

"Everything's fine," I said. Ever since seeing David here, things were a slight degree off with Sister Niema. Or was my entire life in total upheaval and *everything* was off? There was just this funny feeling that I couldn't shake.

I turned off my notifications so she wouldn't have more reasons to be in my business. From time to time, the phone would light up with big emoji. I always messaged back. Pictures of books. Pictures of food. Was I too boring? Or was my day just boring? I scrolled the emoji collection for something that said *I like you* but didn't include hearts. Nothing was quite subtle enough, so I left it alone.

Finally, I got a text with words and even a picture. I eagerly snatched up the phone.

My heart sank when I realized it wasn't from Dexter but leaped again when I saw it was from Dad.

> Hey, honey. Your mom has me up-to-date on all that's been happening. It's almost too much to take in, right? Wish I could be there. But I know you two are safe with Sister Niema. Sounds like they mentioned a few of the travel problems I've been having. But I'll get there as soon as I can. Mom says you're a total trouper. I'm proud of you. Love you. Miss you. See you soon. Love, Dadiki

I had started to compose a response when I got a second message. More from Dad!

No. Not from Dad. From Mom. She'd be home late. Did Sister Niema need anything from the store?

I relayed several grocery-related messages, but by that point, my phone was almost out of charge. I plugged it in and texted Dexter to let him know that I needed to do homework and asked:

U free after school tomorrow?

After I sent it, I realized it was bold. Did I just ask him out on a date? I wished I could take it back, saying instead, "I'm free after school." I had heard somewhere that girls are supposed to hint.

Before I could panic, I got back a *YES!!!* message, which reassured me considerably.

I saw Dexter again the following day in fourth-period English class. We smiled at each other when he walked in, but his seat was way across the room from me and a few desks toward the front. I stared at the back of his head. His neck was so graceful as it rose out of his pale green T-shirt. His hair was cut in a short fade, but I could see the tight swirls of the curl pattern where it was longer on top. His shoulders were broad, and he had good posture. I unconsciously sat up straighter.

The teacher was explaining that we would be studying "point of view" and "context." She put a list on the overhead of the books they'd been studying, mostly memoirs. They spanned from Homer's *The Odyssey* to the recent *A Long Way Gone: Memoirs of a Boy Soldier* by Ishmael Beah.

Then she asked us to pick one of the books to look at for context and point of view and present to the class. Students were to raise their hands for their first-choice books. *A Long Way Gone* was popular, second only to *The Autobiography of Malcolm X*, followed by *Brown Girl Dreaming*.

I watched Dexter's back carefully, hoping we'd get to work together. His hand didn't go up.

"Extra credit for anyone willing to present on a book written before the twentieth century." She got a few takers for *Narrative of the Life of Frederick Douglass* and *Incidents in the Life of a Slave Girl*.

"A bunch of you haven't selected yet," the teacher complained. She was a short-haired woman with an ASIANS IN SOLIDARITY WITH BLACK LIVES T-shirt stretching against her pregnant belly.

I hadn't chosen yet. I wished I could see Dexter's face. Was he waiting for me to say something? He was usually the type to volunteer in class.

"Won't anyone take a shot at *The Odyssey*?" she asked.

Dexter turned around and reached to get a pen

out of his backpack. When he did, he glanced over his shoulder at me. A glance so quick, I thought I might have imagined it.

"Please, people, will someone take *The Odyssey*?"

He had glanced at me, though. He definitely had.

"I'll do it," I said to the teacher, feeling bold.

"Thank you," she said. "Who will join"—she looked down at her roll sheet—"Imani and work on *The Odyssey*?"

For a moment there was silence. I could feel my face flush.

"She can't have a group by herself," the teacher said.

Clearly, I had read the sign wrong. Now I had revealed myself as some kind of nerd. Or worse yet, a teacher's pet.

"Okay," Dexter said. "I will."

"Great," she said. "Now I just need one more taker between the eighth century BCE and the eighteen hundreds."

Eventually, she gave up, and we got into our groups.

Dexter went to the shelf that had the class set of each of the books and got us two copies.

"Hey," I said as Dexter sat in a desk next to mine.

"Hey," he said, smiling. He handed me a paperback with a painting of an ancient sailboat being menaced by a sea monster.

"Thanks for letting me drag you back into the eighth century BCE," I said.

"Are you kidding me?" he said. "I'd love to hang out with you in the eighth century. You got my signal, right?"

"I wasn't sure it was a signal," I said.

"Of course it was," he said.

"Then why did you leave me hanging?" I asked.

"Come on, Imani," he said. "The pretty new girl, and I jump to join her in presenting on the book nobody wants? When I could be doing Malcolm X or a boy soldier from Sierra Leone? I had to sell it like I was reluctant. Otherwise, the teacher would know it was just a ploy to spend time with you in class."

I could feel myself blushing a little, from both the word "pretty" and the fact that he was, in fact, plotting to spend time with me.

"Also," he said, "I needed you to volunteer because I didn't read that book. I tried a few times but got nowhere. Ella helped me fake my way through the quiz about it."

"Oh, I *got* this book," I said. Penfield had forced the classics down our throats last year. "I could write about context and point of view with one hand tied behind my back."

"And maybe do a no-handed flippy-flip thing at the end of the presentation?" he asked.

Now I was really blushing. "That's just for certain people to see," I said. "I can't let everyone here at this school know about my special skills and my secret weapons."

"So you're saying that information is classified?" he asked.

"Definitely on a need-to-know basis," I said, nodding sagely.

"So glad you told me," he said. "Because I was just about to put a notice in the school bulletin: 'Attention, students.'" He mimicked Mrs. J's voice. "'We have a new student, Imani Kennedy, who is a total badass. Students should report to the gym immediately to see her flip over with no hands. This move may come in handy when sneaking off campus and avoiding our security guards.'"

I smacked him playfully in the shoulder. "You've obviously forgotten that I never mastered the aerial."

He sighed. "I guess we'll have to practice some more."

The teacher came by our desks. "Are you two focusing on *The Odyssey*?" she asked.

"Yes," I said. "We were debating whether or not the context was the Trojan War and its aftermath or the Greek cosmology."

"I was pro-cosmology, because I really like all the mythical creatures," Dexter said.

"But I was connecting it to some of the other books on the list as a war memoir," I said.

"Okay," she said. "Clearly you all don't need my help." She moved on to another group who was laughing way too loud. The Malcolm X group was so big, she had to break it up into three subgroups.

"Can we focus on the book?" she asked the loudest group.

"We were," one of the boys said. "We were laughing about the time he had that lye perm on his head and the water went out and he had to put his head in the toilet."

Another boy put his head down and made a flushing sound, and the group of boys cracked up.

"A funny scene," she said. "But can we focus on *context* and *point of view*?"

Dexter leaned in toward me when she was out of earshot. "Nicely done," he said. "You are so smart."

"Thank you," I said. "But you did pretty good for someone who didn't read the book."

"Not really," he said. "I just went off the picture on the cover."

We were interrupted when the teacher dinged a chime. "Listen, folks," she said. "Make sure you have a follow-up plan with your group. And put the desks back."

"So what's our follow-up plan?" I asked Dexter.

He put his pen to his temple and made a face that parodied thoughtfulness. "I think we need to get together after school and discuss this in depth."

"Good thing we already have a date," I said. Before the word was even out of my mouth, I regretted it. We were hanging out. We were doing homework. How had I put so much on it? I could feel the heat rising to my face again, and I kept my head lowered under the pretext of scooting my desk back into place.

"Yes, we do have a date," Dexter said, rescuing me from mortification just as the bell rang.

After school, the two of us sat at the kitchen table in Sister Niema's house. We were each flipping through our copies of *The Odyssey*, and I was taking notes.

"You know," Dexter said. "People often focus on Homer's battle with the gods and the monsters, but I think the biggest deal here is about his girl."

"'His girl'?" I asked. "You're calling Penelope 'his girl'?"

"Okay, my bad," Dexter said. "His wifey. But what I'm trying to say is that some things from that context in the eighth century BCE haven't really changed that much. Like, she was there without her man, and all these other guys were trying to holla at her. Which is, you know, kind of like being a new girl at a big school. There might be, like, a lot of interest in that girl. And a brother might, you know, have a lot of competition in getting to know her."

Competition? I must have just blinked at him in confusion. What planet had I just landed on?

"Wow," he said. "You really don't know, do you? I can't believe you have no idea how beautiful you are."

Just as he leaned forward to kiss me, I heard the office door open, and he sat up straight with his book in his hand.

We heard several footsteps in the hallway, and then Sister Niema walked across the kitchen. She was muttering about "the good old days of microaggressions, when these racist folks had some shame."

She put on the teakettle and was staring out the window. The traffic zoomed past. We heard a couple of people greeting each other on the block.

"Dexter," she said. "Can you help me get this teapot down off the top shelf? I can't seem to find my step stool."

"Yes, ma'am," he said, and stood up to help.

"Sorry, Sister Niema," I said. "I borrowed it. Lemme get it out of the bedroom."

Turned out I hadn't left it in the bedroom but in the hallway outside the bedroom. I was back in less than thirty seconds.

In the kitchen, the two of them had their hands on the teapot and their heads together. Sister Niema seemed to be whispering something to Dexter.

When I walked in, they both looked up quickly.

"Thank you, baby," Sister Niema said.

I sat back down at the table. Dexter slid into the chair next to me.

What was that about? I wrote on the paper between us.

Somebody wants to make sure my intentions are honorable, he wrote back.

I could feel my face flush.

I flipped a page in my book. Dexter flipped one as well. But I could tell he wasn't really reading it.

Sister Niema's gaze sharpened, and she looked directly at me and Dexter. "You know what?" she said. "I shouldn't work on this stuff alone. I'm gonna join you." She walked across to the hallway. "Sometimes I lose my perspective when I'm all cooped up in that office."

Dexter leaned over and whispered, "She's like Poseidon in the book, hampering my journey toward you at every turn."

Now I was really blushing. I hid my face in my book as Sister Niema walked back into the kitchen carrying her laptop computer. She set it down at the other end of the table.

Both of us continued to flip through our copies of *The Odyssey.* I took a few more notes.

Did I call this a date? Dexter wrote on my lined paper. *I meant sitting next to you trying to covertly hold your hand while under surveillance.*

I stifled a laugh.

Sister Niema looked up from her laptop.

"Say what you want about the European canon," I said. "But Homer has some funny moments."

She went back to her computer.

How about a recel date? he wrote.

I looked up at him. Recel? I was so out of it when it came to slang. Recel? Resell? I tried to reason it out, but I couldn't.

I underlined "recel" and put a trio of question marks.

He smiled and connected the *c* to the loop of the *e*, and it made a cursive letter *a*. *A real date.*

I put my hand over my mouth and managed to laugh silently.

Tomorrow after school? Dexter added, writing slowly enough that it was legible.

Okay, I wrote back. Then I wondered if that was too wishy-washy. But I didn't want to look too excited.

Triángulo? he wrote.

Yes! I replied. Then it would be clear I was excited, but not just about him.

We went back to flipping pages in our books. Dexter held his copy in one hand, and his little finger reached across the table to casually land next to mine.

A couple minutes later, the kettle whistled. Dexter moved his hand away about an inch as Sister Niema got up.

She poured herself a cup of tea and offered us some. We both shook our heads.

I couldn't stand pretending to read *The Odyssey*

anymore. I put it in my backpack and saw the corner of my cipher notebook.

"Hey," I said to Dexter. "Can we take a break from serious literature to work on something different?"

"Hallelujah," Dexter said in a deadpan. "I've been saved."

"Do you know anything about code?" I asked.

"Computer code?"

"No, cipher code," I said.

"A little," he said. "I know it's really cool."

"I think so, too," I said, flipping through the pages of my notebook. "My dad sent me this." Suddenly, it occurred to me that the whole code depended on the spelling of my name, which I had changed. How was I going to explain the cipher if I couldn't explain the A-M-A pattern in my name?

"Can I get a couple of pages of blank notebook paper?" I asked him. I had plenty, but I needed to stall.

He handed me the paper, and I copied down the ciphers, but I changed the name in the message to reflect IMANI.

I slid the paper across to him. "See if you can solve these," I said.

JNBOJ J DBOU XBJU UP HFU IPNF UP TFF ZPV9 I51CCP D9MM RFN 9D1E9

While he stared at the ciphers, I tried to figure out how to change the new one. If I suspected that BLBMJ said AMANI, then logically I should be able to use the *I* at the end of the AMANI to be the *I* at the beginning of IMANI.

I revised the code on another sheet of paper. BLBMJ became JLBMJ.

JUF BKVBXR AFFM RP OQPVC PE XPV JLBMJ RSBX RSQPMF

"Wait," he said. "You're giving me another one? I haven't even got the slightest idea how to solve either of these two."

"Okay," I said. "I'll give you a hint." I leaned over the paper. "In this first one, JNBOJ is my name."

He grinned. "Okay," he said. "Looks like they moved it up one letter in the alphabet. So your dad is saying . . ." He took a minute to figure on the paper, then said, "'Imani I can't wait to get home to see you.'"

"Yes!" I said. "And here's my name in this one . . ." I pointed to 9D1E9.

"Hmmm . . ." he said. "The numbers are throwing me off."

I left him to work on that one while I worked on the latest one. If JLBMJ was IMANI in this one, then the *I* seemed to turn to *J*, and the *B* was where the *A* should be. But the other letters didn't work out correctly. The consonants in the word didn't seem to follow the same rule.

Wait! What if the rule was different for vowels than for consonants? The vowels seemed to be a letter later in the alphabet. But if *L* was where the *M* should be and *M* was where the *N* should be, then the consonants were a letter *earlier* in the alphabet.

"I'm stumped," Dexter said, still looking at the second cipher.

"It's a tough one, right?" I said. I showed him the letter/number code.

"Nice!" he said. He worked it out and wrote I REALLY MISS YOU IMANI.

"Exactly," I said. "Now here's the new one." I showed him the decoded IMANI in the new cipher where the vowels and consonants followed a different pattern.

"I know just what this needs," Dexter said. "A chart to organize it." He pulled out some graph paper and filled it in.

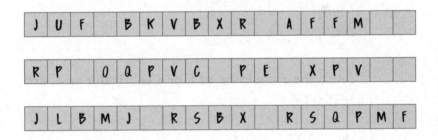

J	U	F		Ƀ	K	V	Ƀ	X	R		A	F	F	M		

R	P		O	Q	P	V	C		P	E		X	P	V		

J	L	Ƀ	M	J		R	S	Ƀ	X		R	S	Q	P	M	F

"I'm gonna assume that each block of letters is a word. So here's the first one."

	J	U	F
VOWEL			
CONSONANT			

"Let's fill in what it would be if it was a vowel and if it was a consonant," I said.

The *J* would be an *I* if it was a vowel and a *K* if it was a consonant, so we filled that in.

	J	U	F
VOWEL	I		
CONSONANT	K		

"But in the next column, the *u* can't be a vowel, because the letter that comes before *U* is *T*, which isn't a vowel," said Dexter.

"Right!" I said. "So *U* is definitely *V*." I filled that in.

	J	U	F
VOWEL	I		
CONSONANT	K	V	

"And the *F* could be an *E* or a *G*," Dexter said, and filled that in.

	J	U	F
VOWEL	I		E
CONSONANT	K	V	G

"Yes!" I said. "So the word has to be 'I've' because 'ivg' isn't a word."

"I was thinking of 'kvg,'" he said.

"Actually 'ivg' could totally be a word," I said. "I think this guy down the block was using it just the other day."

"Oh, really?" he said. "So use 'ivg' in a sentence."

"'Ivg' is African American slang for an Ivy League girl," I said. "You know, 'ivg.' Like 'Wassup, girl, you can't talk to me? You some kind of stuck-up ivg?'"

Dexter cracked up. "I stand corrected."

"I may have only lived in this neighborhood a short time," I said. "But I'm really picking up the local slang very quickly."

"Can I call you an ivg?" he asked.

"No," I said. "It's considered derogatory. Only us ivgs can use it on each other."

"I see," he said. "Now quit stalling and let's figure out the rest of this cipher."

J	U	F		B	K	V	B	X	R		A	F	F	M	
I		E		A		U	A				E	E			
K	V	G		C	L	W	C	Y	S		B	G	G	N	

I'd never shared the ciphers with anyone else before.

R	P			O	Q	P	V	C		P	E		X	P	V
	O				O	U			O				O	U	
S	Q			P	R	Q	W	P		Q	F		Y	Q	W

Just like with IVG, the choices quickly became obvious.

J	L	B	M	J		R	S	B	X		R	S	Q	P	M	F
I		A		I			A						O		E
K	M	C	N	K		S	T	C	Y		S	T	R	Q	N	G

I strung the words together.

IVE ALWAYS BEEN SO PROUD OF YOU IMANI STAY STRONG

Suddenly, I felt myself tearing up. My dad was proud of me. He wanted me to stay strong.

I cleared my throat and reached for a napkin.

"Dexter, honey?" Sister Niema asked. She had a wok in her hand and was taking a container of tofu from the fridge. "It's getting close to dinnertime," she said. "Are you staying for tofu stir-fry? Should you call home? It's almost six."

While Dexter turned to answer, I quickly wiped my eyes.

"No, ma'am," he said. "I didn't realize how late it was. I should go."

He began to load up his backpack.

Sister Niema had put on the wok and began chopping the tofu into cubes.

As her back was turned, he pressed a finger to his lips and touched my cheek with it.

"See you all in the morning," he said, and was out the door.

I stared at our notes on the graph paper. The teary feeling about my dad's message mixed with the fluttering feeling in my stomach. My cheek tingled where Dexter had touched it.

"Your mama messaged that she'll be home for dinner tonight," Sister Niema said. "Will you set the table for three places? This'll be ready in a few minutes."

I went to the cupboard and got the plates.

"So," Sister Niema said. "Looks like Dexter and Ella are helping you to really settle in at Roosevelt. Maybe you like it a little more now, huh?"

I didn't dare take my eyes off the plates as I set them on the place mats. "Yeah," I agreed. "I think it's gonna work out okay."

She didn't reply, just dropped the tofu into the wok of hot oil and let it sizzle.

TWELVE

The next day in school crawled along. The classes hadn't been too boring before, but with the date to look forward to, suddenly they were excruciatingly slow.

There was nothing interactive in English class, so I just stared at the back of Dexter's head, which wasn't even that interesting because he had on a hat. And Dexter didn't sit with us at lunch because of a chess club meeting. I tried to focus on Ella but was texting Dexter at the same time. We decided to walk back to Sister Niema's after school and tell Ella on the way that we wanted to hang out just the two of us. In other words, we would be *telling her*. I guessed if we were on our way to being something like boyfriend and girlfriend, I'd have to tell Mom and Sister Niema, too. But

I wasn't ready to say anything to them, so it was good that we weren't there yet.

Finally, the last bell rang, and I went to my locker before meeting up with Ella and Dexter to walk home.

Ella had gotten her history test back and was not happy with her grade.

"It's an essay exam, but she grades it like it's multiple choice. What were the factors that led up to the Civil War? Apparently, she didn't want me to dig into colonial history in Africa and the primogeniture in Europe."

As we walked, Dexter and I kept brushing our hands across each other. I smiled each time. He tickled my palm, and I giggled out loud. How was Ella going on about this test and not noticing anything?

We walked past a brightly colored mural of Black heroes: tall faces of Malcolm, Martin, Sojourner Truth, and Obama in rich brown hues, with gold lettering that said BLACK IS BEAUTIFUL.

Finally, we turned a corner and could see Sister Niema's house across the street a block and a half down.

I glanced up at Dexter.

"Hey, Ella," Dexter interrupted her monologue. "I need to tell you something."

My heart started to hammer in my chest.

"Huh?" Ella asked, looking at him for the first time since we'd started walking.

"I'm sorry your test didn't go well, but I have some—ah—news."

"What is it?"

"I'm—" Dexter began. "I mean me and Imani—" He looked down at his sneakers. "After I go home to check in, me and Imani were gonna hang out today together. You know? Just the two of us."

"Okay. Whatev—" Her eyes suddenly flew open. "Oh. You want to hang out *together*?" she said. "Cool."

At this point, we were standing in front of Sister Niema's house.

"Can you give us a moment?" Dexter asked.

"Sure," Ella said. She stepped away from the porch and started looking at her phone. Suddenly, she looked up from it. "Hanging out together, huh? My name is Ella Lewiston, and I approve this message."

Dexter smiled. I didn't know why, but her blessing meant a lot to me. I guess she was my best friend by default, so I was glad it wasn't weird. Definitely awkward, but not weird.

We stood on the porch together. He reached for my hand.

"That went well," he said. "So . . . I guess . . . I'll go home and check in, then come back and meet you. We can walk to the comic bookstore together."

"Does that make this an official Black nerd date?" I asked.

Dexter smiled. "Yeah," he said. "Also, uh, the Winter Dance is tonight. Do you like that kind of thing?"

I laughed. "Not really," I said. "But you make it sound like a root canal."

He laughed, too. "Whew! I was ready to go if you wanted to, but I'd rather hang at the comic bookstore. We could go get something to eat after that. If I had some money, I'd suggest that miniature golf place that just opened."

"How much does it cost?" I asked.

"More than Sister Niema is gonna give you," he said. "Especially when it was probably built for the hipsters moving into the neighborhood. 'We need to keep our money in the community,'" he said, mimicking her voice.

"Don't worry," I said. "I can get some cash from my mom."

"I thought she was at work," he said.

"I have my ways," I said.

I looked at Ella. She stood a few feet from us, engrossed in her phone. I leaned forward and kissed him quickly on the lips, then let myself into the house with my key.

I felt bold, having initiated the kiss. I wasn't just a girl who let a boy kiss me. Sometimes I started it. But I also felt a little mortified. What if he didn't like it? I hadn't stayed to see. Roosevelt Imani was the one who kissed him. But Penfield Amani was still around, casting doubt on every interaction with Dexter and telling me not to get my hopes up.

"Hey, Sister Niema," I called. "Just stopping off to get something, and then I'm going back out."

She was working on the computer in the hallway alcove. "No problem, honey. You want some food? I made protein bars."

Her protein bars weren't bad. They had nut butter, honey, and crispy rice. Sometimes they had raisins, which I picked out. No raisins today.

I grabbed a bar for now, then wrapped two to go: one for me and one for Dex. I had begun to call him Dex in my mind like Ella did, even though I wasn't brave enough to try it out loud yet.

Was I just gonna wear my same clothes from school? I looked at myself in the mirror. I was pretty cute in the T-shirt and maxi skirt. I grabbed my hooded jacket and tied it around my waist in case it got cold later. But my eyes strayed to the open closet where I could see a bit of the fabric of that magenta sundress from the mall. Did I dare? Maybe it was too much. I laid it out on the bed. Just in case I got bold. No, I definitely wasn't going to wear it tonight. But even seeing it was sort of a reminder that nothing was out of reach for me. Not beauty. Not bright colors. Not being liked.

I went into the bedroom and began looking through

the boxes for the books. Years ago, I discovered that Mom kept a secret stash of cash in a hardcover copy of the book *Assata* by Assata Shakur. It was a cross between an ATM and a library. I'd borrow money from it, but then I'd give the money back to Mom within twenty-four hours, so she never missed it. When she got home tonight, I'd ask for the money and put it back tomorrow.

When I opened the book, there was a stack of twenties, maybe three hundred dollars total, and when I pulled out the bills, there was a cell phone underneath. It was slender and flat. I took it out and saw a message on the screen:

Miss u tons Dadiki!

It was my message to Dad. I stared at it in disbelief. From me. To Dad.

Why would Mom have Dad's cell phone? No. Wait. That was impossible.

Why would Mom be pretending that Dad was messaging me? A wave of cold passed over me. Was he dead? Was he dead and she was covering it up? Wild possibilities began to run through my head. Was she telling the truth about him being in some spy agency? Was the stalker thing actually true, after all? Was David really a good guy? Wait, was David the stalker?

Or worse, was *Dad* the stalker? Had our house even really burned down?

Everything felt surreal. I felt a buzzing in my chest. But then I realized it was my own cell phone in my pocket. It was Dex:

Headed back to Sis Niema's now.

I blinked. Suddenly Dexter and Triángulo and miniature golf seemed a million miles away. I messaged back:

Can't. Something came up. Call u later.

I pocketed the flip phone and grabbed the cell phone Mom had that was supposed to be Dad's. I tucked all the cash into the pocket of my jacket, and walked out the door.

My chest felt tight as I walked to the bus stop on the corner. On the side of the bus shelter, there was a map of the LA transit system. Through permanent marker and scratched-in graffiti, I figured out I could take a bus to a train to two other buses to get to my old house.

I didn't know what was true about the stalker, so outside the train station I stopped at a drugstore and bought a ball cap and dark glasses.

On the next bus, I scrolled through Mom's phone. She hadn't bothered to put a code on it. There it was.

All the messages back and forth between me and "Dad" since the fire. Or did I mean "fire"?

All through the trip, I felt like I had a vise grip in my chest. Nothing was what I thought it was. It took three hours, a train, and three buses, but I finally got to the bus stop near our old house.

I pulled my jacket's hood over my head and stepped off the bus.

It didn't matter that I had the idea in my mind "house burned down." As I turned the corner, I still expected to see the squat blue bungalow in the middle of the block. Instead, there was a misshapen, blackened thing. A bit of blue showing in the corners. Sure enough, it had burned to the ground.

I didn't stop walking as my tears began to slide down beneath the dark glasses. I shoved my hands in my pockets and walked past my own burned-down house.

At the corner, I went into a mom-and-pop store and hunched in the chip aisle, wiping my eyes on the sleeves of my hooded jacket.

I pulled a bottle of spring water off the shelf, careful to buy glass, not plastic, like Dad always said. Doing my part to fight the global warming that he wasn't actually involved in researching. Dad. Dadiki. More tears started to come down. I breathed until the crying wave passed.

I paid for the water and stepped out onto the street. As I drank, I looked around to see if anyone was lurking nearby, maybe watching the house. The street was pretty quiet.

I walked back to the bus stop, but on the way, I pulled out my cell phone and pretended to be messaging or maybe looking for directions. I saw that I had three missed calls from Dex and a worried face emoji:

Hope yr ok

And my mom had texted me:

Want me to pick up some pizza on the way home?

I stared at the phone. Pizza? How could she just lie like that? Act like everything was normal?

I was so mad. I picked up the flip phone to make a call, but to whom? Dex? I really liked him, but I didn't know him well enough to spring all this on him. Ella was the same. We had been friends for only two weeks. I couldn't talk about this with either of them.

I just put in my earbuds and blasted dance music into my eardrums for the ride home—or I should say, to Sister Niema's, because my last real home had burned to the ground.

By the time I got there, it was dark. I opened the door with my key, and the place smelled of pizza. On the coffee table, I could see the open box, but none of the slices had been touched.

My mom spun toward the door. "Where the hell have you been? We've been out of our minds with worry. Sister Niema's been out combing the neighborhood looking for you."

"I went to our old house," I said.

"You *what*?" she asked between clenched teeth.

"Yeah," I said, my jaw tight. "I just felt like a walk down memory lane."

"Are you kidding me?" she demanded.

"I don't know," I said. "Am I? I just wanted to make sure it had really burned down. It seems like I can't quite trust my perceptions lately. Like, I thought I was getting messages from my father who was lying low while working for some spy agency, but it turns out that I was getting messages from my mother right here in Los Angeles." I casually tossed the phone onto the couch. My mother froze.

"Imani," she said.

"Amani!" I yelled. I didn't realize I had started crying. "Where's Dad? Is he dead? Did he leave us? Is *he* the one stalking you?"

"No, my love," she said, reaching for my arm.

"Don't touch me!" I yelled.

"Baby, wait," she said gently.

"Don't call me baby," I demanded. "I'm not a baby. I'm fifteen and a half, and I'm old enough to know the truth about what's really going on."

She sank down onto the couch. "Sit down," she said.

I sat down. Her expression was so solemn, I almost wished I could go back to not knowing. "Is Dad really dead?"

She sighed. "Your dad's alive . . . as far as I know. He didn't leave us. He's not stalking me."

I waited for her to say more. In the distance, we could hear a man and a woman arguing on the street.

"What's going on, Mom?" I asked.

"It's complicated . . ." she began.

"No, it's not," I said. "Whatever it is, there's a simple version. Just tell me the truth."

"The truth is . . ." she said in a whisper, and I strained to listen.

Mom opened her mouth to finish, but several emergency vehicles drove by, engines roaring and sirens screaming.

In the relative quiet after the sirens, I could make out the words of the arguing woman: "Oh, you got money for gas, liquor, and getting yo new girl's hair done, but can't pay child support for yo son?"

Apparently, the man had no response for that, because I could hear my mom when she spoke, barely above a whisper.

"The truth is," she breathed, "your dad and I are both spies."

THIRTEEN

I blinked in disbelief.

"Spies?" I asked. "You *both* work for this spy agency?"

She nodded. She put her arm around me and adopted the tone she had used when telling bedtime stories. Except this story was true. And not something you'd tell a kid before bed.

Apparently, the organization was started by a Black woman secretary at the CIA named Charlene Thomas. At the time, they didn't usually hire Black support staff, but she had been selected because she was the fastest typist they had ever seen.

One night, on her way home from work, she was approached by an African man who had information about one of the CIA's cases. He shared his story with her, and she gave the information to her bosses. But after they got the information, they totally cut her out of the operation. At the time, they didn't think a Black woman was capable of anything more than typing.

And they totally botched the case. They brought the African man in for questioning, but he didn't trust them, so he recanted his story. He said he was just making something up to talk to a pretty lady. But after they released him, he was killed.

Charlene Thomas began to investigate on her own, and that led her to one of his colleagues. She realized that if she wanted these Black operations to be done right, she would need to do them herself. So she began to develop her own network of Black operatives on the side, covertly. They would gather intelligence in political situations that directly affected people in Africa and the African diaspora and use it for the sake of justice.

Charlene kept her post and eventually hand-selected her replacement. She also managed to plant someone in the FBI.

My mom looked at me with tears in her eyes. "Charlene Thomas was your great-grandmother."

"Really?" I asked.

"I never met her," Mom said. "She died of cancer in the nineties. But she made sure her legacy lived on. Your dad works for them. He recruited me."

"You've been spies this whole time?" I asked.

Mom nodded. "It's an international network of

maybe a few hundred people worldwide," she said. "There are several different subunits, but the umbrella organization is just . . . we call it the Factory."

I shut my eyes tight and opened them again. Was this really happening?

Mom continued, "We're a covert squad of operatives of color who operate nonviolently. We're the good guys. You remember that hijacked flight in Kenya that was taken down by a civilian and nobody was hurt? Or that Chinese factory that was shut down because it was operating with trafficked labor from Congo? Or that prosecutor in Mississippi who was exposed for sending young Black people to for-profit jails for a financial kickback, even when there was evidence that the young folks were innocent?"

"That was your organization?" I asked.

"Your dad worked on those cases personally," she said. "We gathered critical pieces of evidence that made the difference, because that's what we do. We focus on injustices that affect people of African heritage. Various governments will tell one story about what happened. But we investigate and get the evidence to reveal the truth. Then we leak it to the press, to whistleblowers, to activists. We're nonviolent and we try to stay under the radar. We work for the Black bureau, but there are other bureaus for different people of color."

"Then what happened?" I asked. "Who's coming after our family?"

"The operatives in our organization have made some enemies," Mom said. "Mostly among the other intelligence agencies. The US. Russia. Israel. British MI6. We're not exactly sure who's responsible for this latest set of attacks. We just know that some of the families of operatives have been getting targeted."

"So they burned down our house?" I asked. "Are we the only ones they came after?"

Mom shook her head. "Unfortunately, we knew there was a problem when the family of another operative was targeted. They narrowly escaped being car-bombed."

My eyes widened. "Really?"

Mom nodded. "Everyone was okay, but that family went into hiding. That was three months ago. In response, David started doing security checks on the families in the area. The day we ran to Sister Niema's, I returned from dropping you off at school and saw a copy of the *New York Times* on the porch. That was our signal that something was wrong, that our family had been compromised. So I got out of there as quickly as possible, made sure no one followed us, and fled here, to Sister Niema's."

I didn't know how to feel. The facts kept changing. Was I finally getting the whole story?

"So you and Dad are both agents for this Factory spy group?" I asked. "Are you finally telling me the real truth?"

Mom dropped her eyes. "Yes," she said quietly. "I hated lying to you. Sister Niema did, too."

"You both lied right to my face," I said.

"I lied to protect you," Mom said. "Do you have any idea how much danger you're in now that you know?"

"So we don't know where Dad is? Or if he's okay?" I asked. I still couldn't believe she had sent me fake messages from him.

Another thought occurred to me, and I felt my chest tighten. "How will Dad know where we are?" I demanded.

"This has always been our safe house," she said. "That's part of why we sent you to Harambee: so if anything ever happened to us, you'd have a connection with Sister Niema."

"I can't believe you were *both* spies this *whole* time," I said, feeling slightly light-headed. Somehow it hadn't been so bad when it was just Dad as an analyst for some group. He could still be essentially the same person. But Mom? With her cheesy sayings and perfect cookies? She was a spy? Plus, she was the one who was always there. Dad was away half the time. He could've been a spy or a country singer or a trapeze artist with the circus, and it wouldn't have been such a big deal. But *both of them*?

"So you were making spy decisions about my after-school programs?" I didn't quite feel the rage until I heard the bite of the sarcasm in my own tone.

"We were in love and dedicated to a cause," she said. "The cause of Black freedom all over the world."

What could I say to that? *No, Mom, I don't care about Black freedom. I just want a normal family?* But that was exactly what I wanted. I wanted parents who didn't lie to me, except about regular things. *No, honey, I never used marijuana, and you shouldn't, either.* Not that I wanted to use marijuana, but everybody knew parents lied about stuff like that.

I was mad. And I was scared for Dad. But I was honored that she trusted me enough to tell me all of it, and also resentful to be burdened with it.

And I still had so many questions about the organization, about our family. I couldn't even formulate any of them, because my mind had looped into a review of every odd thing that had ever happened in my life, wondering if it was somehow spy related. The questions were popping up faster than I could even articulate them. *That time you went to Cleveland for a "Doctors in the Community" conference in third grade, was it for spy stuff? Is the reception on my cell phone sometimes staticky because the Factory is listening in? Did Dad get that broken leg last year in some spy battle? Have you ever killed anyone? Has Dad?*

Mom's brow was furrowed. She had on her listening-doctor face, where she had something to say but was waiting for the patient to tell her more. Yet the questions had clogged my mind beyond speech. Meanwhile, the cell phone with my message lay faceup on the table, like a smoking gun.

Suddenly, the door opened, and Sister Niema came in with Dexter and Ella.

Dexter took one look at my face and rushed over to me.

"Imani, are you okay?" he asked.

I could only shrug and start crying again.

"She just got some upsetting news," Mom said hurriedly. "It's about her dad. He lost contact with his base in the Arctic and they're worried about him, but I'm sure they'll find him. It's happened before. Their equipment is so antiquated—"

"She knows, doesn't she?" Sister Niema said. "I can tell. Come on, Carmen. Don't just tell pieces of it, tell it all."

"You're part of it?" I asked. I knew already, but I wanted to hear her confirm it.

"Yes," Sister Niema said. "We all are."

For a moment, I thought she meant our whole family, but then I realized she meant Ella and Dexter as well.

"Wait," I said, looking at the other teenagers. "Both of you are in the organization also?"

Dexter and Ella nodded.

I could feel my face getting hot. "So, what?" I asked. "You were assigned to protect me?"

"Something like that," Sister Niema said.

My heart was beating as fast as it had when I saw the message from me to the fake Dad phone. "You were supposed to be my fake friend and my fake boyfriend to keep an eye on me?"

"Boyfriend?" Mom asked sharply.

"That's not how it is at all," Dexter said. "I really like you."

I looked at his handsome, chiseled face, his tall, long-limbed body. Ella, too. They could have been a pair of athletic models for some Afrocentric sports company. Who had I been kidding? From the moment he had kissed me, Penfield Amani had been waiting for the other shoe to drop, the moment it would come out that it had all been a joke, a prank, a mistake. This was worse. Penfield Amani had been right all along.

"I always liked you," Ella said. "Even when we were kids. I even remember that birthday party—"

"Just stop it, okay?" I said, jumping up from the couch. "I don't need the people who've been lying to me for a couple weeks or"—I looked at Mom—"or my entire life to try to reassure me right now of their good intentions."

"Y'all should go," Sister Niema said.

Ella moved toward the door and pulled Dexter to join her.

"No," Dexter said, yanking his arm away. "You gotta believe me—"

"Get out!" I spat, pointing to the door.

He took a breath and closed his eyes. When he

opened them, he looked pained. "I'm just glad you're all right," he said. He opened his mouth to say something else but then let Ella lead him out the door.

"So what was the real reason you never let me go to the doctor?" I asked. "Is it a spy thing?"

Mom glanced at Sister Niema, who nodded once.

"Yeah," Mom whispered, near tears herself. "We didn't want you in the system. No record of you at all. That way . . . if anything happened to us, you would have options. Infinite options."

"And two dead parents," I said. "You were risking your lives and didn't even tell me? What? I would wake up one day with you dead and Sister Niema talking about my infinite options? This is—this is effed up, Mom. Everything about my life has been a lie. Is that why we moved to DC?"

She nodded.

"What about all those private schools? Was that to keep me off the grid?"

She nodded again.

"Aaaauuughhh!" I yelled, and threw the pizza across the room. It hit a pot of iron implements in the corner.

I stormed into the bathroom and locked the door.

Mom was knocking on it a second later.

"Leave me alone!" I screamed.

"Give the girl some space," I heard Sister Niema say through the door.

I looked around at the sparkling white ceramic and

cobalt-blue tiled sink top with the neat rows of cosmetics. I wanted to topple the tropical plant, punch the mirror, rip off the row of affirmations on sticky notes. I was not the cocreator of my universe today. I wasn't beautiful, powerful, and attracting just what I needed.

Through the door I could hear Mom and Sister Niema talking.

"Sorry about the mess," Mom said.

"Leave the pizza," Sister Niema said. "The Orisha don't mind a little food."

I paced back and forth for the three steps in front of the shower/tub in the small bathroom. I couldn't go back into the living room, but I had to get out of there.

I pulled aside the shower curtain. Above the tub was a big sliding window. I put the plant down on the sink counter and checked out the stand. It was made of some heavy wood. I tried balancing on it, and it held my weight.

Usually, no one wore shoes in Sister Niema's house, but I had come in from the bus ride in my sneakers. I put the plant stand in the empty bath and stepped up onto it. My shoe left a big print on the edge of the tub. I reached up for the window, then pulled out the screen and climbed down into the side yard.

I had my phone and plenty of cash in my pocket. I had my hooded jacket to keep me warm. I just started walking.

I passed a couple of guys standing in front of a

liquor store, drinking forties inside paper bags. My eyes saw them, but they didn't register.

"Hey, big girl," one of them said.

"Nice ass," the other one said as I passed. "I'd like to—"

In a split second, I whirled around.

"You'd like to what?" I asked, wild-eyed and furious. "'Cause you touch me and I will kill you. I will KILL YOU!"

He staggered back. "What the hell?"

"That girl crazy," his friend said, and pulled him into the store.

My heart was beating fast, and I felt unhinged. All the anxiety from the past month. The fire, the idea of the stalker, the new school, the boys talking mess to me. And all the heartbreak of knowing my mom and dad had lied to me. And then, the first two people outside my family who I thought really understood me were just—just babysitters? My first kiss? My first almost-boyfriend? And it was all a lie?

I didn't know what I was gonna do. I had no plan. So it felt weird when I looked up and realized I had walked to school. But of course I had. It was the only other place I knew. And it was even weirder when I realized that it was the Winter Dance. The walkway was lit up, and there was music coming from the gym. In that moment, it felt like I'd been hit with an avalanche of despair. I was fifteen and a half. Suddenly, all the stupidness of a dance looked right. Maybe I *should* be at a dance. Or out at the movies with my friends. My parents had made a decision about their lives, and it had totally taken control of *my* life. And they had lied about it, and that made my whole life a lie. Now what the hell was I supposed to do?

"Hey! Homeschool girl!" I heard someone call to me. I turned around and saw Katanya, from my Yoruba class, along with another girl I'd seen before, Cherisse. They both had on high-heeled shoes and bright-colored dresses that showed off their figures.

"Girl, you can't get in dressed like that," Katanya said, looking at my casual maxi skirt and the fleece hooded jacket. "But don't bother. It's so tired up in there. We 'bout to have a real party."

"Where?"

"Over behind the gym," Cherisse said. "Come on."

"What's your real name, Homeschool?" Katanya asked.

"Imani," I said.

Katanya pulled a giant lotion bottle from her purse and offered it to me.

"No, thanks," I said. "I moisturized this morning."

Both girls laughed uproariously.

Katanya said, "No, girl, it's gin."

So I stood around with them, drinking. There wasn't enough liquor in the bottle to get drunk, but it was my first time drinking anything, and I definitely got tipsy. The alcohol warmed me up, and I had to take off the jacket and tie it around my waist.

Finally, I wasn't feeling alone. The two of them were hilarious, doing impressions of some of the teachers.

"And then the dance teacher was like, 'Both feet on the floor, ladies. This is not a rap video,'" Cherisse said.

We all cracked up.

"Man," she went on. "I wish we were at a real show tonight. Not this stupid dance."

"Hell, yeah. That Deza concert is tonight," Katanya said.

"Oh, snap!" I said. "I won tickets to that concert!"

"You what?" Cherisse asked.

"Yes! Four tickets! I totally won four tickets."

"Well, then, what the hell are we doin' here?" Katanya asked. "Let's go!"

"Yaaaasssss!" I said. "I just need to get to my email so I can get the code to claim the tickets." I pulled out my phone, but then I realized it was just a flip phone and I couldn't get on email.

"Here," Cherisse said. "Use my phone."

I opened a browser window and pulled up the email program. But then I hesitated. Mom had said not to go into my old email accounts. What if—? But then I shook the idea off. To hell with all that. I was supposed to trust what Mom told me? After all that had happened? And miss the Deza concert? No way. I opened the program and went into my account. I had 325 new emails, including several reminders about the concert.

"Yes!" I said. "It has a smart thingy. We just bring this to the concert to scan, and we can get in."

"Yeeeah, baby," Katanya said. "I'm gonna go see Deza."

"How we gonna get there?"

"I got cab fare!" I said, pulling several twenties out of my pocket.

Cherisse called a taxi, and the three of us stood out in front of the school singing and rapping Deza songs.

"Everyone said I was smart for my age
Smart enough to know high school was a cage . . ."

"See," Katanya said to Cherisse. "I told you she was cool."

Fifteen minutes later, a dark sedan drove up.

"You girls waiting on a Lyft?" the driver asked. She was a middle-aged blond woman with gray-tinted glasses.

"No, we waiting on a cab," Cherisse said.

"Good luck with that in this neighborhood," the driver said.

"We don't have a Lyft account," I said. "We only have cash."

"I can work for cash," she said. "Where to?"

"The Central Arena," Katanya said.

"Oh, you're going to see Deza?" the woman asked. "Lots of folks going there tonight."

"Let's go!" said Cherisse.

I was the last to get in. I slammed the door shut, but it closed on my fleece jacket. I tugged on it twice, but it wouldn't pull free, so I opened the door a crack to pull in the dangling sleeve.

As I looked down at the sliver of gutter outside the car, I saw a broken forty-ounce bottle of malt liquor and several crushed cigarette butts.

We were deep in the hood. Why would a white Lyft driver suddenly appear outside of a Black high school?

I darted a glance back at the woman. The interior light had come on, and I saw her reach for the door-lock button.

Before I could even think another coherent thought, some survival instinct took over, and I leaped out of the car and took off running toward the school.

"Where you going?" Katanya yelled after me. "We can't go to this concert without you."

I heard her door rattle as she tried to unlock it.

A split second later, the driver's side door had opened, and the blond woman was chasing me onto the school grounds.

FOURTEEN

I ran across the school's cement entryway and turned toward the gym's noise and lights. Ducking around a corner, I ran past the outside of the gym, down toward the chain-link fence.

It was dark, but I could hear the footsteps of the woman running behind me, steady and gaining. Then, as we came alongside the gym, a door opened somewhere, and we could hear a loud DJ voice, over a driving beat, blaring out into the night.

"Yes! Yes! Roosevelt High, it's your favorite DJ, I came to slay . . ."

As he prattled on, it drowned out the sound of our footsteps. I still had a bit of a lead on her as I turned the next corner. I came to the split in the fence and wrenched it open. No longer caring about how it looked, I didn't stop to wonder if I'd fit. I just gripped onto the fence like it was parallel bars in gymnastics and heaved myself up. I stuck both my feet through the split and jammed my butt through. The gravity pulled my whole body free, except my skirt, which caught on the fence, but fortunately, it didn't catch the leggings I wore underneath. In an instant, I pulled the skirt out and heard a tearing sound. Hopefully, none of this had been loud enough for my pursuer to hear.

I crouched down in the dark corner behind the fence, my heart thundering in my chest.

A second later, I heard her running footsteps, and she ran right past me, along the fence that marked the perimeter of the football field. When I could no longer hear her, I began to walk as swiftly and quietly as I could in the other direction—back the way Ella and I had come on the day of the shooting.

The building was mostly dark, but there were lights ahead. I came to a hallway that was dimly lit, and through the window, I saw a couple kissing up against the lockers. I banged on the door.

Eventually, they looked up. I banged harder, and they reluctantly came to let me in.

"You can't use the front entrance like airbody else?" the boy asked.

The girl looked at my torn skirt. "You okay?"

I nodded and ran into the gym.

The large square room was decorated with crepe-paper streamers and twinkling strings of lights. Beside one wall was a long table with snacks and punch, and near the stage was the DJ area.

They were playing a clean radio version of an old Thug Woofer song, and a thick mass of couples danced on the floor. On one end, a group of girls danced together, showing off their different moves in succession. Apparently, they were doing old-school hip-hop dances. One did the running man, and another did the butterfly.

What was I planning to do here? Try to blend in, wearing my torn skirt and hooded jacket?

I walked slowly toward the punch table, untying my jacket from around my waist and folding it over my arm. My T-shirt wasn't much more dressy. I poured myself a cup of punch and grabbed a handful of chips. The moment the food hit my mouth, I realized I was starving. I ate several handfuls of nuts, as well as the carrots and cucumbers on a veggie dip plate that apparently nobody wanted.

I looked around. No sign of the woman who had been chasing me.

Could she find me? And who the hell was she anyway? Lyft drivers didn't work for cash, and they certainly didn't chase their customers into school dances. My parents were spies. Someone was after us. Someone had burned our house down. Somehow, they had found me. And we had been so careful—

The Deza tickets.

I had gone online and claimed the Deza tickets. Mom had said I couldn't use the email account. Had I brought this on?

My legs felt shaky, and I had to lean against the refreshment table.

I saw the gym door open, but it was only Mr. Iroko, the history teacher.

Should I call my mom? Should I use someone else's phone? I didn't know what was safe to do now.

I thought about car bombs and houses burning down. I began to spin out, convinced I had brought certain doom on to my family. If Dad wasn't already dead, maybe this would get him killed. I leaned against the table for support and made my way to the far end of the room, where there were some chairs set up.

A student walked up and set out a tray of cookies and cupcakes, but the sugary smell turned my stomach.

I slumped into one of the chairs. What the hell was I going to do?

I had been sitting there for a five-minute eternity when Mr. Iroko came up to me.

"Imani!" he said brightly. "Are you okay?" He had to shout a bit over the music.

I opened my mouth to speak but couldn't. I pushed the sides of my cheeks up into a smile and nodded.

"You're not exactly conforming to our dress code,"

he said with a laugh. "Was it a last-minute decision to come?"

I nodded but then suddenly panicked. "You're not throwing me out, are you?" I stood in case I needed to run again.

He looked at my torn skirt. "Imani, what's going on? Are you okay?"

"It's j-just . . . I'm n-not—" I stammered. "Can I use your phone to call my mom?"

"Sure," he said, and handed me his cell.

I called the number I knew by heart, and it went straight to voice mail. I tried twice more and got the same result each time.

Throughout it all, I kept my eyes on the gym door, flinching every time I saw it open, looking for the blond head of the woman who had chased me.

I didn't have Sister Niema's number memorized, so I went to my phone to find it, but for some reason, my contacts were empty. In fact, the whole phone memory had been erased. The call log. The messages. Everything was gone.

WTF? I began to shake.

"Imani, what's going on?"

"Something's wrong with my phone," I said, powering the flip phone off then on again. It was still blank.

"Do you need help finding a number?" he asked.

"Sister Niema," I said. "Do you have Sister Niema's number?"

I held the phone in my hand, faceup. The screen was as blank as when my mom had bought it.

"Did your phone just get wiped clean?" he asked.

"I don't know," I said. "It had numbers a while ago, and now it's got nothing."

He looked around the dance, then leaned down close to my ear.

"I know who you are," he murmured. "You're Amani Kendall."

I just sat there frozen, the sound of my teacher's voice saying my name—my real name—looping in my mind.

"Amani?" he said it again. It was jarring but also reassuring. I felt tears pressing against my eyes but blinked them back. And then I had a moment of horror. What if he was one of the bad guys?

"It's gonna be okay," he said. "You probably don't remember me from Sister Niema's years ago. I was at one of the Harambee events."

I relaxed a little when he said that. Maybe that's why he had seemed familiar when I first saw him.

"I've known your parents for years," he said.

"My dad," I said. "Do you know my dad? Have you heard from him?"

"None of us have for a while," he said.

"I just tried my mom three times," I said. "It went to voice mail."

"You won't be able to reach her right now," he said.

"If your mom has wiped your phone, it's because your cover is blown."

"It's all my fault," I said, the tears streaming in earnest now.

"No time to blame yourself," he said, taking my arm and walking me toward the gym door. "We need to get you out of here."

The moment we stepped out into the hallway, I saw the couple who had been kissing at the lockers. They broke apart, as if waiting for the history teacher to admonish them. But Mr. Iroko took firm hold of my shoulders and steered me down the hall, away from the main entrance.

And that was when I heard the helicopters.

Mr. Iroko sped up. Behind me I heard the boy from the couple complaining. "We never get to have any fun without the cops coming to break it up," he said. "Let's go home. This dance about to be over."

Mr. Iroko and I turned the corner out of sight of the couple in the hallway. He took my hand, and we started running.

FiFTEEN

As we sprinted down the hall, Mr. Iroko pulled out his keys. We lurched to a halt outside his classroom, and he unlocked the door to let us in. He didn't turn on the light, so when he closed the door behind us, we were in total darkness.

"Wait here," he said. "I can't risk the light because they're looking for you. But I promise, I'm going to get you to your mom." His voice was disembodied in the blackness.

Your mom. An hour ago, she'd been the world's biggest villain. Right now, there was nothing I wouldn't have given to see her again.

I heard the helicopters grow even louder overhead. There had to be several of them.

My leg bumped a desk next to me. I pressed my hands out through the blackness to feel the shape of it, orienting myself so I could sit down.

I felt my body shaking against the plastic chair. The helicopters sounded like thunder. I heard the shuffle of Mr. Iroko's feet and the occasional thud and grunt as he bumped into objects in the dark.

My panic was rising. It sounded as if the helicopters were right on top of us, and then suddenly—one by one—the sound dimmed a bit.

"They've landed on the roof," he said.

Helicopters were on the roof of my high school?

"You're going to have to trust me," he said. "You know about the Underground Railroad, right? The fugitive enslaved Africans just had to trust each person along the way. That's how this goes. I don't know who the folks will be, but on the other end is your mom, okay?"

In the distance, I heard voices yelling: men barking orders over the beat of the helicopter blades.

"Amani, are you listening?"

I felt frozen. I opened my mouth to speak, and my "yes" came out as a whisper.

"They're going to come looking for you soon," he said. "And they're not going to find you."

I heard the creak of metal grinding on metal.

Then suddenly, there was a tiny pool of light, barely more than the dot on the plug of a laptop charger. He brought it close to a curving piece of steel at the front corner of the room.

"Come quickly," he said.

I got up from the desk, stumbling my way toward him in the dark.

For a second, he made the light brighter, and I saw that the curving metal was an open hot-water heater.

"I hope you're not claustrophobic," he said. "Because you'll be hiding in here. Not only will it hide you from view, but it's specially equipped to hide your heat signature if they use heat-sensing technology."

In the distance, I continued to hear shouts and even running footfalls. Outside the school, through the cracks around the window shades, I saw the occasional swinging beam of a flashlight.

The next thing I knew, I was stepping up into the heater.

"There's plenty of ventilation so you can breathe, and even a tiny slat here so you can see," he said, pressing my hand against a seam in the metal.

I climbed in but couldn't see anything in the dark.

He began to close the door, but my skirt caught on the edge of the metal.

"Hold on," I said. "My hem is stuck."

"Can you take off the skirt?" he asked. "You don't want anything to slow you down."

"Sure," I said, and peeled out of it, handing it to him.

"Wait here," he said. "It might be minutes. It might

be hours. They'll have to get you out at some point tonight. Your code name is Nightingale. Whoever calls you by that name, be ready to go with them, no questions."

He swung the door closed.

"You're going to be okay," he said. And then I heard him walk out of the room.

I tried to calm my breathing. There did seem to be plenty of air, and I trusted him that I would be able to see when it mattered.

It was awkward in the heater, and the metal was cold. At first, I stood rigid in the center, without letting my body touch any of the sides. But eventually I got tired of holding myself up, so I leaned against the heater's inner wall and waited.

Maybe five minutes later, I heard boots thudding down the hallway and doors opening and closing.

The crack of light around the classroom door went from dim to bright, as they must have turned on the main light in the hallway.

The incoherent voices became punctuated by fully articulated shouts of "Clear!" I realized they were searching, classroom by classroom.

The voices and thudding of boots came closer. I could hear them in the classroom next to mine.

Then suddenly, two guys in uniform burst through the classroom door. I was nearly blinded by the overhead fluorescents, and they had flashlights as well. As my eyes adjusted, I saw the classroom, looking so ordinary. Rows of desks. A time line of US history on one wall, and on the opposite wall, a large map of Africa marked with various languages. A lost-and-found box on the counter by the door, with a grimy jacket, a few notebooks, and a trio of plastic water bottles.

The two uniformed men searched around in the closets and cupboards, as well as behind and under Mr. Iroko's desk.

One of the men came up right next to me, peering into the alcove next to the heater, his helmeted head only inches from my face. He even put one hand on the heater as he leaned into the alcove. I held my breath, certain he would be able to hear my heart beating.

"Clear!" he yelled to his partner, and they left, not bothering to turn off the light.

For half an hour, I listened to the sounds of boots running down the hallway and bursting in and out of classrooms, searching. Finally, another uniform entered the classroom. She pulled off her helmet, and I could see it was a Latinx woman with short hair and sharp eyes. She looked from side to side and walked straight to the hot-water heater.

"Nightingale," she whispered. "In thirty seconds, I'm going to let you out. You'll need to exit quickly and climb a ladder. Can you do that?"

"Yes," I said breathlessly.

I heard a thud over my head and a rattle behind me.

As the metal-on-metal scrape of the opening door freed me from the water heater, I saw that she had loosened a ceiling tile and that a rope ladder hung down from it.

I jumped out of the heater. My left leg had fallen asleep. I loped the couple of steps to the ladder unevenly and scrambled up.

"Crawl to the end of the passage. Someone will meet you. Good luck, Nightingale."

She replaced the ceiling tile, and I heard her radio crackle to life.

"Commander, we found something," the voice said. "Hole in the fence, and suspect has apparently escaped. Suspect presumed to be on foot."

It was dim in the crawl space above the ceiling tiles.

I had the panicked thought that I would be too heavy. Just as the uniforms were ending their search, I would fall through the ceiling, right into their custody. I shook my head to banish the thought and kept crawling forward.

At the end of the passage, I was in total darkness again. I lay down on my side for a moment, feeling simultaneously exhausted and wired. My body shook and twitched from the adrenaline. My mouth felt dry. I noticed I had gotten the feeling back in my leg.

The panic gathered at the back of my throat,

threatening to unleash itself. I kept breathing and waited, again, in the dark.

"Nightingale." I heard a whisper.

Suddenly, up ahead I saw a flashlight beam coming from above. I crawled closer to it and saw that it illuminated a shaft with a ladder against the wall.

As I stood up in the shaft, the helicopter beat was louder, emerging from the background noise into my conscious mind.

Again, I climbed up, and the ladder led to a trapdoor. I couldn't see where I was going, only the blinding beam of the flashlight.

Then the light disappeared, and I saw a hand reaching down for me, silhouetted against the glow of the Los Angeles sky.

The hand belonged to a man in uniform. He pulled me into a crouch beside him on the roof and flipped up the visor on his helmet. It was David! I blinked at the stitches on his temple.

"When I give the signal," he said, "we're going to run over to that helicopter. I'm going to shove the pilot out, and we'll get in. You'll need to run fast."

"Okay," I whispered.

"Take this," David said, and handed me a gun.

I gasped. "I can't shoot anybody."

"Don't try to act all helpless with me," he said with a smile, touching the wound at his temple. "Besides, it's fake. It'll just look and sound like gunfire to cover our escape. Got it?"

"Got it," I said.

David handed me the gun, and even though I knew it was fake, it felt cold, heavy, and terrifying in my hands.

At the other end of the roof, someone barked an order, and at least a dozen uniforms disappeared through a door that led down into the school. Thirty seconds later, I heard the helicopter engine change. The sound became stronger, louder.

"Now," David said, and I followed him across the roof, running in a crouch.

He lunged into the helicopter and knocked the pilot over the head, peeling off his headset as he fell down onto the roof.

"Get in!" he yelled over the noise of the blades.

I fumbled to figure out how to get in with the gun in my hand and heaved myself awkwardly onto the seat.

"Buckle up!" he shouted, and pulled some levers that lifted the copter off the ground.

A pair of uniformed officers stepped through the door onto the roof in heated conversation. They glanced up without concern at our departing helicopter. Then I saw the pilot slowly beginning to stand, catching their attention. The two uniforms looked from the pilot up to us.

"Shoot now!" David commanded.

I put both hands on the gun and shot it straight out the window. Four blank rounds, each bucking in my hand, like the gun was a live animal.

All three of the men on the roof ducked down for cover as we hung left and swooped into the sky.

They soon looked like little action figures, and we kept rising.

The helicopter ride was incredibly brief. I could still see the uniformed officers' shocked faces in front of my eyes when we landed in a nearby abandoned lot. The ambient light from the city illuminated the patchy, scraggly grass and dirt, which was covered with broken bottles and heaps of trash. In one pile, I saw a mound of used diapers and broken furniture.

I handed David back the gun. "Sorry about your head," I murmured in the quiet after the copter had stopped.

"Twelve stitches," he said with a smile. "My first thought was that it was gonna leave a scar. The second was that I couldn't wait to tell your dad what a good job you did at self-defense."

I was opening my mouth to ask about his connection with my dad when a woman appeared from behind the furniture/diaper mound and walked toward the copter. David didn't seem concerned, so I assumed she was okay.

She was maybe sixty and full-bodied. Her head was

covered in a brightly patterned nylon bonnet. A fringe of straight hair stuck out behind her ear. She was carrying something, but I couldn't see what it was in the dark.

She approached David. "This is for Nightingale," she said, and heaved a large duffel bag into his lap. He handed it over to me, the movement awkward in the small copter.

"Good luck, baby," she said in my direction, then hurried away across the vacant lot in the dark.

"Can you strap that bag into the front seat and climb into the back?" he asked.

Before I could ask why, the thunder of blades started up again. I strapped in the bag and climbed in back, where there was a bench seat and belts for four people. I buckled up.

And then we were lifting off again and rising into the Los Angeles sky.

SIXTEEN

The next thing I knew, I was stirring awake and looking through a curving window onto a predawn sky. It took me a moment to remember and understand where I was. Spies. On the run. Helicopters. Shooting a fake gun.

Had I fallen asleep in the loud copter? Maybe my body was depleted by the adrenaline and had finally crashed.

The helicopter was still and empty now. I tried to sit up, but something was pulling on me. I realized the seat belt was holding me across the middle of my body. I unclipped it. As I sat up, I felt the chill of morning air. I had half thrown off a quilt that had been covering me. It was hand sewn, with a pattern of intricately looping rings. I pulled it up around my shoulders, snuggling into the soft, worn cotton and trying to get my bearings.

We were in some sort of quarry, maybe. I looked around and spotted David in a jeep nearby, talking on an oversize black phone. I couldn't make out any of his words. He was nodding, and then he climbed out of the vehicle and headed toward me. He had the phone in one hand and a black rectangular thing in the other.

"Copy that," he said as he got close to the copter, and hung up. "Time to go," he said to me, and swapped the black rectangle thing for the duffel bag in the front seat of the helicopter.

He carried the duffel, and we walked to the jeep. I trailed after him, wearing the quilt like a cape.

He slung the duffel into the back and started the engine. "Don't be alarmed," he said, "but when we get far enough away, I'm gonna need to blow up the helicopter."

"You *what*?"

"We'll be way out of the blast range," he said. "It's totally safe."

"How can you be sure?" I asked.

"Because I'm gonna detonate it."

"Is that really necessary?" I asked. I didn't like for anyone to put a coffee lid into the garbage without recycling it. How was I going to sit by and watch him trash a whole helicopter?

"We don't want the FBI to find our DNA in their stolen copter," he said.

I couldn't argue with that.

"Actually, you'd be okay," he said. "Your parents have kept you off the grid, so there wouldn't be a match for your prints or your DNA on file. But the FBI would have no trouble tracking me down, and I'd rather avoid that."

I was beginning to realize how useful it could be for a spy—or a spy's family member—to fly under the radar.

The wind was blowing through the open windows and top of the jeep, and I buried my hands in the pockets of my hooded jacket. And then suddenly I grinned and unzipped the inner pocket. "You've done so much for me," I said. "But I have a present for you."

From the pocket of my hooded jacket, I fished out the three plastic bags I had stuck in there what felt like a lifetime ago.

"These are three pieces of DNA evidence, including one that I removed from a certain gas station bathroom trash can down the street from a certain house that has since burned down," I said, my smile turning a little sheepish. "I would like to return them to their rightful owner. Had I known his identity at the time, I would never have weaponized any roller skates in his direction."

I offered him the bags with a flourish. The blood was now a dark magenta brown.

David laughed and took the samples from my hands. He made a little bow of thanks. "I know just what to do with these," he said. "Wait here." He jogged over to the helicopter, tossed the samples inside, and returned.

As he climbed back into the jeep, he smiled at me. "You did what you thought you had to do," he said. "Which is why you're definitely going to make a great spy someday."

I smiled and looked out the window. The quarry was wide, and we drove to the far end, where the jeep used all four wheels to climb up the sloping side. The sun was starting to rise over terrain that was being revealed as scraggly brushland. As we drove across the land outside the quarry, the copter got smaller in our rearview mirror.

A few minutes later, we were up on a dusty paved road. Nothing around for miles. In the distance, the helicopter looked like a toy.

David stopped the jeep and pulled out a device that had a few buttons.

"Wait!" I said, grabbing his wrist. "Let me do it."

His eyebrows rose. "Okay," he said. "Fair enough."

He indicated the button I should push.

I swallowed hard, and my finger hovered over it for a minute. I was both thrilled and horrified to be in charge of so much destructive power. But if I was up against an enemy that would send a hundred armed operatives to hunt down a teenage girl, I needed to be a little more ruthless.

I clenched my whole body and pressed the button.

The blast was instant. I didn't realize I had closed my eyes, but they flew open with the booming sound and the thundering vibration in my body. The explosion looked just like in the movies, but it wasn't a movie. It was me, damaging millions of dollars in property to make sure we got away clean. The fiery ball rose over the desert, and then it was just the helicopter burning and melting, and the jeep was speeding down the road, away from the blaze.

Fifteen minutes later, we were driving on an empty desert highway, the burning helicopter far behind.

"How do you know my dad?" I asked.

"We worked on some operations together," he said easily.

"Like where?"

"You know I can't tell you that, right?" he said.

I nodded.

"But I can tell you he talked about you all the time," he said. "When I met him, he'd just gotten that bow and arrow for you."

"I was four!" I said, the memory jumping back into my mind. I used to practice for hours in the backyard.

Shooting at targets. Hunting imaginary prey with rubber suction-tipped arrows.

"He was so proud," David said. "I used to help him find polar bear pictures on the internet. Everyone did."

I choked up a little at that. So I just nodded and didn't say anything else for a while.

Slowly, the occasional house or ranch popped up along the empty desert road. Maybe half an hour later, we drove into the parking lot of a general store.

David opened the duffel bag we'd gotten from the woman in the vacant lot. He stuffed the quilt in it and pulled out a paper shopping bag.

"This is for you," he said. I glanced inside and saw that it was filled with food.

"I can't eat all of this!" I protested.

"Take it," he said. "You don't know how long it'll be until you have another chance to eat."

I clutched the bag to my chest.

Beside us, a gray van pulled up that said ROBESON ELECTRIC.

The driver stepped out and nodded to David. Then he greeted me. "Welcome, Nightingale." He was middle-aged, Latinx or Black, and light-skinned.

"Take it easy, Nightingale," David said. "You're gonna be okay."

I nodded but didn't trust my voice to speak. I just climbed into the back of the van and buckled in. There were no windows and lots of electrical equipment.

I missed David. With him I felt not only safe but also connected to my dad. I was kind of glad to be in the back of this van so I didn't have to make conversation with a total stranger. As we drove, this new guy played the radio. I've never been so grateful for '80s soft rock.

We drove continuously for a while, and then things changed. From the stopping and starting, I couldn't tell whether we were on city streets or a crowded freeway. Eventually, however, I got the feel of it. The stop-and-go was at longer intervals, more likely stop signs and red lights than traffic. Finally, one of the stops was longer than a stoplight. I snapped out of my Smokey Robinson daze. Senses alert now, I felt the front door open and close. And then nothing.

I felt a shadow of panic. I was in the back of an electrical van with no idea where I was. I didn't know the names of the people who were helping me. Was the door even unlocked from the inside? What if something had happened to my companion? Would I be locked in here and suffocate?

I unclipped from the seat and carefully tested the door handle. It worked. Okay. At least I wasn't locked in.

I tried to feel relief, but I couldn't. I had no idea how much danger I was in. It all seemed unreal.

I heard footsteps outside the van. I crouched, ready for anything.

The rear door handle turned, and the door opened.

The woman had turned around to look over her shoulder, so all I saw was a head of straight brown hair and a pair of bedazzled designer jeans. If she was an assassin, it was a convincing disguise.

And when she turned to face me, I realized it was my mother.

It took a moment to register. At first it seemed like a hallucination. It was just so bizarre to see her dressed like that, almost like one of those wooden stands at an amusement park, where you could stick your face through to be a cartoon cowgirl or an astronaut.

But even as my brain couldn't process the reality, I inhaled to call her name. Before I could make a sound, she had a finger across her lips.

I just froze there, arms reaching out to her, as she quietly closed the door behind her and came over to me, peeling the wig off and tossing it onto the floor beside some copper wire.

She gathered me into her lap like she used to do when I was little.

I collapsed onto her and sobbed.

"Mom, I'm so sorry. I'm so, so sorry," I wailed.

I don't know how long I cried. At some point, I realized that the van was moving. I hadn't even felt it start up.

"Mom, I can't tell you how sorry I am," I said through tears.

"No, my love," she said. "It's not your fault. We

should have told you sooner." I looked up and real-ized she was crying, too. "We shouldn't have taken the chance you'd find out some other kind of way. We kept putting it off. If only we had told you, you would have known why David was there, and you never would have made that police report."

My eyes bugged out. "Mom, are you saying the police report started this whole thing? Is it my fault that our house burned down?"

Mom shook her head quickly, like she was rattled. "No, love. If everything had been fine, David never would have been doing security checks at our house. Put that idea out of your mind."

"But the police report did trigger something, didn't it?" I insisted.

"Not at all," she said.

"Don't lie to me!" I said. "Did the police report start something or not? I want the truth."

Mom shook her head and looked down. "Old habits die hard," she murmured. She faced me squarely. "We have no way of knowing for sure," she said. "But it's a good bet that the police report triggered something, because our cover was blown the next day."

My tears started up again.

"Oh, please don't blame yourself, my love," she said. "It's my fault. I never should have left you alone with Valerie. But above all, I should have listened when your dad said we should be honest about—"

Suddenly, I snapped out of the self-blame. "What about Dad?" I asked. "Have you talked to him? Is he okay?"

Mom opened her mouth. She seemed totally calm. "I'm sure your father—"

"Tell me the truth!" I said, my eyes burning into hers.

She held my gaze and her face fell. "I don't know," she said, a tear falling off her cheek onto the bright green fabric of her designer sweatshirt. "I promise I'm not going to lie to you ever again. I pray that he's fine. But he's gone dark."

"He's gone what?" I asked.

"Gone dark," she said. "It means he's disappeared from all communication."

"For how long?" I asked. "And what was he working on?"

Mom took a deep breath and wiped her eyes. "Amani, I can't tell you everything. A lot of things are 'need to know.' But I promise not to lie. If I can't tell you, I'll just let you know I can't tell you. This is one of those times."

"Well, what *can* you tell me, Mom?" I asked.

Mom sighed. I could feel the van slow down and go over a speed bump. I buckled my seat belt again, and Mom did the same.

Her gaze rested on a big spool of red and black wire

in front of us. It was quiet for so long, I thought maybe she wasn't gonna tell me anything. But then I heard her take a breath.

"Well, as I said before, we're a Black intelligence agency that gathers information."

"I know," I said.

"Like I told you, we engage in operations that affect people in Africa and the diaspora. We have secret operatives within the CIA and FBI who let us know where to investigate. But someone has started to target people inside our organization. Our CIA officer turned up dead. One of our foreign assets is afraid for his life. And here's the unexpected danger: somehow, several of our operatives have been swapped in the Homeland Security database with international terrorists. There's a leak somewhere in the pipeline, so we're afraid to pass information through the regular channels."

Mom pulled up a tablet. She showed me a picture of an African American man walking a dog. "This was one of our operatives in Dallas," she said. Then she showed me a photo of the same man, dressed as an ISIS operative. There was an Arabic name below the photo and it said REWARD. "They put our guy's photo and fingerprints into the database in this ISIS operative's file."

"What happened to him?" I asked.

"He's in Guantánamo," she said. "He doesn't speak

a word of Arabic, but they don't believe him. This happened last year. Your dad and I were worried, but we took extra precautions."

"What does this have to do with Dad?" I asked.

"A week before our house burned down, I got a message that your dad had been detained at a checkpoint in Colombia, under suspicion of being a terrorist." She pulled up a photograph. There was Dad's face, photoshopped onto some ISIS fighter.

I gasped as Mom handed me the tablet.

The man wearing Dad's face was gripping a gun. I blew up that part of the photo and could tell at a glance that those weren't Dad's hands. Nails not quite the right shape. Too much hair on the knuckles.

"We realized your father had been targeted," she said. "He was able to escape, but he's been in hiding since then."

"Is he still in Colombia?" I asked.

"We don't know," she said.

"Then how do you know he's okay?" I asked, hearing desperation in my voice.

"Our organization is connected to a broader network of sympathizers around the world. Some of them work in strategic locations within the system. Day to day, they function as cops or prison guards or highway patrol. But if our people are in crisis, we can reach out to the network. We believe Dad is getting help just like you and I did."

I thought back to the woman who had helped me from the water heater to the rope ladder.

"What about Dexter and Ella?" I asked, feeling a bitterness rise in my chest. "They're spies, too?"

She nodded.

"Were they assigned to me?" I asked.

"Well . . . yes," she said. "But they weren't spying on you. In our world, they're called handlers. They liked you. They were happy to spend time with you."

"Did they report to anyone about how I was doing at the school and stuff?" I asked.

Mom looked down. "Yeah," she said. "But—"

"They *were* spying on me," I said.

"They were just giving us information so we could support your transition," she said.

"I didn't want handlers," I said. "I wanted friends."

She turned to me sharply. "Dexter . . ." she said. "Did something happen between the two of you. I mean, did you maybe . . . ?"

"Maybe what?" I said. "Please, Mom, don't. You and Dad have some romantic spy history, but don't put that on me. Ella and Dexter befriended me under false pretenses. I'm upset about it. Period. Don't make it weird."

"Sorry," she said.

I thought back to the kiss. Kisses, if you counted the quick one I gave him. Well, I guess everybody in our family had secrets. This could be mine.

• • •

It was getting hot in the van. We were definitely on the freeway now, and the temperature must have been rising outside. Mom unzipped the sweatshirt to reveal a top that said HOT MAMA in glittering letters.

I busted up laughing. Mom didn't care much about her clothes, but she never wore anything like this.

She shook her head. "You like the new look?"

"Let me see it again with the wig," I said.

She reached down to retrieve it and put it on.

I adjusted the bangs.

"You look . . ." I stared at her. "Like someone else."

"Mission accomplished," she said.

"Let me try it on," I said.

I pulled the long sandy hair over my cornrows. Mom handed me her phone. There was no camera, but the darkened screen worked a bit like a mirror. I had tried on wigs in a wig store once as a kid. But now I looked different. In the light trickling in from the milky skylight, I looked eerie yet glamorous. Like those creepy skinny models who look like they're sort of zombies. It was definitely not me.

"It's so itchy," I said.

Mom nodded. "They say beauty is pain," she said. "But they don't tell you how much beauty is itchy."

I laughed and took it off, glad to see my cornrows again.

Something about playing with the wig cut the

tension between us. I leaned against Mom, and she put her arm around me. It was the first time I could recall feeling close to her in a long time.

"Do you know where we're going?" I asked.

"South," she said. "That's all I can tell you."

SEVENTEEN

For a few hours, I sat close to Mom and we didn't talk. After all the time I'd spent with strangers, I just drank her in: her smell, the rhythm of her breathing, the softness of her skin.

When we got hungry, we ate the food from the paper bag. The two of us sat in comfortable silence, the fried chicken crunching in our mouths.

By the time we were finished eating, it had become unbearably hot. Mom just sat there and sweated like it was no big deal, but I thought I was going to melt. Mom saw the stressed expression on my flushed and sweaty face. She leaned forward and tapped some kind of code on the back wall that connected with the driver. I heard a whir, and cool air began to circulate.

I felt immense relief, not only for the cool air but also because Mom knew the codes. I felt safe with her. Whatever this spy thing was, she must be good at it. She had kept me in blissful ignorance for fifteen and a half years. I didn't want to think about where we were going or where my dad might be or exploding helicopters. I just wanted to be here with Mom, like it was when I was little. I wished the ride would never end.

But it did. Sort of without warning. We had been on a freeway, then on some kind of in-between road, and then we were riding on a rough road for a few minutes. Mom and I bounced up and down on the seat, grateful for our bodies' natural padding.

Then the van came to an abrupt stop. I heard the door open and close. And when the driver came around to the back, he opened the doors to the brightest sunlight I'd ever seen.

We stepped out onto a patch of desert dirt. Above us was the world's widest sky. Next to us was a luxury sedan with a type of license plate I'd never seen before.

My mother nodded to the van driver and headed toward the sedan. I followed. Tiny clouds of dust rose with each step.

I expected the driver to come out of the sedan, but no one did. I couldn't see through the tinted windows.

The van driver came over to us, handed something to Mom, and then climbed back into the van and drove away. For a moment, I followed the twin trails of dust behind the vehicle. As it receded into the distance, I realized there was really nothing and no one else around. Unlike the area where the helicopter had touched down, the land we were standing on now was almost entirely sand.

I looked more closely at the car's unusual license plate. It was white with four blue letters and numbers. Below that, in small capital letters, it read SRE DIPL MEX.

"See that?" Mom asked, following my gaze. "Those are Mexican diplomatic plates. That way no one can stop us."

When we opened the doors, there was an elderly Latinx man in a chauffeur's cap in the driver's seat. He nodded to us, and we climbed into the back and put on our seat belts. The sedan had a wide, smooth leather back seat.

The driver eased the car onto the highway. No one was talking, so I watched the scenery go by.

On the floor of the car was a bag. Mom picked it up and poured the contents out onto the seat beside her. Candy bars and junky chips. The kind of stuff she usually never let me have. What I wouldn't have given for one of Sister Niema's sandwiches. I could have left a trail of tiny hard grains to follow back to Los Angeles.

It had been a couple of hours since the fried chicken. I ate two candy bars, and Mom didn't object. At the bottom of the bag was a receipt from a gas station convenience store. Whoever had bought the snacks had paid cash.

I followed the candy bars with a small bag of chips and fell into some sort of junk-food coma. I guess I dozed off because I was jolted awake when the car stopped suddenly. At my side, Mom's body was tense. I could feel her clenching and unclenching her fist, the knuckles pressing against my thigh.

I looked out to see a heavily fenced area. We were at the Mexican border.

"They weren't supposed to stop us in this direction," Mom whispered to no one in particular.

A thickset white guy in a US border patrol uniform was standing beside our car.

"This is a diplomatic vehicle," the driver was saying in a smooth voice with a Spanish accent. "We should be allowed to pass."

"I'm going to need to see everyone's identification," the man drawled.

Mom pulled out a pair of passports and flashed both at me. I saw a smiling picture of myself and the name Terra Jordan. Mom was Clarie Jordan. The driver added his passport to the stack and handed them to the agent.

Okay. If anyone asked, I was Terra Jordan. The passports looked so real. How had they pulled it off?

The border patrol agent took the IDs and punched

them into his tablet. Nobody was freaking out, so I assumed the IDs were good.

"Sir," the driver said. "This is a diplomatic vehicle. By law we should be allowed to pass without incident."

"Now, how do I know that this vehicle isn't stolen?" the agent said. "How do I know you all are who you say you are?"

In the back next to me, I could feel Mom's body go completely rigid.

"What is the nature of your visit to Mexico?" the border patrol agent asked, peering in and back at us. He was chewing gum with a chomp-*smack*-chomp-*smack* sound. "You're not smuggling anything, are you?"

"Sir," my mom said pointedly. "What on earth would we be smuggling *into* Mexico?"

Mom was talking back to a cop? She had taught me never to do that. That it was dangerous. And she was snapping at him while we were *fleeing the country*?

"I don't appreciate your tone, ma'am," he said, clearly irritated. The chomp-*smack*-chomp-*smack* sound got louder and faster.

If she didn't calm down, I would need to do something. Say *something*. Maybe he wouldn't suspect that she was a spy—wouldn't traveling with a teenage girl make someone seem less suspicious? I rolled my eyes and tried to look like more of a teenage stereotype.

"Well, I don't—" Mom began.

"Oh, settle down, Mother," I said in an affected,

bored voice. Like I'd heard girls use at Penfield. I huffed out my breath. My heart was hammering in my chest, but my voice and movements were languid.

I wasn't sure what to say, so I just blurted out, "This is why we should have built the wall. So men like him wouldn't have to work so hard to keep problems out of our country."

The agent seemed startled. "That's right," he said. "I don't want to be here in the hot sun, day after day."

"He's just keeping us safe," I said. "Can you just cooperate so this man can go back inside where it's air-conditioned?"

I turned to the agent. "We're going to a destination wedding. My dad is getting remarried—"

"And I'm just fine with it!" Mom snapped.

The agent pursed his lips and nodded.

"Come on, Mom," I said with an eye roll. "Just breathe deep and think of the alimony."

The agent glanced down at his tablet. "All right," he said. "This all checks out."

I could feel the clench in my stomach release just a bit.

Mom nodded. "I apologize for my tone before," she said. "And I want to thank you for your service."

"Thanks, ma'am," he said, and waved us through.

EiGHTeeN

The next hours—or days—were a blur. Mom gave me a sleeping pill, and then we rode in the trunk of the car. I had hazy recollections of being shaken awake and staggering out to pee alongside rural roads, once at dusk and once in total darkness. I recalled my mom giving me bottled water and some kind of protein drink.

I woke up in Cancún, Mexico, sometime around midday. The car was pulling into an alley, and Mom and I climbed out of the trunk with a shoulder bag and a six-pack of sports drinks. I stood on shaky legs and gulped fluids as the diplomatic sedan sped away.

Inside the shoulder bag were some fresh clothes, a couple of baseball caps that said SAN DIEGO PADRES, and two pairs of shades. Mom handed me an over-size T-shirt that read I DIDN'T COME HERE TO MAKE FRIENDS, AMIGOS. I put it on, along with the cap and shades. She put her cap on over the sandy-brown wig, and we walked to the end of the alley. I didn't exactly walk, more like staggered.

"I can't go anywhere like this," I said. "I'll attract too much attention."

"Don't worry about it," Mom said. "You just look like another drunk American college student."

Soon we were sitting at a US fast-food franchise, and I was eating French fries, drinking bottled water, and wondering why there was a row of American fast-food restaurants in a country that surely had much better food than this.

"Hey," I said suddenly, as the fog of the drug was wearing off. "You think I look like a college student?"

"What?" Mom said.

"You think I could pass for twenty-one?"

"Don't push it," Mom said, smiling. "Eighteen, maybe."

"What happens now?" I asked.

"We're going on a boat," Mom said. She glanced up at a pair of older white tourists walking by. "It goes with our travel package."

"Sounds good," I said. "I'm looking forward to a bit of boating."

She smiled, but I could tell she was nervous. She looked at her watch.

"Come on," she said. "Let's go wait at the dock."

El Cid Marina looked like any other harbor. It was next to a strip of beach, and the water looked warm. I realized with a pang that I wished I really were a carefree student on vacation, not a girl from a spy family on the run. Yet I had to look relaxed as we walked down the unfamiliar piers and passed the sunburned tourists and their bright white boats.

El Chupacabra was the slightly shabby boat docked at the slip number that Mom had been given. We were early, so we walked by, giving the boat a sideways glance. A lone man on the craft was screwing a long hose onto a spigot on the dock.

"What's he doing?" I asked quietly.

"Probably filling up the boat's water reserves," Mom said. "For showers and stuff. You still can't drink it."

"How soon do we leave?" I asked.

"I'm not sure," she said. "I'm waiting for a signal."

We walked to the end, where we could see a few fishing boats anchored a little ways out. A man on a small craft seemed to have caught something. He stood up and began to reel it in.

"Do you know where we're going?" I asked Mom.

"No," she said. "I could only guess."

The man on the boat seemed to have caught

something big. He leaned back as he reeled, the end of the pole arching and bouncing.

"Terra," Mom said sharply. "There's the signal. Let's go."

I turned and followed her eyes to where both the Mexican and the American flags were rising on *El Chupacabra*. Mom and I walked briskly toward the craft.

There were two men and one woman on board now.

In the slip next door was a group of country-club types on a much bigger craft.

We walked up to the crew on *El Chupacabra*. "Hola," Mom said. I noticed her American accent was particularly pronounced.

"Don't worry, señora," one of the men said with a thick Spanish accent. "We speak English."

"Thank goodness," Mom said.

He helped us aboard as the woman pulled up the rope that held the craft to the dock.

"And the fees are taken care of as part of our tour package?" Mom asked.

"Absolutely, señora," the man said. "You won't owe us a thing. Tips are always welcome, of course." He grinned.

"Of course," Mom said as the motor began to hum and we pulled away from the dock. "Just let me see where I put my pesos." She pretended to rummage in her shoulder bag.

A moment later, when we had moved out of view and earshot of the other boat, Mom stopped rummaging and grabbed my hand. She took me below deck.

There were several large crates, and the other man was sitting on a small bench against the wall. He had on a faded blue T-shirt with TRIÁNGULO printed in gold letters.

"Juan Carlos?" my mom called, pulling off her wig.

"Carmen?" The man lit up, and they ran to each other and hugged. But that surprise was nothing compared to what happened next. The two of them broke out into Spanish so rapid that I couldn't make any sense of it. Not even after six years of Spanish in school. I'd had no idea my mom spoke Spanish at all.

At first it was all smiles, but then she looked really serious. I caught him saying the word "esposo." Spouse? Male spouse? Husband? Was he talking about Dad?

Mom nodded. He put a hand on her shoulder.

"Juan Carlos!" the other man called from above deck. Juan Carlos patted Mom on the shoulder as he walked toward the stairs.

Mom's brow was furrowed, and she looked like she was a million miles away.

"Mom?" I asked, dazed.

Suddenly, she seemed to see me.

"Amani," she said. "Mi amor. Desculpa . . ."

This time she spoke slowly enough that I could

understand. Mi amor. My love. The term of endearment she had always called me that was so unlike all the other Black people I knew, calling their kids "baby" and "honey" and "sweet pea." Those southern endearments sounded foreign on her tongue because her tongue was foreign.

"Mom," I said. "What the—"

"I'm from Venezuela," she said. The words just fell from her mouth. A confession.

I stared at her, dumbfounded. "But—but—" I sputtered. "You always said you were from Virginia."

"I picked a state that began with *V*. To help me remember."

"I don't believe this," I said.

Mom slid down, her back to the big crate.

Then she was sobbing, and I was the one comforting her. Within the next hour, the whole story came out.

"It was after the two thousand and two coup attempt," she said. "Your dad was in Venezuela investigating. He was injured. I was working with Hugo Chávez's people. I treated your father, and we fell in love. He recruited me for the Factory. I got a new identity and moved to the US. We were married. And a few years later, we got pregnant with you."

I tried to picture those two bright-eyed parents in my baby picture as a wounded spy and medic falling in love in Venezuela. In a regular hospital? In a military tent? Not only was I unable to picture it, but I couldn't wrap my mind around it.

"This is unbelievable," I said. "This whole time you were someone else? You were from somewhere else?"

"It wasn't safe for you to know as a little kid," she said. "And since our cover was blown, it wasn't safe for you to know until we got out of the US and out onto the water. If any of our enemies looked into my past in Venezuela, it would compromise my people back there."

"I have family in Venezuela?"

Mom looked down. "No," she said. "Most of my family was killed. And my dad was originally from Nicaragua. I meant . . . the people I worked with."

"Mom," I said. "This is more than I can deal with."

"I know it's a lot," she said.

"But it explains so much," I said.

"Explains what?" she asked defensively.

"There was always something wrong about you."

She looked stung. "What do you mean, 'wrong'?"

"Something off," I said. "Something fake. There was some way you weren't like other Black people, but I could never put my finger on it."

"How can you call me fake?" she asked. "Black people come from all over, not just the United States. And all immigrants have to figure out how to make things work in this country. Just because I'm not originally from the US, that doesn't make me fake."

"Of course not," I said. "But most immigrants aren't pretending they grew up here and developing an elaborate backstory. All your cheesy sayings? Who talks like that? And there were things everyone else's parents knew—things Dad knew—that you didn't know."

"Like what?" I had never seen Mom this defensive.

"Silly things," I said. "Like, you knew Queen Latifah was a rapper and Brandy was a singer, but you didn't know either of their sitcoms from the nineties, when you would have been a kid and everyone would have been talking about those shows. You never gave me a straight answer when I asked you about your high school years. And then there were times when I'd ask you things and there'd be these big pauses. Now I realize you were either remembering your cover or making things up. You were never a Delta, were you?"

"I pledged the sorority in med school," she said, sounding hurt.

I was half furious and half bewildered. "Mom, was my whole life a lie?"

She stood up and threw her arms around me.

"No, mi amor," she said. "Your father and I love each other, and we love you. All the values we taught you, everything we said we believed in and were working for as a doctor and a scientist are what we really do. We just do it as . . ."

"Spies," I said.

"Yes," she said.

"Was I even planned?" I asked. "You talk about how much you prayed for a baby, even though you were still in med school. Was that true?"

She let out a big breath. "No," she said quietly. "You weren't planned."

"Did you even want to have me?" I asked. "Since I was obviously very inconvenient to your espionage lifestyle?"

"Don't ever say that!" she said. "Everyone but your father urged me to have an abortion. I'm pro-choice, and I had even had an abortion earlier in my life. But I was so in love with your father. I knew any child that we created together would be a joy and a blessing. And you have been. I used to sing to you in Spanish when you were a baby. Those were some of the happiest times of my life."

I just couldn't deal with all of this. Mom was Venezuelan? Or was she Nicaraguan? All her family had been killed? I was unplanned, and she'd had an abortion before me?

"I need some air," I said, and pushed past her and ran up the stairs.

Of course, it was a small boat, so there really wasn't anywhere to go.

"Nightingale," I heard a voice behind me say. "I don't know your real name." It was Juan Carlos. He came over and shook my hand. "I owe your mother my life," he said in heavily accented English. He introduced me to the other two sailors. The woman was from the Dominican Republic, and the other guy was from El Salvador.

"I'm sorry I didn't have better news about your father," he said. "But no news is really good news. I'm sure he'll surface soon."

I nodded, not trusting my voice to speak.

We stood there awkwardly for a moment, and then Mom came back up above deck and the three others found things to do.

Mom just sat down next to me and didn't say anything. When I didn't get up or turn away from her, she took my hand.

She was always like that. Without words, she had always felt just right. Only in English was she awkward and somehow forced. I felt her warm fingers close over my hand, and I leaned into her shoulder. We felt the gentle roll of the water beneath the boat.

After a while, I asked her, "Where the hell are we going?"

"Nobody's said anything," she said. "But at this point, I figure it has to be Cuba."

NINETEEN

Sure enough, several hours later, after night had fallen, we pulled into a harbor in the Havana area. Mom and I said goodbye to the boat crew. She hugged Juan Carlos tight before they all went back below deck.

A middle-aged woman was walking toward us down the dock. She was stocky, with short gray hair. "Nightingale?" she asked, her accent as thick as the boat crew's had been. My mom nodded, and she walked us to a dark, boxy van. The front passenger seat was missing. I sat down next to Mom on the torn upholstery of the back seat and reached for a seat belt that wasn't there.

Through the window, I saw a procession of women in white walking along the harbor. They had candles in their hands that bobbed with each step toward the waves, which crashed against a low seawall. The lead woman threw a bundle tied in white cloth out over the waves. As it hit the surface of the churning water, it came loose, the cloth opening. I could see an explosion of white petals in the candle- and moonlight.

"Welcome to Havana," the woman said.

We drove through the city, along wide streets filled with bicyclists and pedestrians, and arrived at a square cement building. It was sparsely decorated, with a few desks and pictures of Fidel Castro and Cuba's new president on the wall. The air inside was humid and cool.

The gray-haired woman invited us to sit, gave us water, and exchanged some rapid words with Mom in Spanish. Then she stepped out and brought us a couple of bags of plantain chips, along with several pieces of sweet bread. After she said a brief goodbye and left, I ate and drank hungrily. I hadn't eaten a real meal since the fast-food restaurant in Cancún.

When the food was gone, I stood and paced a bit, not certain of what to do with the energy that had finally returned to my body after the drugs had worn off.

"What happens now?" I asked Mom.

"I don't know," she said. "Our guide told us that someone would be here soon."

"Soon as in five minutes or soon as in a few hours?" I asked.

"Cuban soon," she said. "Which probably means

between an hour and a day. But I suspect they'll feed us again if it's too long."

Everything felt so surreal. This woman had given birth to me, had lived with me all my life, but she was a spy? She was Venezuelan?

"Mom, are you even a doctor?" I blurted out.

"Yes," she said. "I went to medical school twice. In Venezuela, then again in the US. And your dad is really a researcher, except instead of researching global warming, he researches for our organization."

"Which probably takes him to the Arctic much less than I've been led to believe," I said.

She ignored my sarcasm. "We never know where it'll take him."

"And what about you?" I asked. "Do you just work a regular job now?"

"Mostly," she said. "But sometimes they fly me places around the country to give medical attention to someone who can't go to the hospital."

"Like David?" I asked.

She nodded. "Who do you think put in those stitches?"

"Well, doesn't being a spy violate your doctor oath not to kill anyone?"

Her eyes flew open. "Kill anyone?" she exclaimed. "No, my love. I told you: we're a nonviolent organization."

"Why should I believe you?" I asked. "If you were a secret assassin, it's not like you'd tell me."

"Consider this," she said. "A group of Black spies going around killing people wouldn't last for decades, believe me. The US government has always targeted so-called Black Extremists, the latest version being 'Black Identity Extremists,' a label they won't even define. No, we just gather data. Yes, we engage in some spycraft to get it. We have experts at forging documents, computer hacking, theft—obviously—but our organization is also guided by the principle of nonviolence. We defend ourselves in the few instances where it's necessary, but by building strong relationships, we don't need violence. In movies, when the hero is alone with a gun and surrounded by a hundred people, of course he'll have to shoot his way out. But when we had to escape from LA, we counted on our allies. And they got us out. Quietly. No big gun battle."

I thought back to the gun I'd shot from the helicopter. It was true; David could have pulled out a real gun and shot the other guys, but he'd just wanted me to create a distraction.

"We're strictly an intelligence-gathering group, with a few top people in the FBI and CIA. In situations that compromise the rights of African or African diaspora folks, they try to place operatives to gather intelligence."

"What you're saying sounds good," I said. "And I want to believe it. But I just—I don't know."

"We lied to you, and we damaged your trust," she said. "I can't say anything that will make you trust me right away. But I believe that our family can repair that trust over time."

I looked at her, hoping to feel some resolution, but I didn't. By then it was after midnight, but the time change and the sedatives had me off-balance. I wasn't sleepy, but I felt lethargic and foggy.

I wasn't sure if I believed in gravity anymore. Or the sunrise, or rivers running toward the ocean.

My senses sharpened, however, when I heard voices and footsteps down the hallway. I looked expectantly toward the door. I don't know who I expected. But nothing could have surprised me more than the pair who walked in.

It was Dexter and Ella.

TWENTY

The last time I'd seen them, I'd been furious with them. But I didn't feel any anger now. Their betrayal seemed so minor compared to everything that had happened since.

"What are you guys doing here?" I asked.

"The same thing you are," Ella said. "Making sure we're safe."

"But I thought . . ." I started.

"Our organization works in cells," Mom explained. "If one member of the cell is in danger, the whole cell is in danger. We didn't know what the trail would lead back to."

"Someone came to school asking about a 'new girl,'" Ella said. "They didn't have a picture of you, but they had a description. Kids in school will be able to put us together."

"What about Celeste?" I asked. "What about Sister Niema?"

"Celeste isn't part of the cell," Ella said. "And no other kids came to Sister Niema's."

"But what about the vice principal? And Mrs. J?" I asked.

"No problem," Mom said. "Folks from the school know to keep quiet about the connection to Sister Niema."

The short-haired woman came back in and began to converse with my mom in rapid-fire Spanish.

Mom turned to us. "Looks like the coast is clear enough for us to go out and get some food."

"Thank God," Dexter said. "I haven't eaten since the fake grandma's fake rest home."

I looked across at him. He had on cargo shorts, a white Thug Woofer T-shirt, and flip-flops. I would have been shocked if I'd seen him wear any of that back in LA. But I didn't know what to make of him anymore. He was a stranger now.

Mom got directions, and the three of us walked to a nearby cafeteria that was open all hours. It was really just a few tables on the sidewalk and a small cubby of a restaurant that mostly did takeout.

Patrons drifted in from a nightclub nearby. When

the door opened, I could hear salsa or reggaeton music blasting out into the street.

Mom ordered for all of us in Spanish.

"Wow," Dexter said. "Your mom speaks like a native."

"Yeah," I said. "Apparently she's from Venezuela."

"She what?" Ella asked.

"Not just a spy but a foreign spy," I said. Somehow, I couldn't be as bitter with other teenagers around. "What's next?" I asked, suddenly desperate for comic relief. "She wasn't really baking all those great pound cakes? They were from a mix?"

The line wasn't even that funny, but I think it was the angst-filled face I made that sold it. We all cracked up.

"I'm glad you've still got your sense of humor," Ella said. "It helps."

The man at the window served up four heaping platters of food. We carried them to the table, and for about fifteen minutes, the only sounds among the four of us were of eating.

It was the opposite of Sister Niema's cooking. The rice was white and oily. The proteins were meat, either chicken or pork. And the vegetables were the smallest part of the meal.

I could get through only a third of my plate before I felt stuffed. Mom and Ella had slowed down, too. Only Dexter was still eating.

"I'm going to stretch my legs," Mom said. "I won't be far." She stood up and strolled out of earshot but not out of sight.

I set down my fork and took a deep breath. "I'm so sorry I brought this down on all of us," I said.

"We knew the risks," Ella said.

"I'm just sorry I didn't say anything to your mom or Sister Niema when I—when we started—whatever," Dexter said. "There are rules about that. To avoid this exact type of thing. If someone finds out you're a spy . . . or a handler—if there are also . . . feelings. It just . . . it can be that much harder to know what's real or not. If it had just been finding out about your mom and not about us, and if you and I hadn't been . . . whatever . . . you might have been willing to listen and not run off."

"It was partly my fault, too," Ella said. "I should have pushed Dex *to* say something. I just didn't really think about the implications. I have my spy life and my teenage life. I just thought this was a strictly teen thing. Teenagers keep secrets from adults. Spies can't afford to keep secrets from their team."

"How do you do it?" I asked. "How do you have this secret life and then just go function in classes with people whose biggest concern is their hairstyle?"

"I don't know," Ella said. "Lots of teens have heavy things going on in their families that they block out during school."

"Sometimes it helps," Dexter said. "Like, when guys

in school were hassling me, or when I didn't make the cross-country team, I'd just tell myself: *This isn't my real life. My real life is being a spy for my people.*"

A trio of girls walked up to the cafeteria, skin glowing from dancing in the nearby club. When they got closer, I realized they were transgender girls. They looked elated as they got bottles of water and ordered at the window, flirting with the young man who worked there.

"At first I really envied the two of you," I said to Ella and Dexter. "Like, you were in on the big secret, and I wasn't. But now it seems it's been a privilege to be sheltered from all this."

"When I first found out, I was so mad," Ella said. "I just wanted to be a normal family. But slowly I stopped blaming my parents for standing up for what they believe in. I started blaming the system."

"In the beginning I thought it was cool," Dexter said. "But the Factory's missions are serious. It's not a game."

The trio of girls sat down at the table across from us and dug in to their plates. I realized I might never be like them—just going out to a club with a couple girlfriends. Normal.

"I feel so bad, though," I said to Ella and Dexter. "You had to leave LA and everything because of me."

"It's probably just temporary," Ella said. "We've been messaging photos of us visiting our sick grandma in Texas."

"Let me guess," I said. "You don't have a grandma in Texas."

"Nope," Dexter said. "She lives in New Jersey."

Mom got take-out containers for the three of us, and she'd also gotten the address of a guesthouse where we would be staying. We caught a taxi and crowded in. Dexter was the tallest, so he sat in the front. Mom was the shortest, but Ella had the narrowest hips, so she sat in the middle of the back.

The cab sped through Havana's dark streets. We stopped in front of a single-story pale yellow bungalow. The cabbie accepted US dollars from my mom.

Mom knocked on the door, and a woman with a compact build answered it. She was wearing a lightweight robe, and she introduced herself as Doña Iris. She showed us to a pair of rooms that each had two double beds.

Just looking at a bed, I felt suddenly exhausted, like the distance of ten feet between me and the mattress was longer than the entire trip from LA to Havana.

I think I bid Ella and Dexter good night as I face-planted onto one of the double beds.

I woke just before dawn. I could see a thin strip of light coming from the hall as Mom slipped into the room. I turned over on my side to go back to sleep and saw Mom in her bed. I froze as I realized it wasn't Mom walking into the room but someone else.

I turned quietly, carefully, as the unknown person crept farther into the room.

From the height and silhouette of the figure, it looked to be a man.

I kept my eyes half closed, faking sleep. As he moved toward me, I coiled my muscles.

He was nearly leaning over me when I sprang with a howl, driving my shoulder into the man's chest and knocking him back. He yelped.

Mom leaped up from the other bed, prepared to pounce.

I had knocked the wind out of him, but I expected him to reach for a weapon or try to run away. I tensed myself, ready to react.

But instead, he just sat there on the ground, wheezing. One hand on his chest, the other hand flung out as if to protect himself.

Mom circled around the man, his form dark and nearly indistinguishable in the dim room. He didn't seem to be getting up, so Mom reached for the light switch.

At first, it was too bright for me to see, and it took my pupils a moment to adjust.

"Forrest?" Mom said. "Is that you?"

I just stared at him with my mouth open. "Dad?"

TWENTY-ONE

The man in front of me was clean-shaven, with a wild Afro. I had never seen my dad without a beard. When beards had become fashionable, Mom teased Dad that he was a hipster, but Dad said they were all just trying to copy him. Now I saw that he had a dimple in his chin and higher cheekbones than expected. With the clean-shaven face and big puff of hair, he looked younger, like some sort of pop star.

I gaped at him as he stood up to hug me.

And then the three of us were all hugged up in a clump, each of us crying and clinging on for dear life.

A couple hours later, we were sitting with Ella and Dexter, eating a breakfast of fruit and toast at the big kitchen table.

"I can't believe how big you both are," Dad said. "Ella, I still remember you with those huge two front teeth. It's like you've finally grown into them."

"We used to call her Bugs Bunny," Dexter said.

"Thanks for bringing that up," Ella said, her mouth full of guava and mango.

"So, Dad, where have you been?" A heaviness settled over the table, like I had committed a faux pas. "What?" I asked.

"Let's finish breakfast, my love," Mom said. "Then maybe the five of us can go out for a walk, no?"

"Okay," I said.

We settled back into eating, but the playful nature of our breakfast had vanished. I hurried up and finished my toast. I wanted to know what the hell was going on.

Half an hour later, we had finished breakfast and washed the dishes, and we were walking down the residential street where the guesthouse was located. Havana was so different from LA. People hung out on their porches and talked. There were more bicycles than cars, and lots of people on foot.

Dad smiled, but the brightness didn't reach his eyes. "I was crossing the border from Brazil into Colombia when I got stopped, but I managed to bribe one of the guards. I was able to get to a safe house in Venezuela."

"Tío?" my mom asked.

Dad smiled for real for a moment. "Tío."

I knew "tío" meant uncle. Must be a pretend uncle because Mom had said she didn't have any family left. Assuming she was telling the truth.

Dad pointed to an old 1950s car going by. "Look, kids!" he said loudly. More quietly he murmured, "We're supposed to be tourists, remember?" Ella and Dexter grinned and watched the car.

With his eyes on the retreating vehicle, Dad went on: "I waited there for weeks, until they smuggled me onto a ship going to the Dominican Republic, and then from there to Cuba."

"So what set it off?" Mom asked. "They had a photo of you?"

"No," Dad said. "I got detained at the border, and they fingerprinted me. When they ran my prints, they matched a suspected ISIS terrorist."

Dexter's and Ella's mouths dropped open. "Remember, kids," Mom said. "We're happy tourists."

They both smiled again. I realized my own face had become a mask of anxiety. I grinned and linked my arm through Mom's. We looked cozy, but I was really clamped on to her arm with a death grip.

"Somebody must have gotten into the system at the highest level," Dad said.

"What's our next move?" Ella asked.

"I haven't been able to make contact with anyone

else from our cell," Dad said. "As I traveled, I didn't share any particulars. It's just a network of progressive safe houses across Latin America. Some of it is still in place from the dictatorships of the seventies and eighties. I knew the passwords, but some houses had been bought by new people who had no idea what I was talking about. Other people opened their houses for the first time in forty years."

Dad sighed. "So far, everyone in the Factory who was targeted was in the same cell. It looks like they only have the identities of our small group of operatives. But we don't know where the mole is. We don't know how close they might be to identifying more operatives in our organization to target. When I got away, I initiated the protocol to destroy every trace of information on the servers."

"All of it?" Dexter asked. "How will the Factory be able to operate without that information?"

"It can't," Dad said. "But I downloaded it all before I destroyed the info online. We have to get this drive to our network."

Suddenly, I heard the sound of a wave crashing. I looked up, and there was a seawall, a low partition of concrete separating the city from the ocean.

"Kids," Mom said. "Can you all walk ahead? We need to talk for a minute."

"Come on!" Ella shouted, and ran toward the ocean.

Dexter and I ran after her, fake smiles on our faces.

Ella got to the seawall and leaned out over it. A wave crashed and sprayed her with salt water. She laughed, the first genuine smile on her face since breakfast.

Dexter and I pressed against the wall beside her. I stared out at the expanse of ocean. Somehow, the power of the sea and the delightful unpredictability of the waves helped me rise above the anxiety of the moment.

I glanced back at my parents. Mom had her hand on Dad's shoulder and had thrown her head back, laughing. I couldn't hear her voice over the crashing of the waves, but the image was familiar.

Had it been like this at home sometimes? Me in the kitchen and Mom and Dad chatting happily in the living room, a portrait of lightness, when they were really worried about some spy business?

A wave crashed and sprayed the side of my face, pulling my attention back.

Dexter and Ella laughed uproariously. Ella stepped back from the wall, her whole upper body drenched, her Afro puff drooping down with the weight of the water.

"You look like a drowned mouse," Dexter said.

Ella shook her wet puff at him, splattering him with some more water.

He took off his T-shirt and swung it at her in

retaliation. She jumped out of the way, and it hit the wall with a hard slapping sound.

The sight of his naked chest took my mind off my parents for a moment. I watched the two of them playing. She loosened the tie of her hair and shook her head at him, the tight coils having sucked up the water like sponges, sending it back his way in a spray. He kept flicking the wet shirt at her, managing to make contact one out of every few tries. I was mesmerized by the muscles in his torso and how they moved as he swung the towel.

"Kids!" Mom called. "Time to head back."

The three of us turned toward them. Mom and Dad stood with their arms draped casually around each other as they pivoted and headed back to the guesthouse.

Dexter put his soggy T-shirt back on, and it stuck to his chest. Thank goodness Ella and I had on layers. I wrung out my top and pulled it forward so it would hang loose and not cling to my own skin.

We jogged to catch up with my parents.

"So let's think about where we might want to go for lunch," Mom said. "There are some amazing Chinese Cuban places. And Forrest and I would like to talk to our daughter alone, okay?"

Ella and Dexter nodded and fell behind us, just out of earshot.

"What is it?" I asked, and remembered belatedly to smile.

"Your father and I know this has been a lot to take in," Mom said.

"No," I said. "I'm okay now. Just happy Dad's back."

"Yes," Mom said. "But we have to figure out how to get the disk drive to our people in the States."

I thought back to the series of people who had helped me get from LA to here. I imagined an envelope traveling to Cancún on the boat, up through the desert in the diplomatic sedan, back to Sister Niema's in the Robeson Electric van and the helicopter.

"Will Juan Carlos be back?" I asked.

Dad took a big breath. "One of us will need to go."

"Dad!" I said. "It's not safe for you."

Dad smiled. "You're right. I can't go."

"Will you go, Mom?" I asked. "Or Ella or Dexter?" I glanced over my shoulder at them. "Aren't they in the system?"

"They are," Dad said with a shrug. "Which is why we need you to go."

"Me?" I asked.

Mom sighed. "You know how you were born at home," she reminded me. "And how you've always gone to alternative schools until Roosevelt."

I nodded.

"No fingerprints," Dad said. "No photos. No medical

records. All your immunizations were done under an alias. No data."

"I-I'm really not in the system at all?" I stammered. "That's . . . wow."

"If anything happened to us," Mom said, "we wanted to be sure you could get away clean. That no one could track you down."

Mom and Sister Niema had told me this already, but suddenly I put it all together. "Of course," I said. "You didn't know what to do when it was time for me to get a driver's license."

"We have a fake passport for you," Mom said. "We just need you to fly to the US and call our operative in the FBI. Meet with her. She can take it from there."

"Oh, that's all?"

"Amani," Mom said. "Your father's life is at stake. You're the only one who can possibly go."

"And afterward, do I come back to Cuba?" I asked. "Is this our new home?"

Mom and Dad looked at each other. "No, my love," Mom said. "Cuba has an extradition treaty with the US now. It's not safe. Dad'll be traveling to—it doesn't matter where he's flying through. His final destination is on the African continent. Someplace where the government isn't obligated to send him back to the US."

"And then that will be our new home?" I asked.

"If your mission is successful," Dad said, "it won't have to be. We can meet up again wherever we want."

I looked at Ella and Dex. They were chatting with their regulation smiles in place but had anxious eyes fixed on me.

I looked up at Dad, his clean-shaven face still a shock. Yet it fit somehow. My parents were different people than they had been a week ago. Everything was different now.

"Okay," I said. "You need me to fly back to the States and call someone from the FBI? Am I flying to Washington, DC?"

"Actually," Dad said, "I got word that our contact isn't at FBI headquarters in DC. She's on assignment in San Francisco."

I nodded. "Burner phone?" I asked.

"Pay phone."

"Do I fly direct?" I wanted to know.

"Via Houston," Dad said.

"Oh, no," I said. "No movie."

I looked up at them with a cheesy grin. The joke hadn't gone over well.

I let my face relax and fall somber for a moment. "Okay," I said. "I'll do it."

Mom's and Dad's faces split into twin smiles of anxiety and relief.

"Come on, kids!" Dad yelled to Ella and Dexter. "Let's go get some lunch."

TWENTY-TWO

Later that afternoon, I was sitting in the living room when Dexter came in. "Wanna go for a walk?" he asked. He had on a plain T-shirt now, with sneakers and the cargo shorts.

By this point, I knew that "a walk" meant having a conversation that wouldn't be overheard.

"Sure," I said.

We were finally alone, walking together on a beautiful tree-lined street in one of the safest low-income neighborhoods in the Western Hemisphere. No one was going to jump us for Dexter's sneakers. No cops were going to shoot us because we were Black. No men hassled me on the street, even though I had a pair of short shorts on because it was so damn hot and my only other choice was a pair of leggings that felt like wearing a sauna.

And yet I would have given anything to go back in time, to be walking with him down a sidewalk with broken glass and even the occasional dirty diaper. As much as I hated the hissing and kissing sounds from guys on the street and the comments that followed my rear end down hallways, it was worth it to be at a school with my people and to be making new friends and even maybe having a boyfriend.

Instead, I would be going back to the US alone. None of them would be with me. And there was a danger much more lethal and calculated than obnoxious creeps on the street.

"You leave tomorrow?" Dexter asked.

"I guess," I said. I'd be flying to the US with a message for the FBI, using a fake passport. When it came to my legal identity, I was a ghost.

"I can tell it's a lot," he said. "But, Imani, I know you can do it."

"Amani," I said, not sure what he already knew.

"Huh?" he asked.

"My real name is Amani," I said. "Amani Kendall."

"It wasn't just because we were assigned to you," he said. "I liked you for you."

I couldn't help but notice the past tense. How was that supposed to make me feel any better?

"I was so excited that I might be able to have a

girlfriend," he said. "We don't really get to . . . date. If I liked a girl and was lucky enough that she liked me back, I knew eventually I'd have to start lying to her about what mattered most to me and my family. So what was the point? Why get close enough to get my heart broken or to break hers, you know?"

"I guess," I said.

"Ella seems to have the romance thing worked out," he said.

"So why didn't you just do whatever she did?" I asked.

He shook his head. "We each go to athletic summer camps. Mine is all male, hers is all female. She has a girlfriend there. They call and text all during the school year, then spend the summer together. It's way easier to be a spy in a relationship that's long distance."

"Wait," I said. "Ella's gay?"

He looked surprised. "Yeah," he said. "We thought you knew."

"She and I were friends for only a couple weeks," I said.

"I thought Sister Niema had told you," he said.

"I didn't get a spy briefing about the two of you," I said. "Did you get one on me?"

"Sort of," he said. "I mean, yeah. They showed us your picture, and I thought you were really cute. But they also told us you'd gone to Penfield. So I expected you to be . . . I don't know. Stuck-up or something.

Or, like, whitewashed. And then I met you and . . . it was like . . . I mean, you're the coolest girl." He smiled. "Even if you weren't part of all this, I would have liked you. So when your family was in the network—I was just, like . . ."

He put a fist to his temple and then lifted and opened his hand, making an explosion sound.

I nodded. I didn't know what to say.

"So, I mean, you know, everything's different now," he said. "But I wasn't pretending or anything back in LA. What I felt was real."

"I don't know what to do with that, Dexter," I said.

"There's nothing to do with it," he said. "Our cell is blown. We'll end up scattered in the US . . . if we're even able to go back."

"So what you felt," I said, "you don't feel anymore?"

"It's not that," he said. "I just can't let myself get my hopes up. It's not that I don't like you like that anymore. It's that I won't let myself. I only wanted to let you know that I did. I really did. In a way I'd never felt before."

I could feel the tears welling in my eyes. "I felt that way, too," I said. "And I'd never felt that with anyone else, either."

I swallowed back the tears and stuck out my hand. "Well, Dexter," I said in a fake chipper tone. "It was nice liking you."

He laughed and shook my hand. "Nice liking you, too, Amani."

Then he pulled me close to him and kissed me on the lips—lingering a little more than the pecks we had had before. "I really wanted to do that back when I liked you," he said.

I smiled and kissed him back. "I see what you mean," I said. For a moment, with our lips pressed against each other and my eyes closed, I could have been surrounded by enemies and wouldn't have even known it. Or cared.

We pulled apart gently and he nodded. "Glad we understand each other."

"We should head back," I said. "Before we let ourselves get our hopes up."

"That would be a terrible idea," he said.

We didn't kiss again, but we did hold hands as we walked back to the guesthouse.

A few blocks from our destination, we passed a house where four teenagers sat around a table on someone's front porch. As we passed, I realized they were playing Triángulo. The cards they had were color copies on paper, DIY laminated with clear packing tape. Their board was also homemade. For game pieces, they used bottle caps and shells. And in the middle, they had an actual triangle-shaped stone.

Dexter squeezed my hand, and we smiled at each

other. We just strolled casually and held hands until a block before the guesthouse. The moment we turned the corner and the small bungalow was in sight, our hands spontaneously disentangled. I smiled to myself. My timing was the same as his. Apparently, my spy-craft was finally getting up to speed.

TWENTY-THREE

The summer-weight suit and pantyhose felt strange against my skin. I also felt unsteady in the heels, even though they were low by any standards. I had never before worn any type of bra that wasn't athletic, and I kept worrying that as I moved, my chest would strain against the buttons, and people would be able to see my bra.

My head also felt strange. My hair had been done in extension braids for the first time. The synthetic hair felt heavy, scratchy against my neck and shoulders, and way too hot. My own hair was shorter but much silkier. According to Mom, my usual cornrows or Afro puffs were too noticeable. I needed to look more mainstream, like a young professional. I wore lipstick and eye makeup, as well as a little blush to create contours on my baby face. The mascara was waterproof. I had to keep reminding myself not to rub my eyes or rub my lips back and forth against each other like I usually did with clear lip balm.

In other words, being a grown woman was precarious and uncomfortable. Still, I didn't complain about the "Wow, you look . . . wow" I got from Dexter. And the way Mom cried about how grown-up I was nearly broke my heart.

The four of them came to the airport to see me off for my 6 a.m. flight. I had barely slept the night before, and everything felt a little like a dream. I hugged each of them in turn. "You can do this, baby," Dad whispered in my ear. "I'll be flying out later today, and one way or another, we'll all be back together soon."

Ella didn't say anything while she hugged me, but afterward she took my hands. "You're gonna do great in that job interview," she said. "I know it."

Mom just cried and hugged me, then cried harder as Dad put an arm around her.

Dexter held me tight in a different way from the others. It was the closest we had ever been. Even when we'd kissed, it was just our lips touching. I wanted to hold on forever but began to feel self-conscious with my parents and his sister watching. As we pulled apart, he pressed a tiny piece of paper into my hand.

I tried to put it in the pocket of my suit jacket, but

the pockets were fake. So I palmed it, pressing it against the suitcase handle as I wheeled the bag behind me.

"That's your flight," Mom said. She was the only one who spoke Spanish well enough to catch all the announcements by Cubana de Aviación.

I turned and followed the line of people walking toward the gates. I kept looking over my shoulder and waving, leaving my other hand clamped solidly on the suitcase handle. Even in the early morning, the day was already warm and humid. The last pink rays of dawn were fading, and the sun was beginning to beat down in earnest. It was going to be a scorcher of a day. I was certain that by the time I finally peeled my palm off the suitcase handle, the paper would have turned to pulp.

Inside the terminal, I went to the bathroom and wheeled the bag into the stall. I slid my palm from the suitcase handle. On the paper was an email address: oldjazzguyname@yeemail.com.

I smiled. Old jazz guy name. Dexter, like the musician Dexter Gordon. I would never forget it. I tossed the paper into the toilet and flushed.

I sweated my way through the passport line in Havana, but they just waved me through. In Houston, however, they looked at me like I was a criminal. It was the same passport that I'd used to cross into Mexico. It said I was Terra Jordan and had a date of birth that would make me nineteen.

"What were you doing in Cuba?" the older woman agent asked.

I started to panic. If I got selected for additional searches, would they find the disk drive? Would we lose the only copy of the network contacts? Worse still, would the whole network be compromised and subject to attack?

"I'm with an international epidemiology team doing research on Zika virus," I said.

"And you're only flying one way?" she asked.

"We went in via Mexico," I said. "Cancún. By the way, here's the latest update on Zika, particularly if anyone in your family is pregnant or planning to become pregnant."

I handed her an updated pamphlet that Mom had printed off the CDC website. I kept my face neutral.

"Thanks," she said. "My daughter wants to start a family."

"Is she here in Houston?" I asked. "She should really read this." It was so different to talk to adults this way.

But it seemed to be working. She stamped my passport and waved me through.

The flight to San Francisco was uneventful. It was early afternoon when I landed. From the airport, I took a shuttle to the hotel Mom had reserved for me.

I dropped my wheeled bag and put on more casual clothes. Then I took a cab to downtown San Francisco and went in search of a public phone booth.

Dad explained that this protocol had been put into place before cell phones. Back then, there were phone booths everywhere. But not now. I looked around for a while before I managed to find one next to a gas station. I put coins into the phone and dialed.

"Eve Henderson," a smooth voice answered.

"Yes, Ms. Henderson," I said. "We seem to have found your library card. We don't usually call, but I see that you're a former librarian."

"Yes," the voice said. "I used to work in the main branch. Thanks so much."

"You can pick it up anytime," I said. "We're open until eight today."

"Perfect," she said. "I get off at five. I'll head right over."

We said goodbye and hung up. It was already 4 p.m. I paid cash at an internet café and got directions to the main branch of the library. I also got a new email account and sent oldjazzguyname a YouTube video that I thought he should really watch. It was of two Brazilian kids, a boy and a girl, doing capoeira.

TWENTY-
FOUR

I walked into the main branch of the San Francisco Public Library and went directly to the African American literature section. Mom had told me the signal was that I should be reading a book by Toni Morrison. I asked Mom why Morrison, and she said because she had won both the Nobel and the Pulitzer Prizes for literature and her work would be in any library.

I picked *Song of Solomon*. I started at the beginning, but I couldn't understand it, probably just because I was so nervous. I flipped through and read a page in the middle over and over again.

And talking about dark! You think dark is just one color, but it ain't. There're five or six kinds of black. Some silky, some woolly. Some just empty.

*Some like fingers. And it don't stay still. It moves
and changes from one kind of black to another.
Saying something is pitch black is like saying
something is green. What kind of green? Green like
my bottles? Green like a grasshopper? Green like
a cucumber, lettuce, or green like the sky is just
before it breaks loose to storm? Well, night black is
the same way. May as well be a rainbow.*

I looked up at the clock. It was 5:23. With every
second that ticked by, I became more convinced that
something was wrong. The words started to swim
before my eyes. I was getting a headache. I put the
book down and pinched the bridge of my nose.

Then I saw a woman walking toward me. She was
medium brown, with bright eyes and high cheekbones. Her hair was pressed straight, and she had on
a cream-colored suit. The lines of her suit were so
smooth, it made mine look like some kind of amateur
sewing project.

She smiled at me. "I love Toni Morrison."

"It's no easy read," I said.

"It's worth it," she said. "*Sula*'s my favorite."

And that was it. That was the code, word for word,
as we were supposed to say it.

I put the book down. "I really did used to work in
the DC library," she said. "Let's go to someplace a bit
more quiet."

She led me down a corridor and to a back office. The door said EMPLOYEES ONLY.

She slipped a set of lock picks out of her pocket, and in a few seconds, we were inside.

I realized I had been holding my breath, worried that a real employee might be in there. But it was empty. Apparently, this was like a hospital for books. There were several with raggedy bindings and torn covers. There was also a microwave with a coffee pot on top.

"You did good, sis," she said. "As you know, I'm Eve Henderson."

"Amani Kendall," I said. Mom had told me to be totally honest with her. But nothing would have prepared me for what happened next. Her hand flew over her mouth, and her eyes grew wide.

"What is it?" I asked.

She was crying.

"Please," I said. "Is everything okay?"

She nodded through her tears. "I'm—" she began, but broke off in a sob. "I'm your aunt!"

"You're what?" I was confused.

"I'm Forrest's sister," she said. "Half sister. We have different fathers."

She was what? I looked at her, shocked.

"I haven't seen you since you were a baby. I didn't think I'd ever get to see you again." She rummaged in her big designer bag. From inside a large wallet, she flipped to a color photograph in a plastic sleeve. It was a picture of her looking younger. Her hair was in an Afro, and she had on a Queen Latifah T-shirt. She was holding a baby. It was me, in a yellow onesie, in a room with periwinkle-flowered wallpaper. It was from that same set that Mom had saved from the fire.

I looked at Eve. She had the same high cheekbones that I had finally seen on Dad's clean-shaven face. I could feel the emotion welling up in my chest, and then someone walked past in the corridor. I pushed down the feelings as she spoke hurriedly.

"Are your parents okay?"

"They're in Cuba," I said. "They sent me because—"

"You're the ghost," she said. "But last I knew, you all were in Los Angeles. And Forrest was in South America. What happened?"

I took a deep breath. "Well, to start with, let me give you this." I handed her the disk drive, and immediately I felt a huge weight lift off my shoulders. I told her about how Dad had to wipe the servers, and then I went back and filled in all the details. I explained about the trip out of the US, about ending up in Cuba, and that Dad was traveling to the Continent. I told her about the family that escaped the car bomb. The fire. I even told her about shooting the fake gun and the helicopter explosion. Then I told her about the ISIS photo and fingerprint swap. She hadn't known about the assassination of the operative in the CIA.

She shook her head. "If the other operative is dead, and the terrorist files have been tampered with, then there are only a few agents who might know about our cell and have that kind of access. I have a suspicion about who the leak is."

"Who?"

She shook her head. "An agent I thought was sympathetic. It's safer if you don't know yet," she said. "And in the meantime, I can't trust anyone. Not even my own team. But what *he* doesn't know is that we've added a second CIA operative. The new guy can put those files right and can leave a cyber trail that leads back to the leak. He'll be exposed, and your dad will be safe. And we can get the list of operatives into the right hands. But we need to hurry."

Eve looked around the room and saw a few jackets and sweatshirts hanging on a coatrack by the door. She sorted through them quickly and handed me a plain black hoodie. Then she reached into her purse and pulled out a shopping bag. She handed it to me with the hoodie.

"Put these on," she said. "Be quick. I'll be in the hallway making sure no one comes in."

She slipped out, and I opened the bag. It had a blue wig, a pair of glasses with turquoise-tinted lenses, and a tube of black lipstick.

I pulled the sweatshirt over my head. Then I used

the microwave door as a mirror for the lipstick and put on the wig.

When I came out, she was hanging up from a whispered call on her phone. She rushed me out of the library and into a taxi that was waiting for us at the curb.

For the next twenty minutes, Eve was on her phone. She seemed to be setting up some sort of videoconference. Apparently, there were a lot of people who needed to "sign off" to make it happen, and she was getting all of them to do it. We drove through the city evening to an office building without any signage.

Without stopping her call or looking at me, she handed me a smartphone with earbuds. She tapped her ear, motioning for me to use the earbuds. When I put them in, she nodded.

Eve paid the cabdriver, and we walked into the building. After she used her badge to enter through a secure door, she murmured in my ear, "If you see or hear anyone you recognize, don't react, okay?"

We walked in through a lobby. The only other instructions she gave me were "Be sullen."

I slouched down into the hoodie and trailed slightly behind her.

The office was boxy, nondescript, and windowless. I immediately felt anxious when I walked in.

Several men in suits were conferring in a tight knot.

Eve strode into the room and asked, "Who's in charge here?"

"And you are?" one of the younger men asked.

"Eve Henderson," she said. "FBI." She flashed some kind of credentials.

The guy's eyebrows rose. "Assistant Director Henderson," he said. "What can we do for you?"

"I was in the area with a charge to be transferred to WITSEC," she said. "She can wait here. Where can we talk?"

He led her away to another office. Suddenly, I could overhear the conversation on the smartphone earbuds.

"I heard you had a hit on an ISIS operative," she said. "My director asked me to stop by and observe the interrogation. I happen to have information on a domestic link."

"Of course," he said. "Right this way."

There were bagels and cream cheese on the table. I helped myself.

I chewed quietly as I listened. There was a woman's voice, not Eve's. It sounded more distant, a little distorted. "Mr. Kendall, you say you're employed as a researcher, but we don't have a work history for you since 2002."

I could feel my body twitch. Eve had said not to react. Was this recording from before Dad left? Was it recent? Wasn't Dad supposed to be on his way to the Continent?

"That's correct," I heard Dad say over the earbuds. His voice was equally staticky. "I've been working as a contract employee since then. Just look at my tax returns. I'm a scientist. I don't have any connection to ISIS. I've never even been to the Middle East."

"Has he been telling this same story the whole time?" It was Eve's voice now and much clearer. "Has someone pulled the tax records to corroborate his story?"

"Waste of time," a man's voice said, clear like Aunt Eve's. "He's lying. But DNA evidence doesn't lie. We're just waiting for the lab tests to come back. I'm not sure how he evaded the authorities in Bogotá, but it won't happen again."

It was quiet for a moment, then I heard a faint *ping* in my ears. I looked at the phone, and it seemed to be some sort of Zoom call. Dad was in one of the windows, labeled "Miami TSA." He sat at a table with handcuffs on. His face, in five o'clock shadow, wore a grim expression. A female FBI agent stood behind his chair, looking down toward him. Eve was in another window, labeled "SF satellite." My heart was in my throat. That was the suit Aunt Eve was wearing today. This was no recording. It was happening in real time. They had Dad in custody.

In the third window, a Black man in a suit smirked, looking at his large designer watch. It was labeled "LA." The display changed to speaker view, and it was just the smirking man's face.

Through the earbuds, I heard a door open and close.

"Did the DNA evidence come through?" the smirking man asked someone off camera.

"It was inconclusive," another man's voice said.

"What?" It was the same man who had accused my dad of lying, but the smirk was no longer in his voice or on his face.

"Then shouldn't Mr. Kendall be free to go?" Eve asked. "If there's no conclusive DNA evidence, what evidence are you using to hold him?"

"Assistant Director Henderson," someone off camera said. "You should see this."

I could see Eve scrolling through something on a tablet.

"Mr. Willis," Eve said. "The San Francisco team here will need to ask you some questions about a connection between your personal computer and some Homeland Security files—"

Suddenly the screen went blank. I tried pressing buttons on the smartphone, but nothing worked. When I rebooted the phone and tried to join the meeting, I got the following error message:

THE CURRENT USER DOES NOT HAVE SECURITY CLEARANCE FOR THIS MEETING.

So I waited anxiously for almost an hour without any idea of what was happening inside. Finally, Eve walked back into the room. "San Francisco can take it from there," she said to the other man in the suit.

"Come along," she said to me, taking the smartphone and depositing it at the desk. I stood dutifully, and she strode out with me trailing behind her.

Eve hailed another cab.

"So . . ." she began. "I'm not sure when your father will be getting off work." She seemed to be choosing her words carefully. "I thought he was coming home early, but his boss seems to have asked him to work late."

I assumed this was code to tell us Dad hadn't been released. "Okay," I said. "But he'll be home in time for a late dinner, right?" My heart was pounding hard as I asked the question.

"I'm not sure," she said. "I certainly let him know that the family would be holding dinner for him, but we're not sure if he's gonna be able to get away from the office."

I could feel my stomach drop. Dad was still in custody?

"Do you and your dad like to play word games?' she asked. "He loved them when he was a kid."

"Word games?" I asked. Was she trying to cheer me up? Shouldn't we be trying to figure out how to get Dad out of custody?

"Games," she said, her voice more pointed now. "You know. Playing with letters and numbers?"

Oh! She meant ciphers. I looked at her, and she

looked from me to the cabdriver. He looked oblivious to me, but I guess you never know.

"Yes," I said. "Dad and I love word games. We play them all the time."

She smiled. "Good to know."

I hesitated. Could I give her more information? "Word games are always more fun when there are patterns," I said. "Like your name, Eve—it's a palindrome."

"Yep," she said. "The same backward and forward."

"Right," I said. "My name is only part palindrome. The first three letters. That can be fun . . . in word games." Did she understand what I meant? That I used my name as a key? I hoped it was okay to allude to my real name like that.

She nodded and gave me a knowing look. "Smart," she said. "I like it."

"So do you think Dad will be home tonight after I'm already in bed?" I asked.

She gave a shrug as her phone chimed. She looked at it, then looked up at me.

"Did you bring any club clothes?" she asked.

"Club like . . . country club?" I asked.

She gave a dry chuckle. "Club like nightclub."

"Nightclub?" I asked. Then I whispered to her, "I'm only fifteen."

"Fifteen and a half," she whispered back. "And I'm sure you have ID that places you at over eighteen."

I nodded.

"Do you have something at your hotel that you can wear?" she asked me.

"I guess . . ." I said, thinking of the uncomfortable suit. Did that count?

"Where are you staying?" she asked.

When I told her, she shook her head. "It's too far," she said. "We need to get to the mall before it closes."

When we pulled up to the downtown mall, she paid the driver and we got out.

"I have a drop spot to the new CIA operative," she said.

"In a nightclub?"

"On Fridays, yes," she said, looking at my leggings and sweatshirt. "And that outfit will definitely not cut it."

Two hours later, I was sitting in a cab next to Eve in a glittering miniskirt and an off-the-shoulder black top, with a pair of chunky-heeled black boots. We had ditched the sweatshirt. I whispered an apology to whatever library employee it had belonged to.

During our trip to the mall, she had been on her phone constantly, mostly tapping the screen furiously. Finally, while we'd waited for the cab, she had looked at me with a relieved smile. "When I meet with this contact, we should be able to pass on the evidence that will free your dad."

I was heartened to know that Dad was gonna be

okay, but now I had a different (and, admittedly, lesser) problem. A fashion crisis. In the taxi, I kept trying to tug the miniskirt down over my thighs.

"Are you sure this is what I should wear?" I asked. "I feel so conspicuous."

"I'm sure," she said. "You look perfect."

She had bought an outfit as well: a skintight jumpsuit. She'd explained that it wouldn't do to bring me to her apartment, just in case.

Eve—Aunt Eve—had a build like Dad's, long and slim.

In the store I had tried to get her to buy me a dark maxi skirt and loose blue blouse, but she insisted that *those* clothes would make me stick out.

The miniskirt had looked really cute in the mirror at the store. I was getting more comfortable with my body. But it's one thing to pose in a mirror in a short skirt and another thing to walk around in it or sit down. Lesson learned. I told myself to focus on the strength in my thighs rather than the size and to see my curves as sexy—but still, I would have preferred something I could *move* in.

From the mall, we headed over the bridge to Oakland, to a club that was mostly Black.

I stepped out of the cab and saw a line of glamorous girls standing behind a rope below an awning.

"Looking good, ladies!" a guy said as we walked in.

The place was dim, and there was a steady pulse

of bass. I felt a bit unstable in the heels and wanted to spend the rest of my life tugging down the skirt.

But I had to admit Eve was right. In the maxi skirt, I would have looked like a Black member of the Amish. Most women were dressed like us in here. And the men were offering compliments—respectful and enthusiastic ones, not like the catcalls from boys at school or creeps on the street.

"Looking beautiful, sisters!"

Was it flattering? Scary? I didn't know. Maybe if I were an actual grown-up it would have been nice. As it was, I just felt more fifteen than ever with these guys grinning at me. I trailed after Eve and tried not to react.

We made our way across the dance floor, which was full of people shaking and twirling.

Eve held my hand and pressed through the crowd toward the DJ booth. I could see a guy in the shadows wearing a baseball cap with a big pair of headphones. Was she going to make a song request?

When we got close to the dance floor, she had me stand at a table. "Wait here," she said. "I don't want my contact to see you."

"Okay," I said with a confidence I definitely didn't feel. I watched her head over to the booth and touch the DJ on his arm. They exchanged a moment of conversation.

"What's your name?" A guy had come up and tapped me on the shoulder.

I turned to him in surprise, but then I surprised myself: "Lauren," I said, the lie coming out effortlessly.

He was young and handsome, with a baby face and a low fade.

"Wanna dance?" he asked.

I wasn't exactly sure what to say. I smiled awkwardly and put my hand up in a sort of shrug. But I guess it looked like I was saying yes because he took my hand and led me onto the dance floor.

It was only a few feet away, so I stayed at the edge where Eve could see us. I also stayed where I could keep an eye on my backpack at the table.

He was respectful, dancing a couple of feet from me. I didn't really know quite how I should move my body. The guy looked young, but I had never danced with a guy at a club. I'd never even been to a high school dance, aside from my brief appearance at the dance at Roosevelt. Sometimes, I danced alone in the house or with my mom. Rarely, Dad would join us. But I'd never danced with anyone outside of my immediate family. Never where anyone was watching me. Of course, I had seen music videos, but that didn't help.

In desperation, I leaned on the four years of African dance I had taken as a kid.

As the song ended, the DJ began to mix into another song.

"Gotta go," I said to the guy. "Uh, thank you." I hustled off the dance floor. Eve was waiting by my backpack.

"You're a good dancer," she said when I reached her.

"Really?" I said. "I felt so awkward with that guy."

"That *cute* guy," she said.

"I was just faking it," I said. Dancing with a guy was weird enough. Knowing he was an adult made it even weirder.

"You did great!" she said, her eyes roving toward the door and then around the club.

"The DJ's your contact?" I asked.

"No," she said. "But my contact should be here any minute. Maybe you can find someone else to dance with in the meantime."

She was smiling, but suddenly her face froze. She turned abruptly to me.

"Don't look at me or the door," she whispered urgently. "Look at the bar."

I obeyed, turning toward the rows and rows of illuminated bottles.

"Two men just walked in," she said. "Just glance at them in your peripheral vision."

I gave them a sideways look and picked them out immediately. They stood out in their dark suits. One was white, one was Asian—two of the only people in the club who weren't Black.

"Those are men on my squad, and I'm not sure whom to trust. My contact isn't here? They're here instead? That's not good. So you need to get the evidence to my contact. This is the information that will clear your father." She handed me a flash drive I'd never seen before. "Plus the info you brought." She gave back the other flash drive I'd given her. So much for having a weight off my shoulders. Now I was under double the pressure. "My contact's DJ name is RayBreak. He's not the actual operative, but he can pass information. He should be here in the next couple hours. He's the only person you can trust. Ask if he has the deep house mix of 'Respect'—that's your code word."

"By Aretha Franklin?" I asked, unable to imagine a 1960s song in this current nightclub.

She shook her head no. "By the artist Adeva."

And then she ducked away into the club without a goodbye.

I sat down on a tall stool at the table. I pretended to be people watching, but my eye kept following the two agents as they methodically searched the club. Eventually, they left with Aunt Eve. She swept past me and didn't even make eye contact.

Over the next hour, a half dozen men asked me to dance, but I declined all of them. I kept my eye on the DJ booth, waiting for DJ RayBreak to take over.

By midnight, I was still wired but also exhausted. It was 3 a.m. by my body's inner clock. Had I really woken up in Havana?

Finally, someone moved into the DJ booth, but it looked like a woman. DJ RayBreak? Hadn't Aunt Eve said her contact was a guy?

I moved slowly over to the DJ booth to request my song.

When I got there, the previous DJ was clapping the woman on the back and heading out with a thick messenger bag full of musical tech.

The woman was setting herself up. She had a wild mane of curls and a bright smile.

"DJ RayBreak?" I asked the woman.

She shook her head. "Sorry, love, I'm subbing for him."

So the DJ *was* a man. "Is he coming later?" I asked.

"Nope," she said. "I'll be here till closing."

"Does he have another gig?" I asked.

She shrugged. "I don't know," she said. "The club promoter just called me and asked if I could sub for him last minute."

I thanked her and headed back to my table, but a trio of guys had taken it over. I steered clear and leaned up against a wall to watch. For what? DJ RayBreak? Aunt Eve to come back? I didn't know. But I had no idea what else to do.

About fifteen minutes later, another guy asked me to dance. He was baby-faced and a little shorter than me, with locs in a ponytail.

"No, thanks," I said.

"Come on," he said. "Why did you come to the club if you don't want to dance?"

"I came for DJ RayBreak," I said.

"I know," the guy said. "He's the best, right?"

"Yeah," I said. "This DJ said he's not coming tonight."

"We should look on Insta and see if he's spinning somewhere else," the guy suggested.

"We"? Ugh. Was this guy gonna be hard to get rid of?

"My phone is dead," I lied. "Can you look him up?"

I didn't add that I didn't have Instagram because I was fifteen and my mom wouldn't let me.

"Sure," he said. He scrolled through his phone. "That's weird," he said. "His last post was about how he was all excited to be coming here. No posts after that."

"Can you google him?" I asked. "See if he popped up at some other club?"

He typed a bit and tapped a few more buttons. "Nope." He shook his head. "Nothing. You sure you don't want to dance?" he asked.

"Not if DJ RayBreak isn't here," I said.

"Is he your boyfriend or something?" he asked.

I had no idea what to say. Would it be a good cover?

"Just . . . no thanks, okay?" I said, feeling a little desperate for him to leave me alone.

"Okay," he said. "Have a nice evening."

As much as I was glad to be rid of him, I didn't like being alone with thoughts spinning in my head. All I knew about DJ RayBreak was that he sometimes moved messages for the Factory and now he was missing. Was he dead? Kidnapped? In the hospital?

What was I supposed to do next?

TWENTY-FIVE

I stood at the back of the club, turning down offers to dance and feeling frozen with indecision, until the DJ who was not DJ RayBreak said it was "last call." Call for what? I didn't know, but shortly after that, she said it was the last song. When the music finished, the lights of the club came on. They were blinding after the low lighting of the last few hours.

"All right, everyone," the DJ said. "You don't have to go home, but . . . ?"

"You can't stay here," the crowd yelled back.

Everyone seemed to be crowding around the coat check to get their jackets and bags. Others were on their phones getting rides.

I guessed I would go back to the hotel. My only real choice, right? But how would I get there?

Rideshares were pulling up in a cluster in front of the club. A taxi pulled up and two guys got into it. Maybe I could get a taxi. But how could I call it? Everyone was clamoring for rides. How was I going to get one when my old phone couldn't call or go online?

"No way," one of the guys getting into the taxi was saying. "I'm not gonna show you the money before you take me." He stepped out of the cab. "That's just racist."

As I jogged toward the cab, I heard the guy still complaining. "I bet you don't ask white guys in the financial district to show you their money."

"I'll show you the money," I said, pushing past the guy.

As the cabdriver inched forward in the jam of cars, I pulled out two twenties to show the driver. He was an older white guy, and from the look of distaste on his face, the guy was probably right about the racism. But he nodded and let me climb in.

"How she gonna just stab a brother in the back like that?" I heard the guy complain loudly from outside the cab.

"Don't trip, bruh," his friend said. "Our ride gonna be here in ten minutes."

The taxi took me back to my hotel in San Francisco, which was a little south of the city, near the airport. The room seemed huge but empty, with its bland colors and pale seascape paintings.

I took a shower. I tipped my head back and drank a bit of the shower water, which was when I realized I was insanely dehydrated after the flight and everything with Aunt Eve.

After I toweled off, I drank the half liter of water in the room.

They also had a minibar with sodas and candy. I didn't drink any of the colas, but I did eat the cookies.

Then I lay awake in bed, not knowing what to do. I felt terrified for my dad, and as the day's adrenaline drained away, I also felt spent and lonely. I couldn't stop thinking about Mom and Dad. It was really Mom who fascinated me the most. I hadn't really understood her at all. But now I could see why we had never quite felt totally connected. And I could see her—faults and all—as a real person for maybe the first time. I could see them both. Which might be why I missed them so much.

At some point in the wee hours of the morning, I fell asleep with my pillow soaked in tears.

When I woke up, it was still pitch-black. My watch said it was 8:12 a.m., but it was on Cuba time. That put it at . . . 5:12 a.m. in San Francisco. I felt slightly groggy and disoriented, but worst of all, I had no idea what would happen next.

I couldn't just sit around and wait. Dad was still in custody. My mission was to help get him free. I was the only one who could do it. I was the ghost in the system. I would need to figure out what my next move was.

At 6 a.m. the business center opened. I went down there to use the computer.

I looked at the San Francisco headlines. Thankfully no reports that DJ RayBreak was murdered. Nothing about Eve Henderson. I tried to recall the last name of the smirking agent from the Zoom call with Dad. Wallace? Willis! And when I googled "Willis and CIA," I got a hit.

"FBI to address media in case of rogue CIA officer." There was a press conference this morning. Maybe Eve would be there. Or maybe there would be something that would give me more information.

It was my only lead. I found the location information and looked up subway directions, which I printed out. I needed to hustle, or I would miss my train.

I ran back upstairs and changed into the travel suit I had worn on the plane. As I was exiting the hotel, I grabbed a couple of chocolate bars from a bowl in the lobby. But then I heard the clerk calling me.

"Miss," she said. "Excuse me, miss!"

Oh no! Was I supposed to pay for the chocolate bars? Or worse yet, maybe the room hadn't been paid for? Was I going to get in trouble?

I turned around. *Act confident.* I swallowed the lump in my throat and smiled.

"Is something wrong?" I asked.

"Sorry," she said. "The night clerk forgot to ask you to sign for the incidentals."

My smile stayed pasted onto my face. What were incidentals? I walked toward her with my false confidence.

"Right here," she said, indicating a page where I agreed that they could charge the credit card on file for anything I used in the room: alcohol, snacks . . . even the water wasn't free. Oops. I hoped my mom's credit card could cover it, since she had booked the hotel.

I hadn't practiced Terra Jordan's signature, but I did my best to make my penmanship look sloppy and mature, like my mom—a doctor who signed things all the time—and not like a teenager who hardly ever signed anything.

"Are you checking out?" the clerk asked.

"Not yet," I said. I had no idea. Since I knew nothing about how long I'd be in town, it seemed wise to make sure I had someplace to stay in San Francisco.

I followed the directions on my printed map to the subway. It was called BART, and the train came shortly after I got to the platform.

I found a seat and flipped through a newspaper I found on the seat beside me. I didn't really read it, though. My mind was racing.

I didn't realize how nervous I was until I looked down and saw that I had eaten both chocolate bars without actually noticing.

As the train headed downtown, it picked up lots of morning commuters, and we were soon packed in. Through the train windows, I could see the views of the bay and of San Francisco's suburbs. This included lines and lines of pale and pastel houses even as we first crossed into the city. Eventually, it started to look a bit more urban, and then the train went underground. I got off at the downtown stop, near the Moscone Center.

As I walked the few blocks from the subway, I expected to feel at home. But Northern California was like a whole different place from LA. None of the women looked like bikini models, but more than that, they didn't look like they *wished* they were bikini models, either. I saw several really big women wearing formfitting clothes and seeming happy about it.

Also, the climate was really different. I never realized how much of a desert Southern California was until I was in the upper half of the state, which had twice the humidity. I mean, it was no DC or Miami or Havana, but San Francisco was moist with fog. It was clammy and cold. I shivered in the thin suit as I made my way to the press conference.

It was 8:52 when I arrived, and I got one of the last front-row seats.

"San Francisco?" one of the reporters said to another. "Really? Whatever it was, they couldn't have just had the press conference in DC or online and spared us all the hassle?"

"I have a source who says it's all damage control at this point," another reporter said. "But we'll see."

A few minutes later, Eve came into the room. She wore a royal blue suit and conferred in a knot of men in charcoal and black. I almost collapsed with relief when I saw her. I wanted nothing more than to run up to her and give her back the flash drives, but I couldn't risk it. What if she was being watched? I had to play it cool and figure out what to do next.

The podium in front had at least a dozen microphones set up. The seats had filled up with reporters, and there were camerapeople in all the aisles. Still photographers were snapping pictures, and in a couple of corners, bright lights illuminated sharply dressed reporters for the twenty-four-hour news shows.

"In just a few moments," a woman with stiff blond hair was saying, "we anticipate that the FBI will be making a statement about a developing story in their anti-terrorism division. Stay tuned."

At exactly 9 a.m., a man in a dark suit came up and introduced Assistant Director Henderson.

Eve walked up to the stage with a stack of index cards in one hand.

"Yesterday evening," she began, "at seven thirteen local time, the FBI uncovered information that a CIA officer has allegedly been planting false intel and sabotaging our terrorist database. We do not know at this time if this agent has been working alone or on behalf of another entity. We apprehended our suspect, CIA Officer Bernard Willis, at seven forty-six p.m. yesterday, while he was on an assignment in Los Angeles. Agent Willis was arrested, but his transport did not arrive at the San Francisco FBI office as scheduled, and we have reason to believe he may be at large. We are currently investigating and have a massive manhunt underway. San Francisco police and all local officials are participating."

She turned toward the wall behind her, and a photo of Agent Willis flashed onto a large white screen. I nearly gasped at the sight of him. It was definitely the same man who had tried to get my dad locked up. He was smiling, not sneering like he'd been on the Zoom screen, but there was a trace of that smugness, that arrogance. It was a face I would never forget.

"When Willis escaped, we believe he was unarmed, but he is a trained agent. We are asking the press to circulate this photo and to tell residents not to try to approach or apprehend Willis. I repeat, do not attempt to approach this suspect. Anyone who has any information that may lead to apprehending Willis should call our hotline," she said, and a number flashed across the screen.

"We suspect that Willis may attempt to flee the

country, and we have the cooperation of the TSA as well as the authorities at bus and train stations. We will find him, and we will see that he faces justice." She took a breath.

"We will not be taking questions at this time. Thank you," she said, and gave a brief nod as she stepped back from the podium.

The moment she finished, the room exploded with reporters standing up and calling her name. It seemed like the words "Ms. Henderson" were coming from everywhere.

"Eve!" the guy next to me called. He was an older Black guy, but using her first name? Rude.

"Assistant Director Henderson said no questions," one of the agents next to her said, to the groans of the reporters.

Eve was pulling together her papers and putting them into her briefcase. She took a sip of water and dabbed her mouth with a napkin.

The reporters began to file out, and my aunt looked at the guy next to me, the one who had called her Eve.

"Seriously, Walt?" she asked. "You're gonna call me by my first name?"

"We've worked together for over twenty years," he said. "And I'm many years your elder. I figured I was entitled. And it got your attention, didn't it?"

"We need to go, Assistant Director Henderson," the agent beside her said.

"Just a moment," Eve said.

The agent looked at her with surprise.

"These next comments are off the record," she said to the guy called Walt. "I don't want anyone recording it." She stood to her full height. "I want your word that you will not . . ." Then, for the first time, she shot a quick glance straight at me and continued speaking, ". . . record this."

I nearly gasped. She knew I was there, and her meaning was clear. She *did* want me to record this.

I fumbled in my backpack for my flip phone. I had to be subtle. I slid it nearly out of the pack and leaned over, opening the phone and turning on the record button.

My heart was beating so hard, it was a challenge to pay attention to what she was saying. And when I did tune in, she wasn't making any sense.

"Yes, everyone loves liberty. Ostensibly, Washington has a timeline yielding efforts likely leading our work. Habits are tough. Your eastern logjams limit our work habits. Arbitrate that."

"Oh-kay, Eve," Walt said with a confused look on his face. "I'll see you after you catch him."

"Absolutely," Eve said. "How about we meet in our usual spot in DC at noon?"

"What usual spot?" Walt asked.

"Is someone getting forgetful?" she asked. "Our designated meeting spot. At noon."

She looked at me and handed me the crumpled napkin. "Young lady, do you mind tossing this out for me? Why don't they have a trash can in here?"

I took the napkin. I was almost going to point out the can in the corner when I realized that she was probably passing me information.

I nodded and stopped the recording on my phone. Then I pulled a crumpled tissue out of my pocket. Walking over to the wastebasket, I tossed the tissue while I pocketed the napkin Eve had given me.

"Clear the room," the other agent said.

I glanced at Eve in my peripheral vision. I guessed this was the end of our time together. Maybe I would catch up with her at the hotel? Maybe my instructions were on the napkin?

I walked out into downtown San Francisco. I wasn't sure what to do with myself. I wanted someplace private to inspect the napkin she'd given me, but I had no idea where to go.

The area outside of the Moscone Center was an odd mix. There were lots of restaurants and stores, befitting a downtown area, but there was also a large population of people curled up in sleeping bags in some of the doorways. I was asked for spare change by several people and was sorry that I didn't have any cash to spare.

I walked back to Market Street and looked for someplace to sit where I could find some privacy. I hadn't wandered around for long before I came across the library where Aunt Eve and I had originally met. Perfect!

I found a quiet table and looked around to make sure no one had followed me. I didn't see anyone, so I took the napkin out and smoothed it flat. It had the Bon Genevieve Hotel logo on it.

The rest of it looked blank. Maybe she was just trying to give me the hotel info for where she was staying. But when I unfolded the napkin, I realized that there were light pencil marks on the inside. I pulled out a pen and went over them.

It was a cipher. A mix of letters and numbers. I had told her about the code with my name, hadn't I? Yes! In the cab. I looked for the A-M-A combination. And sure enough, there it was, right up front. It took only a little while to decode the rest. The first line read:

AMANI YOUR BIRTHDAY IS OCTOBER 9.

But my birthday was wrong; it should have been October 7, not 9. I realized that she had applied the same shift to the numbers as she'd used on the letters—I'd have to decrease each by two to get the real answers.

Then there were three more lines of numbers with some periods in them. Then the word NEGATIVE and another line of numbers. Why did it say "negative"? But as I decreased each digit by two, I began to sort the numbers out. The first line seemed to be a date.

Wait, that date was today! But what was I supposed to do, and where was I supposed to go?

The next two lines must give me more information. Could they be latitude and longitude? Thank goodness I was in a library. I didn't know if I would have time to make it to the business center at the hotel to look online.

It took a while for a computer to free up, but I eventually got one and found what I was looking for. Yes! The latitude and longitude directed me to a spot in the Presidio, a former military base in San Francisco. Then I found the bus route that would get me there and printed everything.

I rushed out of the library to the bus stop, my stomach growling. It was only 11 a.m., but the chocolate bars I had grabbed at the hotel hadn't been a very good breakfast. Plus, it was 2 p.m. Cuba time already.

I passed a convenience store on the way to the bus stop and got a sandwich, a few bags of nuts, and some crackers. I had no idea when I'd next get a chance to eat.

I also passed a cheap clothing store. I had my sneakers from Cuba, but I bought socks and sweatpants. I didn't try them on, just held them up. They were big and loose. They'd do.

Sitting at the bus stop, I felt a little self-conscious changing while I waited for the bus. But there were lots of people around who looked like they might find themselves in a position to change clothes on the street as well. I didn't know whether they had housing or not.

When I really thought about it, I didn't have housing. Our LA house had burned down. I was in San Francisco staying in a hotel room, but I had no idea for how long. I didn't know anyone here—not who I could actually call or talk to—and I had no idea where my parents were right now, and I couldn't even call them. Sounded pretty unhoused to me.

Hopefully, when I got to the destination, someone would be able to help me figure out the next steps.

I ate the sandwich and tossed the plastic wrapper into a trash can on the street.

I assumed I would just go to the location and wait around until someone came and called me Nightingale or used some other code. But then I remembered the recording. I pulled it out to listen to it.

"Yes, everyone loves liberty. Ostensibly, Washington has a timeline yielding efforts likely leading our work. Habits are tough. Your eastern logjams limit our work habits. Arbitrate that."

Timeline? Was she trying to be more specific about the time I should go? It was a Washington timeline. Did that mean it was DC time—eastern—or Washington State?

The bus finally came. The directions I'd printed had estimated that the ride would take twenty minutes, or half an hour to forty minutes with traffic.

There was definitely traffic.

I listened to the recording again. But even on the second time through, I didn't get any hidden message. Why had Eve been insistent that I record this? It didn't make any sense. Maybe that glance was just a fluke. Maybe she really didn't want Walt to record it because it made her look bad professionally? No, that didn't make sense, either. Eve was a spy. She wouldn't just ramble to a reporter for no reason. And she had glanced at me so intently.

I played the recording again. Still, I got nothing.

"Yes, everyone loves liberty. Ostensibly, Washington has a timeline yielding efforts likely leading our work. Habits are tough. Your eastern logjams limit our work habits. Arbitrate that."

I wrote the words down to be able to look at them. I took out the capital letters and punctuation to make it easier to look for patterns:

yes everyone loves liberty ostensibly washington has a timeline yielding efforts likely leading our work habits are tough your eastern logjams limit our work habits arbitrate that.

What did I notice? Well, it definitely didn't make sense. There were threads of it that sort of hung together, but overall it was nonsense. If it was scrambled, how was I supposed to know how to put it in order? It was in full sentences, but it didn't communicate a coherent thought.

As far as patterns, my eye and ear kept being drawn to the words that began with *L*. Loves liberty. Likely leading. Logjams limit. Wait. The double *L*s kept repeating. Was that the pattern? And each time, they were followed by a word that began with *O*, then a word that began with *W*.

In fact, as I looked through it, I saw that the first letters of the words were in a pattern that kept repeating. LLOWHATYE. Which made even less sense.

But then I started from the beginning and used the first letters of each word.

YELLOWHATYELLOWHATYELLOWHAT. Yellow hat? I was looking for someone with a yellow hat! Okay. Yes. I had a who: someone with a yellow hat. And a where: latitude and longitude to the Presidio. And a when: today. Should I just wait around all day for someone in a yellow hat?

I played the recording again. After the yellow hat part, I let it run.

Walt: *"Oh-kay, Eve. I'll see you after you catch him."*

Eve: *"Absolutely. How about we meet in our usual spot in DC at noon?"*

Walt: *"What usual spot?"*

Eve: *"Is someone getting forgetful? Our designated meeting spot. At noon."*

I felt a twist in my solar plexus. It was 11:36.

I snapped my head up from the phone and saw that my bus was still crawling through the slow traffic. We hadn't gotten that far.

I hustled to the front of the bus and picked up a schedule that included a little map. We had made it about three-quarters of the way there, but the traffic was getting even more jammed as we moved forward.

"Is the traffic always this bad?" I asked the woman next to me.

"Oh, no, dear," she said. "It's because of the protest."

There was a protest? Was I meeting the yellow hat person at a protest?

"My wife and I are headed there," she said. "If I didn't have this bum hip, I'd get out and walk. It might be faster."

I nodded. That was exactly what I had in mind.

I signaled for the bus to stop, but it was another five minutes before we made it to the next corner.

I leaped off the bus and took off at a fast clip. I had the printout of exactly where I was supposed to go in the Presidio and the bus map. It was a little over a mile, and I was supposed to be there in eighteen minutes.

I needed to hustle.

I was out of breath by the time I had jog-walked to the Presidio. It was a former army base that had been repurposed as a park. There were still army barrack–type structures around, but it also had ponds and grass and trails and recreation buildings.

There was some sort of military event happening there, and what looked like hundreds of thousands of people protesting against it.

DIVEST FROM FOSSIL FUELS AND ORGANIZED VIOLENCE! INVEST IN OUR COMMUNITIES AND A FUTURE WITHOUT ENDLESS WAR! one sign said.

Then I saw people standing behind a big banner: US MILITARISM FUELS THE CLIMATE CRISIS!

The military ceremony was in one of the buildings, but they had erected a huge temporary screen at the front of a massive outdoor parade ground.

I was supposed to meet the yellow hat person in five minutes, but the way was blocked. I found myself having to circle around. I looked at the map, made my best guess, and took it at a run.

A guy in a black armband called to me: "No running, remember?" he said. "This is a nonviolent protest. We don't want to do anything to agitate the police."

I didn't want to agitate any police, but I was *not* going to be late to meet Yellow Hat. I pushed my way between "Divest from Fossil Fuels! Defund the Police!" and "No awards for destroying the earth!" as I closed in on the spot.

As I got closer, I could see that there was a statue

of Rosie the Riveter on the approximate spot from the coordinates in Eve's message. Two minutes to spare. I'd made it.

I reached into my bag and pulled out the tiny flash drives that Aunt Eve had given me. No sooner did I have them in my hand than I looked up and saw a woman in a yellow hat who was looking around.

She had short locs and a shirt that said IT'S NOT TOO LATE TO SAVE THE PLANET. IT'S JUST TOO LATE TO DO A HALF-ASSED JOB. But she looked right past me. Was she the right person? I had just assumed she would approach me, but maybe not. Maybe she didn't know who she was looking for.

I walked over to her, unsure what to say. "Um," I fumbled. "I like your hat."

She looked up at me and smiled. "Yeah," she said. "I know it looks handmade, but actually it's from a factory." She emphasized the last word.

I smiled back and nodded. "Thanks for coming to the protest today."

I reached out to shake her hand, and when we shook, I slipped the flash drives into her hand.

She nodded at me and walked away, the crowd closing over a final flash of yellow.

Yes! I had gotten the evidence to the contact. The CIA would have all they needed to free Dad! I was so elated that I wanted to jump up and down and hug someone. But who? I guess I'd thought the person with the yellow hat would give me some instructions or something, but she was long gone. She'd probably taken off the hat as well.

Then it hit me. I had really done it! My mission was completed. I had no idea how to get ahold of my parents or Aunt Eve. But I had a backup plan. There were three quarters in my pocket and a number I had memorized to call. Supposedly, the Factory could pinpoint my location and would send someone to extract me within forty-five minutes. I just had to tell whoever answered the phone that the dry cleaning was really for pickup. Now, I just had to find a pay phone.

"Excuse me, young lady." An officer stopped before me. He had on a pair of reflective shades and a belt with a nightstick.

I could feel my heart beating. At least he was Black. Maybe he'd be cool.

"Can I see some ID, please?" he asked.

I had been to know-your-rights workshops. Police didn't necessarily have the right to ask for ID. Still, I didn't want to make any more trouble.

I reached slowly into my backpack. "I have my passport right here," I said.

He snatched it out of my hand and riffled through it. "You traveled to this protest all the way from Cuba?" he demanded. "That's highly suspicious. You need to come with me."

"Wait," I said. "I traveled legally."

He grabbed my arm in a tight grip and began to march me toward the entrance to the Presidio.

I felt a clutch of panic in my chest. What could I do? Run away? Would he shoot me?

I figured my best hope would be to go along. See if I could talk him into letting me go before I got processed and fingerprinted. My fake passport had held up until now. Maybe it could hold up to police scrutiny as well.

The officer marched me out through the front gates. There was a line of people chanting:

"What do we want?"

"Peace and climate justice!"

"When do we want it?"

"NOW!"

Between them and the gates stood a line of police in riot gear. Behind them was a row of Sheriff's Department buses with barred windows. Some of the buses were already filled with protesters.

"Listen, Officer," I said. "I'm a medical researcher. I'm trying to prevent the spread of Zika virus. Can't you just let me go?"

"I don't think so," he said. "You're definitely getting arrested today."

He pulled out a pair of zip ties and cuffed my hands in front of me. I expected him to walk me toward the buses, but he walked me in the other direction.

Something was wrong.

I looked up at his face for the first time. Really looked at him. Not looking for *cop* but for something else.

And I found it.

The chiseled jaw and the hard line of the lips: that was the same face that I'd seen on a smartphone Zoom window, the same face I'd seen on the screen during the press conference. The leak in the CIA. Agent Willis.

That was when my insides turned to liquid. I was no longer afraid of just being arrested and having my identity put on the grid. I was afraid for my life and my parents' lives.

"Where are you taking me?" I asked. "You're not really a cop, are you?"

"Don't worry," he said. "I may not be a cop, but I'm definitely going to make sure you get arrested. Not by these riot cops in this low-security protest circus. I'm going to get you out to a real cruiser that will take you directly to one of the precincts in San Francisco and get you processed. Forrest's little ghost-in-the-system fantasy is about to end."

I lost my poker face.

"Yes, I know your dear old dad," he said. "We were roommates in college. Your dad was the smartest guy I knew. He had all these schemes, including a ghost kid who could move all over the world without being detected. He could have had a real career in intelligence, but when the CIA tried to recruit us, he turned his nose up at the whole thing. He didn't trust the US military? What did he know about the military? My dad fought in Vietnam. He taught us kids what life was really about. He would wake us up in the night with helicopter sounds. With gunfire and bomb sounds. It traumatized my little brother. He has PTSD to this day. But I was the strong one. I understood. This is what it looks like to fight for your country.

"Forrest thought he was too good for America. If he didn't like it here, he could have left! Instead, he had the nerve to stay here and work for some rogue agency? George W. Bush had it right. In America, you're either for us, or you're against us. And for us, as Black men, we have to fight to let it be known that we're patriots. Do you know how hard it was for me to be the only Black guy in my cohort of CIA recruits? Your dad was supposed to go with me. Together, we would have had a blast. Shown those white boys a thing or two. But instead, I had to face them all by myself. He spit in the face of everything that mattered to me. And for what? Some Black superhero fantasy?" His mouth turned into the most bitter grimace I'd ever seen.

He was barely looking at me as he ranted. It sounded like a toxic bromance.

"I don't know what Carmen ever saw in him," he went on. "Did you know that I met your mom before your dad did? I thought she and I were hitting it off until he came along. I always acted like it was fine with me that she chose him. No big deal. But it wasn't fine. What? You think I was jealous? It wasn't that he took the woman who might have become my girlfriend. You can find another girlfriend. It was that she was a foreigner, and she took my brother. Her. The Factory. When I met Forrest, I thought you could get another brother. But I was wrong."

Mom had described the guy chasing them down as a stalker, and I'm not sure if even she knew how right she was. This guy was definitely a stalker. But who was he stalking? Mom as a girlfriend? Dad as a friend? Both of them?

"I saw them years later, and she was pregnant. I did the math. That would have been you. The ghost baby. But then you disappeared. I was determined to find him. And Carmen. And you. I made it my mission to destroy the Factory."

A police SUV roared past, siren shrieking.

"So many times I've been close to exposing your family," he said. "Starting with that first time you lived in Los Angeles. Just as I was about to catch up with Forrest, he moved out of town. By the time I figured out you'd gone to DC, he'd moved you all for a second time. I didn't even think to check Los Angeles again. I assumed he'd keep moving. I was thinking maybe the Midwest. Maybe Canada."

I heard more sirens in the distance.

"He got away from us in Colombia," Willis said. "But

then I got that police lead in LA. And I was so close to finding you. Till your mother burned the house and destroyed every trace of you."

For a second, I could only see the wreckage of what had once been our home. *Your mother burned the house.* Mom? *Mom* had burned our house down?

Of course. Fire survivors don't have their kids keep special suitcases. Spies do. In case they need to run. Or burn it all down. Or both.

I snapped myself back from the split second of distraction. No matter what he said, I needed to stay focused. Of course Mom had torched the house. Anything to keep this sociopath away from us.

My sense of panic was rising. This man had stalked us for over a decade. How was I going to get away from him?

"But I got smarter," Willis was saying. "Previously, I'd focused on tracking Forrest. Whenever he got away, I'd end up with a burned alias and an empty desk at a fake biotech startup. But this time I also tracked you and Carmen."

He had marched me around a bend, and there was a trio of police cars ahead on the other side of a wide street that had been blocked off.

"Perfect," he said.

As we approached the corner, I heard a sudden whoosh of water behind us.

We both looked to see that a figure in black with

a bandanna over their face had opened a fire hydrant. Water rushed toward us.

The masked figure with the wrench ran off up the street. Two of the police stepped out of their cars and proceeded to chase the masked figure on foot. The other cop was on his radio, watching the chase and talking animatedly.

Willis yelled to get the cops' attention, but between the sound of the water, the protesters, and the booming voice of the awards ceremony over the loudspeakers, the cop couldn't hear him.

And the water was rushing between us and the police, maybe two feet off the ground.

Willis was off-kilter. He leaned forward to investigate the water, and his nightstick tipped into the stream, the high-pressure current pulling it out of his hand.

For a second, he let go of my arm to grab after it.

That was all I needed.

In that instant, time slowed down. I didn't think. I didn't question. I just bent my knees and hurled myself through the air, every fiber of my muscles fully engaged. And then I was upside down, doing an aerial over the water. Even as I flipped, I retracted my arms over my chest. And the next thing I knew, I had landed on the other side, anything but graceful, but on my feet and running.

I headed down the street, away from the cops and the protesters and the buses.

Over my shoulder, I saw my abductor jump over the water, but his boot got caught when he landed. He tripped and fell but quickly righted himself and gave chase. Unfortunately for him, his cop helmet was washed away downstream.

He chased me down the street, and I ducked into a grove of trees. "Over here," I heard a girl hiss. Behind a tree, I saw a light brown girl with pink hair and a black bandanna over her face. She had a pair of garden clippers. Before I could say a word, she snipped off one of my handcuffs and darted out through the trees. I pulled off the plastic that now hung limp and pushed the other cuff under my sleeve so it didn't show.

When my abductor-turned-pursuer came running into the grove of trees, he wasn't expecting me to bring my arm up and punch him in the face, which I did. Then I took off running up the street. I figured I'd be better off in the open. I didn't know if he had a gun, but if he was going to shoot me, I wanted witnesses.

Without his cop helmet and nightstick, his wet, dark clothes no longer looked like a uniform. He looked like just a drenched guy with a bloody face chasing a young woman down the street.

I didn't want to call for help because the cops might ask too many questions. But I hoped to find a way to get away from him.

When we came out onto the boulevard, there was a huge demonstration heading our way. Thousands of people were marching toward the Presidio from over the Golden Gate Bridge. They were quiet and nonviolent, mostly singing.

> *"Stop the war machine—shut it down*
> *Keep the fossil fuels in the ground*
> *We want racial equality*
> *And a future where we all can breathe . . ."*

It was difficult to get through them, but I pressed forward, hoping to lose myself in the crowd. I hunched down and walked in a crouch for a while.

I peeked up. Had I lost him? I looked around, trying to get my bearings, then ducked back down quickly as I spotted him. The air was full of singing, distant angry chants, and the drone of helicopters.

Somehow, in spite of all the chaos, every time I glanced up, he was coming my way. How could he know where I was? There were literally tens of thousands of people. I was zigzagging through them, and yet he could still find me? How was that even possible? He was a spy, after all, and they had technology. But I wasn't carrying a connected cell phone. There was no other way he could track—

But then I remembered. The handcuffs. I had cut one off, but not both. I pulled the cuff out from under my sleeve and tried to inspect it as people bumped against me in the crowd. It looked like a regular zip tie, but the thingy that the tie went through seemed bigger than it had to be. I looked through the milky white plastic and saw the outline of a chip.

Dammit! I tried to get my wrist out but couldn't. Why hadn't I asked that protester girl to snip both cuffs?

There were several helicopters overhead, and I kept moving through the protesters on the bridge. I stopped crouching, no longer afraid to be seen. As I looked over my shoulder, he was gaining. The helicopters stayed over our heads.

Then a voice boomed from the copters, louder than the singing all around me. "Mr. Willis, we have you surrounded. Get on your knees with your hands behind your head."

I saw cops on foot pushing through the crowd from both sides. I held my breath in fear, but they pushed right past me.

Willis saw them, too. He looked both ways down the bridge, then up overhead. He was on the side now, close to the railing.

Many of the marchers stopped singing. They moved away from him.

He slowly knelt down and put his hands behind his head.

I backed away, toward the other side of the bridge.

Behind the cops, Aunt Eve rode in on a black

motorcycle toward Willis. Protesters scattered out of her way. She made a second of eye contact with me, then skidded to a stop just a few feet from him.

As the protesters backed off, there was a clear line from the cops to Willis.

The police slowed down. They had him hemmed in from both sides and under helicopter surveillance from above.

One cop advanced toward him. "You have the right to remain silent," he began.

And then, just like that, Willis leaped to his feet and scrambled up the barrier on the bridge.

The cops swarmed in, and one grabbed hold of his pants leg. But Willis kicked free and hurled himself over the edge.

In movies, you see the shot from overhead or maybe the wide angle shot of someone falling down. Sometimes they play it in slo-mo. But this was just the quickest flash of black fabric whooshing by. Any sound of a hit or splash was drowned out by helicopters and boots running on concrete.

As I stood on the bridge with my mouth open in shock, I kept listening for that splash, and in my mind's eye, I imagined Agent Willis simply falling and falling forever.

TWENTY-SIX

We huddled in a room at the San Francisco Police Department, Aunt Eve pretending to be questioning me. Then she turned to the other officers in the room.

"So apparently," she said, "former Officer Willis escaped custody by overpowering a guard in transit. As near as we can tell, he was working alone. He seems to have abducted this young woman to use as a human shield to make his escape. We may never know why he was here at the Presidio."

"Our theory," said one of her FBI colleagues, "is that he may have been there to meet with someone."

"Very possible," Eve said.

"Young lady." She turned to me. "We're so glad

you're okay. You managed an incredible job of escaping from him. Really. He's a trained operative, and you're only a teenager."

"Thanks, ma'am," I said.

"We've typed up your statement, and you just need to sign it."

My statement was partly true; it just excluded all the best of my spycraft. And I signed the name Terra Jordan. Eve Henderson had "verified" my ID.

"I guess we're done here," she said, and reached out her hand to shake. She stood up and smiled. "I hope you enjoy the rest of your time in San Francisco. You should take a tour of the city. There's a Green Anchor Line bus in the morning."

"Really?" I asked.

"Yeah," she said. "It leaves at eight."

"Good to know," I said.

It was easier to leave, knowing that I would see her again in the morning. Maybe then she would give me an update on Dad and help me reunite with my parents.

I walked out onto the street. It was evening now.

A pair of young women walked down the street carrying a picket sign that said CLIMATE JUSTICE IS RACIAL JUSTICE. I heard another cluster of folks singing a refrain from one of the songs I had heard on the bridge.

I caught the bus to the hotel and crashed.

• • •

I nearly overslept. By the time I woke up, I barely had time to take a shower and put the sweats back on before I was rushing down to the lobby to catch the tour bus. I grabbed a toaster muffin and two cans of cola on my way out of the hotel.

I hopped onto the bus—which said MARIN—but Eve didn't make eye contact. I took her cue, and the two of us just rode in silence like strangers. The tour guide pointed out different San Francisco landmarks like Coit Tower and a view of the Golden Gate Bridge.

The bridge I was already very familiar with. Were they going to mention the man jumping yesterday? Why wasn't Eve talking to me? Was I ever going to be reunited with my parents? It was about half an hour into the tour, and my heart had begun to thump wildly in my chest. I felt hot. I could hear blood rushing in my ears. I was certain that I was having a panic attack.

But then I remembered the two cans of cola I'd drunk. Maybe Mom wasn't being so ridiculous by always telling me to avoid caffeine. I got hyper when I had chocolate, and this was sort of out of control.

I coached myself to breathe slowly. *This is temporary,* I told myself. *It'll wear off. It'll be over soon.* My heart continued to beat fast, and my limbs still felt jittery, but the roaring in my ears stopped. *You're not going to die. You're just overcaffeinated.*

I was still breathing deeply when the bus stopped at a beach location and everyone got off to take pictures.

Maybe the driver said the name of the town, but I didn't catch it.

Eve got off, so I did, too. She sat down in front of a boutique hotel and began to read the paper.

My heart continued to race. I thought of some of Deza's lyrics:

Breathe deep, brown girl, you got this.
And keep in mind you're flawless.
Old stereotypes are blown.
Breathe deep: you're not alone.

Didn't that speak to my whole life right now?

You got this, I told myself. I wasn't ready to say I was flawless, but everything in my life was definitely blown. And I wasn't alone anymore. I had Aunt Eve.

The bus loaded back up, but Eve made no move to board, so I didn't, either. I just looked out at the water.

After about half an hour, Eve had read all of the news sections. From time to time, she looked at her phone.

Eventually, two gray-haired tourists in tropical print shirts came and asked Eve for the time. They were almost a cliché of old white tourists, except they were Black and kind of sweet because they were holding hands. The woman held a tour bus schedule in her free hand. And she had on a wedding ring just like—wait! It was Mom's hand!

I had to fight to keep from leaping up and hugging her. Instead, I slouched back and gave a bored upward glance.

Yes! Mom and Dad dressed as seniors. How had they communicated with Eve?

"Looks like we missed the bus, Howard," Mom was saying. "I guess we should go walk on the beach a bit before the next one."

"Sure, honey," Dad said in a slightly shaky voice. "There's supposed to be a lovely view to the east."

"It's to the west," Mom corrected.

"Yes, dear," he said, and linked his arm through Mom's. "Thanks, miss," Dad said to Eve, and they strolled out toward the beach.

After about five minutes, there was a brief moment when no one was around.

"Catch up with them," Aunt Eve murmured without turning from the paper. "I'll be ten minutes behind you."

She didn't need to tell me twice.

I got up casually and followed the two figures down the beach to a spot where we could wade in the ocean.

There were a few people around, so I kept my face totally neutral.

"Is it okay for us to be seen together?" I asked without looking at them.

"We think so," Mom said. "But let's just act casual."

I nodded. "Do we get to stay together after this?"

They both smiled. "Definitely," Mom said.

"Do we need to stay in hiding?" I asked.

"Not exactly," Dad said. "But we can't go back to LA. The Factory will develop some new identities for us. And a new home base."

I was so grateful that we would be together that I could have cried, but I had a million questions about what our new identities would be, where we would go, whether I would go to school again, what it meant to be a ghost in the system. Instead, I asked a question that was burning in my mind: "What about Ella and Dexter?"

Mom and Dad exchanged glances. "I promised we'd be honest unless there was some danger," Mom said.

"Okay," Dad said. "Their parents' identities were compromised more thoroughly than ours. They've been reunited, but they won't be coming back into the country anytime soon."

Even through the persistent jitters of the caffeine, my heart sank.

The three of us were looking out at the ocean. I realized that thousands of miles away, in Cuba, Ella and Dexter were probably sitting with their own parents, maybe looking out at a different ocean. There wasn't a ton of free and random internet access in Cuba. I shouldn't expect an email anytime soon.

The waves were gentle in this area and lapped at my

feet. I hadn't realized how much I'd been hoping that maybe . . .

"Look," Mom practically yelled. "Motorboat rentals."

I looked over my shoulder to see Aunt Eve heading our way.

"Perfect," Dad said. We walked slowly down the beach to the boat rental spot, where a bored-looking Latinx guy was sitting at a little booth. I saw he was on his phone, scrolling through Triángulo cards for sale.

Mom pulled out a credit card to pay the guy for the rental as Eve walked up beside us.

"I'd like to rent a boat," Eve said.

"My last one," the guy told her as Mom was signing the paperwork.

"You could join us," Dad offered.

"That would be great," Eve said, and raised her binoculars. "I just need to check something." She peeled some bills off a wad of cash and gave them to Mom.

The four of us climbed into the motorboat, and Eve steered us into a quiet cove.

The feeling of skimming on top of the water was exhilarating, but she had to cut diagonally across the waves. She steered around in a wide circle, and we went behind a rock jutting out of the bay. There was a small buoy behind it. Dad secured the boat with a rope.

The moment we stopped, Mom leaped over and threw her arms around me. I squeezed her so tight.

When I looked at Dad and Eve, they were hugging, too. She had her arms around him, and his head was cradled just below her neck.

"Rescued by my big sister," Dad said. "Again."

I had sort of assumed Dad was older, but I realized that was just because he was taller.

"Story of my life," Eve said. "Getting my baby brother out of messes."

Dad stretched out his free arm, inviting me to sit on his other side. I piled on and almost tipped the boat.

Mom, who apparently was an expert in small boat craft, moved to the right spot on the opposite side and balanced us out.

"Sort of not fair for you to be left out of the group hug," I said.

"I'm looking at the three people in the world I love the most, against the backdrop of the water. I've got an attitude of gratitude."

So we just hung out like that for a few hours. The caffeine left my body, and I dozed for a while, until I felt the boat moving again. Mom was steering us back to land.

We hit ground in a different spot on the beach.

"Are you sure that the three of us can travel safely as a family?" Dad asked.

"Definitely," Eve said. "But I don't know when we'll see one another again."

I hadn't had an aunt before, and I was so sorry to lose her. The tears pricked my eyes and came fast. She had been my anchor for the last couple of days, and now I had no idea if we'd ever cross paths again. I leaned over and hugged her tight.

"Even though you didn't know about me," she said, "I've been loving you for fifteen years."

"Fifteen and a half," I said.

"Nope," she said. "Fifteen. You were six months old when we met, and I fell in love with you."

After we finally let go, she hugged both my parents and then wiped her eyes and took off in the boat.

We watched until it was a speck in the distance, and then we couldn't see it at all.

When I looked at my parents, I was startled again by the gray in their hair. "Didn't you come from Miami?" I asked. "Isn't the fountain of youth supposed to be somewhere in Florida? You all should have visited."

"I'm definitely ready to get some of this paint off my face," Mom said. I could see some of her wrinkles were drawn on, and they were starting to smudge a little.

As we walked down the beach, I realized there was a question I had forgotten to ask.

"Hey," I said. "Do either of you know how Aunt Eve found me on the bridge?"

Mom smiled sheepishly. "I told her where you were," she said.

"How on earth did you know?" I asked.

She looked at Dad and then back at me. "We have a tracker on you," Mom said.

"What?" I asked. "I thought it was just Agent Willis. In the zip-tie handcuff."

"We've had one on you for nearly a decade," Mom said. "It's in the filling in your mouth. We can take it out—our tracker. Your choice."

"How come you let me go to a dentist, but you never let me go to a doctor?" I asked.

"It was our Factory dentist," Dad said.

"Wait. Was it a real cavity?" I asked, remembering how scared I was when I'd gotten my first and only filling.

"God, yes," Mom said. "From all that candy Dad let you have when I was in residency."

"So?" asked Dad. "Should we take out the tracker? You *are* fifteen and a half now. Maybe you've earned a bit of independence."

"I need to think about it," I said. "I guess it depends on whether or not we stay in the business."

"That's got to be a decision the whole family makes," Mom said. "You're old enough now to have a say."

I didn't know what I wanted. I could see that the work they did was important. But I also loved the taste I had had of a normal life. High school. Capoeira. Boys who thought I was cute.

"Meanwhile," Dad said, "guess who's in San Francisco tonight? Well, Oakland, really."

"I don't know," I said. "Sister Niema?"

"Deza," Mom said.

"Really?" I asked, my voice getting a little shrill with excitement.

"Yeah," Dad said. "If you don't mind going to a concert with your parents."

"After all we've been through," I said, "I'm just glad we're back together."

Mom grinned and kissed me on the cheek.

"Besides," I said. "I don't know anyone in San Francisco. So there's no reason to feel embarrassed to be with two people who are so old and uncool."

"Is it okay for me to sing along?" Dad asked. "I know a lot of the lyrics."

"Don't push it," I said, but I linked my arms through theirs as we made our way back to the hotel.

At the concert that night, I stood between my mom and dad, screaming my lungs out for Deza. And the opening act turned out to be DJ RayBreak! I found myself breathing a sigh of relief when he walked out onto the stage. I don't know what had detained him the night before, but at least he was okay.

The stadium concert's massive audience was at least half teens. But there were plenty of adult fans, too, and

I wasn't the only one with my parents. I looked around at the other teens, mostly girls. They had bright smiles and excited voices, but as I walked up the stairs behind one girl, I heard her telling her friend:

"It's not just that he dumped me; it's that he did it right in front of everyone. Like, he didn't just want to break up but to totally humiliate me. I'm so glad Deza's concert is tonight. I really needed this."

A moment before, she had just looked like a happy and excited girl with lank brown hair and freckles. I realized that every girl in here had her own challenges. Some were likely to pass quickly, like a middle-school breakup, but others were probably more serious. When I thought about it, I likely wasn't the only one who'd had a harrowing day.

That being said, I was probably the only one with spy parents who'd escaped from a rogue former CIA officer. And when Deza sang her final number, it felt like she was singing directly to me:

> *"You were a girl*
> *So, so innocent*
> *Grew up too fast*
> *And far too magnificent*
> *The world couldn't handle*
> *Your curves, your smarts*
> *Some people mishandled*

Your precious heart
Haters always
Try to bring you down
You gotta find the folks
You want to keep around
You come from a people
Who are strong and proud
And you can't go back
Because your time is now."

That was the thing about Deza. It always seemed like she was reading my mind. But every girl in the concert probably felt that way. Still, if Deza ever wrote a song about parents who were spies, I would know she really did have some mind-reading abilities.

The bass and drums of the music called to me. I stood up and danced in the aisle, shaking my hips to the rhythm. The moment was so magical that I didn't care what I looked like or who might be watching.

On the way back to San Francisco, we rode over the Bay Bridge. I looked at the lights of Oakland behind us, a sparkling downtown with a glittering landscape of darkening hills that rose up behind it.

Up ahead, I looked beyond the twinkling lights of the Bay Bridge to San Francisco's majestic skyline. We were in transit. Where were we going? To a hotel, yes, but after that? I had no idea where our family would go next.

I saw Dad's profile in the front seat. His beard was growing back, and he looked more like himself. Mom sat next to me in the back and held my hand. My mom—my Venezuelan mom—and my dad, who had a sister. How had my life changed so much in less than a month?

Like Deza said, I missed my innocence, but now I knew more about what was real in my life—these two folks who really loved me, despite their many short-comings. This was my crew, at least for now. And I was ready to go with them on our next adventure.